The Toucan Lodge

A Novel

by

CARLOS MUNDY

ISBN: 9798620221097

3rd Edition 2021 with photographs

Cover illustration by Guillermina Royo-Villanova

DEDICATION

To my father Rodney Meynell Mundy, in loving memory.

To His Holiness the XIV Dalai Lama, my guiding light.

To all the men and women who have sacrificed their lives
in the name of freedom.

ALSO BY CARLOS MUNDY

The Twilight of the Fourth World (with Charis Mundy)

The Lost Romanov Icon & the Enigma of Anastasia (with Marie Stravlo)

Grand Duchess Maria and her justified claim to the Imperial throne of Russia

The Indian King of France: The fascinating story of the Bourbons of Bhopal

The Truth about the Royal House of Anjou and Prince Alexis d'Anjou

ACKNOWLEDGMENTS

Special gratitude to the late Phryne Alabaster Mundy for her recollection of those days and the part of her life she shared with our father; to the late Alicia Balenchana and Sandoval who was very helpful with her memories of Madrid during the second world war, to my sister Charis for her editing work and to my friends world-wide for their constant support and their and their friendship.

FOREWARD

When my father revealed to me in Costa Rica that he had been a member of MI6, I was fascinated. Since then and every time we saw each other, I urged him to write his story to no avail.

However, after his sudden death I found to my surprise that he had been taking notes, and even ventured to write certain passages of what was going to be his autobiography had he not died so unexpectedly. So, I was compelled, in tribute to his life, to take over and finish what he had started.

Borrowing from his autobiographical notes, writings and tales, and Phryne´s recollections I was able to picture a time past and construct the backbone of the story, but the material had many gaps to be a biography so, instead, I decided to write it as a novel. This allowed me the freedom to change the names of certain characters to protect the identity of their descendants, to fictionalise some of the different incidents, and to fill the gaps to the narrative's convenience.

As the Toucan Lodge is a work of fiction based on my father's life, I have made the creative choice of writing it as if the narrator was my father's consciousness remembering his life.

I hope you will enjoy the story as much as I did writing it. Some of the characters were the main players in the history of the 20th Century. After all, they do say that those who forget their history are condemned to repeat it.

Though what is recounted in this book is based on historical facts, some of the characters and situations are fictional and a product of my imagination

Carlos Mundy Tangier June 2009

AUTHOR'S NOTE JUNE 2021

A lot has happened in Spain since The Toucan Lodge was first published in 2009. It is very worrying that the wounds of the past are being reopened when there are practically no survivors left from the years of the Second Republic, the Civil War and General Franco's regime. The drift began during the socialist government of José Luis Rodríguez Zapatero (2004-2011) and his unnecessary Law of Historical Memory of 31 October 2007. An unnecessary law because the transition from dictatorship to democracy had finally closed the old wounds of the civil war.

After the general elections of 10 November 2019, the Spanish Socialist Workers Party (PSOE) won with a simple majority with the promise that it would never govern with the communists of *Unidas Podemos*, a promise it broke, forming a government with communist members whose only objective since its formation has been to destroy the regime born in 1978 that cost so many political sacrifices to make it a success under the leadership of King Juan Carlos I.

On 2 June 2014 the King abdicated in favour of his son who assumed the throne as Felipe VI and finally retired from public life 5 years later. It is Felipe VI who with great tact and extraordinary political sagacity stopped the 2017 *coup d'état* by the pro-independence supporters for which he is not forgiven. Since then, overthrowing the Constitution and forcing constitutional change has programmatically united the Catalan and Basque pro-independence parties and the ultra-left party (*Unidas Podemos*) that is in government. It has become their leitmotiv and their obsession. Any excuse is a good one to try to destroy the monarchy and the King is just the ideal excuse for that higher goal, which is to achieve regime change in one way or another. Independentism pursues it to facilitate self-determination; and the extreme left, among other reasons, to achieve the fantasy of a federal republic.

King Juan Carlos has made some mistakes in the personal sphere that have been recounted and manipulated by the government-subsidised media. This intolerable media pressure made him take one of the hardest decisions of his life and more than a year ago in an act of absolute patriotism, putting the interests of the Crown above his own and as a last great act of service to the country to which he has dedicated his life, he decided to leave Spain temporarily. To date he has not returned.

The long reign of Juan Carlos I (1975-2014) has been the most fruitful historical period Spain has ever known. Heir to the authoritarian powers of General Franco's dictatorship, King Juan Carlos I made known shortly after his accession to the throne his explicit desire to renounce them to promote the Spanish institutional organisation in accordance with the model of Western democracies. King Juan Carlos pledged to be the King of all Spaniards and soon achieved a Spain without exiles and the overcoming of the issues that had opposed Spanish society in recent history. The approval by referendum of the 1978 Constitution, following free elections in which all political parties participated, brought about the reconciliation of Spaniards and a great national agreement, which fulfilled the King's wish for Spain to be a European and Latin American country, in accordance with its historical vocation, and an advanced Western democracy, where everyone could fit in, open to representative pluralism and political alternation. The so-called Spanish transition to democracy was a powerful reinforcement of national self-esteem and, at the same time, a model admired and imitated internationally. Juan Carlos I, played a decisive and indispensable role in this process. It was and still is true that he was described as the "engine of change".

In the memory of all those who lived through it, both in Spain and in all democratic countries, the consolidation of democracy is indelibly marked by the firm intervention of King Juan Carlos and his message of disavowal of the attempted coup d'état of 1981: *"The Crown, symbol of the permanence and unity of the homeland, cannot tolerate in any way actions or attitudes of people who seek to interrupt the democratic process by force"*.

The prestige resulting from this repudiation was recognised by the most important forums and media throughout the international world, thus reinforcing both his image as Head of State of a democratic country and that

3

of the Crown, an institution that guarantees stable development and a stable future.

King Juan Carlos represented Spain with absolute dedication, an attitude of service and love for his country, acting as ambassador with overflowing enthusiasm and resounding success to show a reborn Spain, with a new spirit perfectly integrated into the most important international organisations. His permanent support for European unity and his constant concern and interest in fostering and strengthening lasting ties of friendship and collaboration with other nations deserve wide praise. It is also worth noting that, in the early years of his reign, Spain joined the Common Market and NATO, which led to Don Juan Carlos receiving the Charlemagne Prize for merits demonstrated *"in the service of reconciliation and international cooperation in Europe"*, among countless other awards.

Although Franco's Spain never recognised Israel and always supported the Arabs, it was Juan Carlos I who took this relationship to another level. In 1983 Israel was recognised by the government of President Felipe González and in 1992 King Juan Carlos himself, in a surprising episode, 'apologised' to Israel for the decree of expulsion of the Sephardic Jews in 1492, signed by his ancestors Isabella I of Castile and Ferdinand V of Aragon, while strengthening Arab ties.

In 1992, thanks to the King's discreet efforts, Spain hosted the Olympic Games in Barcelona and the Universal Exposition in Seville, reflecting the image of a young, prosperous and dynamic nation led by a sovereign who had successfully and without trauma installed a true democracy in his beloved country.

King Juan Carlos has been instrumental in promoting Spain's interests abroad, especially in the Middle East, where from the beginning of his reign he has forged bonds of brotherhood with the region's royal families. His charisma and charm have won major contracts for Spanish companies over the years, earning him the admiration and gratitude of the Spanish business sector.

The Spanish Constitution establishes that: *"the political form of the Spanish State is the parliamentary Monarchy"*; and defines the King as the Head of State, *"symbol of its unity and permanence"*, who *"arbitrates and regulates the regular functioning of the institutions, assumes the highest representation of the State in international relations, especially with the nations of its historical community, and exercises the functions expressly attributed to him by the Constitution and the laws"*.

Throughout the years of his reign and in the performance of his constitutional duties, Juan Carlos I has invariably remained faithful to his democratising purposes and to the responsibilities derived from the institutional framework, as was the case on the day of the attempted coup d'état. He has been able to act with permanent attention and care to the political, cultural, economic and social progress of the country and its citizens, to its rich diversity, to the international prestige of the Spanish community and to the peaceful and harmonious integration of Spaniards in their diverse opinions, origins and beliefs.

Under Juan Carlos I, the monarchical institution, as rarely before in Spanish life, has come to play a central and essential role in the arbitration of national political processes and has consequently become a basic element in the functioning of Spanish constitutional democracy. Proof of this was the popularity that Juan Carlos I achieved during his reign and the very broad acceptance that the Monarchy aroused among Spaniards. The Monarchy had become, as the Constitution advocated, a form of government suited to the needs and preferences of the Spanish people, useful for its moderating capacity and neutral behaviour. The current King, Felipe VI, is a vivid example of these qualities, which in essence reflect the best and most enduring legacy of his father, King Juan Carlos I.

It is therefore a gesture of extreme ingratitude and a national disgrace that the best king in our history, who never acted against the interests of his country and to whom Spain owes so much, is currently far from his country and is not expected to return in the near future. We must not forget that he is already 83 years old and that in this last stage of his life he should be receiving tributes all over Spain and not living alone and far from his loved ones and the country for which he has sacrificed so much since he was sent to Spain when he was only 10 years old.

The operation to destroy the regime of 1978 by members of the current social-communist government and their pro-independence partners continues with their campaign against the mode of state established in the Spanish Constitution approved in the referendum of 6 December 1978, as a Social and Democratic State of Law, with a system of government, governed by the Parliamentary Monarchy.

Every public officer holder swears or promises on conscience and honour to fulfil faithfully the duties of the office with loyalty to His Majesty the King, and to keep and uphold the Constitution, as the fundamental rule of the State, and therefore they are obliged to comply with this requirement when they accede to the condition and full rights, to be members of the Congress of Deputies, once they are elected in a fully democratic general election. But in this government of LIES, they fail to fulfil their obligations, and nothing happens. All immoral.

It is tragic that the government presided over by Pedro Sánchez and his ultra-left government partners, joined by the pro-independence parties, are trying to pass the misnamed "Law of Democratic Memory", which would replace the Law of Historical Memory of 2007 and rewrite the history of Spain from the establishment of the Second Republic until the return of democracy in 1978.

Rewriting history is very tempting and typical of authoritarian regimes. Putin's government is doing it to whitewash the crimes committed by the Soviet totalitarian regime. The Spanish left, lacking ideas or a coherent new programme, has partially repudiated the prosperous and largely decentralised democracy born of the 78 Constitution on the grounds that it was tainted by Franco's dictatorship, although it ended it. "Anti-Francoism" has become a central banner, attributing to a dictator who disappeared more than four decades ago the power to dominate Spanish affairs from beyond the grave. More than anywhere else, in Spain polemics about recent history form an important part of the current political controversy. It is of great concern that the social-communist government intends with this law to do the same as

Putin and whitewash the crimes committed by the left both during the Second Republic and the terrible Civil War. The truth is that terrible crimes were committed by both sides and a law like this should cover all crimes and not only those that the government of the day is interested in.

General Franco's regime was not an ideal regime, but neither was the II Republic idealised by the most extremist members of the current Spanish government. The Second Republic was born with good intentions but soon became radicalised and fell under the control of the communists and Soviet influence. Franco's regime had many shadows, especially in the first part but it kept Spain out of World War II as I narrate in this book. It is a historical fact that during the second half of his rule, the Spanish economy grew and in the 1960s economic growth was second only to Japan and a buoyant middle class emerged that had not previously existed. In fact, this middle class was the chore support of the regime between 1960 and 1975. If the new law of Democratic Memory is passed, remembering these historical facts will be a crime!

The majority of 21st century Spaniards do not support the fantasies of the so-called "historical or democratic memory", which is neither history, nor memory and much less democracy. Tragically, in Spain as in the rest of Europe, most of the new generations are ignorant of history and therefore reopening wounds that were well closed is an aberration. Spain does not deserve these politicians who once again want to divide Spaniards, at a time when there are other more serious problems to solve such as the pandemic and the economic crisis.

History is an interpretation by men and women (the historians) of our past and few of them do not fall into the temptation of adding their personal and singular point of view. That said, no government in the world should be able to rewrite history for it is good to remember that peoples who forget their history are condemned to repeat it.

And I conclude by affirming that the defence of the King is the defence of the Constitution.

I

RECOLLECTIONS

London 27th October 1922, the place and date I was born…I do not have too many recollections of my childhood nor of my life but I will do my best to remember. Since I passed away, my memory began to blur and the line between facts and fiction seems to have slowly faded away.

Had I lived, I would be approaching my eighty-ninth birthday…I must confess I never looked forward to old age's tribulations and, with hindsight, I am glad it all happened as it did. I simply died in my sleep

II

CARLOS & I

My second son Carlos and I decided to go to Costa Rica for ten days before our Jamaican holidays where we were going to welcome the New Year with some family friends. We had not spent quality time together in quite a long time.

We stayed for three days at the colonial Gran Hotel in San José, which proved to be an exhausting exercise with all the lavish entertainment in the beautiful homes of friends, who had once lived in Spain, and the non-stop touring of the Central Valley. We visited the Poas volcano and were very impressed by the otherworldly setting. The sight of its sulphur pool surrounded by smoke and steam rising from fumaroles was such a marvellous experience that a whole eternity will not erase it from my memory.

Nothing in our stay hinted that all the phantoms of my past were about to return. But return they did and in the most unexpected way.

Carlos had arranged that we should go on December 21st to Puerto Viejo de Talamanca, a small village on the Caribbean Sea, only a few miles from the Panamanian border. Our friends in San José had told us that a devastating earthquake had hit the area a few months earlier and suggested we should go instead to a resort on the Pacific

Coast. But as Carlos had secured an article for a magazine about Puerto Viejo and its inhabitants, he insisted in sticking to our original plan, having made reservations to stay at the new Toucan Lodge; so, it was that on the morning of December 21st we set off in a rented four-wheel-drive vehicle for the Costa Rican Caribbean.

We took the Guapiles highway to Limón, which goes through Braulio Carrillo National Park. The scenery was one of rolling hillsides clothed with a thick emerald, green mass of vegetation. Carlos was intent on stopping and walking the park's 700m 'Los niños trail', but I was adamant about reaching our destination in daylight. Although I did not confess it at the time, I had done my bit of sightseeing, and I was looking forward to having a relaxing drink at the lodge.

We arrived at about three in the afternoon at the large tropical estate in which the Toucan Lodge stood, facing the beach. Our first sight of the lodge was that of a wooden bungalow with a veranda, dining area, and reception lobby in the basement. Someone told us that the owner, a Costa Rican from San Jose called Martin Jimenez, had bought the land many years ago but had only recently developed it They were expecting us. A small well-built 'tico'[1], in charge of the reception, welcomed us with a broad smile.

"*Buenas tardes, señores.* Did you have a nice trip? My name is José, and I am at your service," he said, ringing a bell.

Willy came into the reception. He appeared so quick that

---

[1] How the Costa Ricans are known.

it seemed he had been standing behind the door, waiting for the bell to ring. He was a good-looking young houseboy, whom Carlos immediately speculated belonged to the Bibri Indian tribe. He showed us to our cabins and left, sporting a broad smile all the time. Amidst lush vegetation were the bungalows, with toucans and parrots flying about the garden. We were both pleased with the relaxed atmosphere and the beauty of the place. An idyllic setting to unwind from the trip. The lodge was quite charming and exuded good taste and refinement with a touch of understated luxury. Built of bamboo with a front porch, the cabins were simple but extremely cosy.

I was unpacking, merrily daydreaming of a pre-dinner whisky, when I heard a chilling scream- an expression of such horror I never thought I would hear again. I ran out of my room and saw Carlos running out of his, white-faced.

"What's wrong? Are you ok?"

"Yes, yes," Carlos replied, still shaken. "There's a large green and orange snake in my bathroom! It suddenly appeared behind me. I nearly got bitten."

By then, José and a middle-aged Indian had joined us. We all went into Carlos' room, but there was no sign of the reptile anywhere.

"These snakes are quite poisonous, but they seldom bite anybody... that is unless they feel cornered," said the Indian looking into my eyes as if anticipating something I could not grasp and showing no intention of hunting the snake down.

After Jose's friendly but long diatribe on the pros and

cons of life in the woods, we decided Carlos would move into a new cabin, and we would try to forget the incident.

Once we had settled in, we went off for a swim to refresh ourselves. We followed a narrow dirt track along the coast to Punta Uva because our friends had told it was the most beautiful beach in the area. It had been a paradise, but the earthquake's devastation was evident: the floods that followed had washed thousands of tons of wood and debris down to the sea, which the tides had thrown back onto the beaches. In our eagerness to swim, we took a long dip in the warm, clear waters while keeping an eye out for floating log.

Back at the lodge, having showered and changed into loose clothes, we went to the bar, adjacent to the open-air dining room, to have a drink before dinner. I was struck with horror when I saw the man standing by the bar. He had a pair of Rottweilers by his side. He held his back tautly straight, had wavy blonde hair, a sour expression, and was slowly sipping a beer as he watched the entrance. I looked straight into his icy blue eyes, and a chill went down my spine. The man, who was the owner of the Toucan Lodge, stood up to greet us. I hardly managed to force a smile.

"You must be *Los Señores* Mundy. My name is Martín Jiménez. I am glad to have you here with us. Jose will shortly offer you welcome drinks," he greeted us in a friendly manner.

I do not think Carlos realized how stunned I was. His face was disturbingly familiar, but I could not pinpoint where I had seen that face before.

That evening I was not very chatty, and I could hardly eat my dinner. The sight of Martin Jimenez had deeply disturbed me. I was unable to sleep that night. My restless mind travelled back and forth, rescuing from oblivion memories, I had decided to forget long ago.

Where had I seen that face before? I tossed restlessly in my bed, sweating with anxiety, unable to resolve the puzzle. My mind was like a wild horse, and no matter how much I tried, I was unable to tame it. At my age, I still remembered a face, but having met so many people during my life, I had difficulty remembering the circumstances that surrounded each one of them. I suppose, under normal circumstances, I would not have complained about this small handicap, but this was different, his face gnawed me, igniting all the fear I had bottled inside during the last decades.

Although there are few things, I hate more than getting up early, I got up just after sunrise. Lying in bed had become a lethally, dangerous exercise.

I met Carlos for breakfast, and we made plans for the day. The fact that it had rained all night and that the morning was wet, did not deter us from visiting one of the three Indian reservations in the Talamanca Mountains. The lands where these ancient people live are protected against all commercial development in a variety of ways: hunting is forbidden except the one practised by the Indians for their survival, and access to the reservations requires special permits. José suggested that we visit Mauricio Salazar, a Bribri Indian, Mauricio lived on a 14-hectare plot of the jungle where he had built three charming thatched Indian-style bungalows. José had told Carlos that Mauricio had permits to visit the Kekodi reservation and could swiftly arrange permits for the other two. I found myself following my son up a steep, slippery path towards the Cabinas Chimuri where Mauricio's lived.

When we arrived, I was ultimately out of breath. A charming German girl greeted us, and we soon found out she was Mauricio's girlfriend. She explained to us the difficulties involved in acquiring permits but insisted that it would be well worth it, as meeting the Indians would be an unforgettable experience and a walk through the rain forest would be thoroughly enjoyable. I had my doubts, as one is none too agile when approaching seventy, but Carlos was very excited. Nevertheless, we arranged that they would notify us at the Lodge when the walk would take place. Mauricio, who was temporarily absent, would be our guide.

Once back in the car, I suggested to Carlos that we arrange a fishing expedition, as I knew that there was good Atlantic tarpon. So, we went to see Willy Burton, a local fisherman and friend of José.

We followed the dirt track back along the coast, past Punta Uva, until we reached Manzanillo. Willy lived on a house on stilts on a riverbank close to the ocean at the end of the coastal track from where you could walk to Panama. He was a small, stocky man in his early fifties who wore shorts and a pair of old Wellington boots and revealed a hairy torso frequently exposed to the sun.

"*Buenos días*, I would like to go fishing one of these days. Jose says you can arrange it for me," I said.

Willy had an amiable expression and a naughty twinkle in his eyes. He indicated that we follow him to a shack under which he kept a boat in need of a coat of paint. Pointing at it, he burst into hearty laughter.

"This is your vessel, *señor*, but the weather is not good now. The sea is rough because of the new moon. However, as soon as the weather changes, we will plunge into the sea. It'll be good for me to earn some bread!" He laughed again, probably at Carlos' expression of disbelief as he looked at the boat.

A striking older man, another Bibri Indian who was probably in his seventies, interrupted us. He was only wearing a pair of shorts, and his long black hair fell over his shoulders. He introduced himself as Roberto, the shaman. While Willy and I discussed fishing, Carlos got into a lively conversation with our new acquaintance, and soon we received an invitation to visit him at the reservation. My son was thrilled and decided that his article would centre on him.

By the time we bade farewell, the weather had not improved; nevertheless, we had gone swimming to Punta Uva. I was adamant in convincing Carlos to go to the Pacific coast as soon as he had his article. It was too wet for my liking, but my desire to get away was more from uneasiness at the sight of Martin Jimenez than because of the weather.

Neither my children nor my wife knew anything about my past. I had never wanted them to be involved. After

1977, I had decided to lay it to rest with great success.

I saw him again that evening. We were on our way to the car to go out for dinner when he stepped out of the lodge. This time, he did not acknowledge us. He pretended he had not seen us, but I felt his piercing eyes set on me as we climbed into the car. As we walked into a small restaurant lit with neon lights, Carlos blurted out, "that man gives me the creeps!"

"I was just thinking the same thing," I muttered.

God knows why we were in such an awful restaurant or why Carlos was asking for someone by the name of Johnny, *el guapo*.[2] We had a mediocre meal and later, as we were drinking tea, Carlos' friend walked in. He turned out to be a dealer in the sacred herbs of the Indians, which Carlos wanted to try. He explained it was part of his research. I did not think this to be a good idea, but I knew my son was headstrong and once he had decided to do something, there was nothing I could say to make him change his mind.

While Carlos spoke to *el guapo*, who needless to say was one of the ugliest guys I had ever seen, I sat in silence feeling a bit dumb. Johnny had a generous smile, though, and did not seem to be a dangerous fellow. He was very dark-skinned, and he explained that his mother was a native and his father, a Colombian. He suggested we drive him to a friend's house where he would collect some pot.

Despite myself, I was quite amused by the adventure.

---

[2] The Good looking

The weed-dealer had a great sense of humour, and, before we knew it, my son and I were enjoying his company and laughing our heads off as if we were high. We drove up to a farm on a hill to find nobody was there.

On our way back to the restaurant, to drop Johnny off, he abruptly ordered us to stop the car because he had spotted his friend, a Spaniard named Gerardo, who was delighted to hop into the car, take refuge from the heavy rain, and sell Carlos six dollars of marihuana.

Back at the lodge, the sight of the two Rottweilers unsettled me again, and I had difficulty getting to sleep. I unsuccessfully tried to calm myself down through reason and logic. It was apparent from his physic that Martin Jimenez was of German descent, but this did not necessarily make him a threat. Nothing appeased my fears, and my only comfort laid on the supposition that due to the heavy rain, Carlos would soon want to leave to the Pacific.

Unfortunately, the morning greeted us with an imposing sun. Carlos came into my cabin urging me to get ready quickly, for he had planned a very tight schedule for the day. I was glad because he was going to get all the information he needed in just one day, but the sunshine destroyed all hope of him leaving on his own accord.

We drove to the path that led to Mauricio's small plot. This time he was in with his girlfriend. He had the permits with him, yet he cautioned us that the trek would not be an easy one and that it would take a good two hours. Nonetheless, we set off on our way through the jungle. The flora and fauna continually called my son's attention, making our march painfully slow. After a good three long hours, we finally reached our destination.

The village was tiny, and the Bribri Indians lived as they had done for generations. Roberto gleefully greeted us the minute he saw us. As the wise man or witch doctor of the tribe, he possessed knowledge passed on orally from one ancestor to the next for many generations. He knew the spiritual and medicinal properties of every plant in the jungle.

Carlos was escorted around the small village while he took pictures and notes. When he finished, Roberto invited us into his hut where we sat around a small fire.

"So, you'd like to know what the Gods have in store for you, would you?" he asked.

Carlos nodded with anticipation. The shaman took my son's hands and started chanting in a language unknown to us. Within minutes, he entered a self-induced trance, muttering words we did not understand. His voice changed, becoming coarse and loud. Mauricio looked worried but said nothing.

"What's he saying?" I whispered. Carlos also seemed to be in some sort of a trance, probably from the pot he had smoked earlier.

"Grave dangers loom over you...you must be careful...."

That was the last thing I wanted to hear. A hair-raising silence followed. Only the sounds of the jungle could be heard, mingled with the laughter of some children outside the hut.

I must have looked as worried as Mauricio when Roberto, opening his eyes, became himself again. He ordered to a young girl, who was sitting quietly by the entrance to the hut, bringing a tray of fruits, which we shared in silence. After a while, Roberto gave Carlos and I, an amulet against the evil spirits, saying that we were to wear it around our necks. We thanked Roberto and the most prominent members of the tribe for their kindness and left for Mauricio´s home.

"What did he mean, Mauricio?" I asked, somewhat concerned and upset at the shaman's economy of words.

"You should not worry too much. He is an old man that speaks in metaphors. His medicine is only good for us Indians. We are quite superstitious, ¨ Mauricio said hoping to calm me down.

"Well, we're OK now. Time is not linear. The dangers that loom over us must be the snake incident, and anyway, we have these now," said Carlos, pointing at his colourful amulet gleefully.

I was dead worried but said nothing.

*

Before lunch, we went to the beach at Cahuita to swim and sunbathe. Only ten miles north of Puerto Viejo and situated in the National Park that bears its name, Cahuita is a charming village with a unique flavour. To the East of the hamlet, a white sandy beach stretches for a mile and a half beside a gently curving bay. Although severely affected by the earthquake, it still offered good swimming and plenty of shade. We spent a couple of hours dipping into the turquoise water, sharing family stories, and soon we forgot the morning's incident. Carlos had given me to read, *"The spy went dancing,"* the best-seller by Aline, Countess of Romanones. The American-born socialite had worked for the American Office of Strategic Services in Madrid before marrying Luis Figueroa, Count of Romanones, and Carlos was a good friend of her son, Luis, Count of Quintanilla, and his charming wife, Inés.

What forces were suddenly at work and determined to make me remember my past? Was it what many new-age writers now call synchronicity? The fact was that this book talked of a period of my life that I had not shared with anybody.

I had not known Aline in those days. According to her book, she arrived after I had already returned to England. What amazed me was that her job description was the same as mine had been. During the war years, she had met most of the same people that I had, and later in life, we had friends in common and had moved in the same circles. I did meet her, though, in 1966 in Seville. I had seen her from behind. Jacky Kennedy, Fermín Bohorquez and Aline were riding on horseback in front of the Marquis of Atienza's carriage, in which Pepita and I were riding. They were wearing the typical *'traje corto'* or short jacket, with Cordobés hats. At the sound of the bells on the harness of our four

Cartujano[3] greys, they turned and smiled at us. Fermín, I knew well. He was a close friend of our host, the Marquis. The two ladies were surrounded by large crowds, as everybody wanted to get a close look at America's First Lady.

We met again that evening. After a memorable bullfight at the Maestranza, Mimi Medinaceli and her husband Rafael[4], invited us to the Palacio de Pilatos, home of one of the oldest and noblest families in Spain. Also, there was Prince Rainer and Princess Grace of Monaco. She was astoundingly beautiful. I noticed that she and Jacky Kennedy did not seem to like each other as they sat side by side the duke and they did not even acknowledge each other's presence.

✳

Having interviewed natives from the different Indian tribes, Carlos seemed quite happy with the material gathered for his article. He thought it convenient to write a travel piece on the area, so for the culinary section, we decided to try the famous local dish, *rondon*[5] at Miss Edith's restaurant. Miss Edith was a large-black mama who exuded so much charisma that she had no difficulty convincing us to return that evening for our Christmas Eve dinner, especially once

---

[3] Breed of Spanish horses

[4] The Duke and Duchess of Medinaceli

[5] Beef soup with potatoes, chayote, pumpkins and cauliflower

she had made us taste her mouth-watering *casado*[6], her deliciously coriander flavoured ceviche[7], and her renowned dessert, *tres leches*, made with three different types of milk.

Back at the lodge, José informed us that a man, who refused to leave his name, had telephoned us from Spain and that he would call again at seven. Not a soul, except for our friends in San José, knew of our whereabouts. The unexpected always creates a sense of unease, and this time was not to be the exception. However, I had not been trained to lose my cool and, seeing Carlos´ worried face, I gaily said: - "Let's open a bottle of Dom Perignon. It's Christmas Eve!"

We sat at the veranda to sip the delicious, chilled champagne, which we had brought from Europe together with a Christmas pudding from Fortnum & Mason's that José was keeping as a treasure for our Christmas lunch. I smiled at the thought of how we English love tradition. I had even bought with me the silver George V sixpence that, since my mother's days, has always gone into the family's pudding!

We had drunk half a bottle and were feeling relaxed and happy at being together when, at 7 o'clock sharp, José answered the telephone and called my son. We both approached the phone, and Carlos picked up the receiver. I asked impatiently, "Who is it? Who is it?" before he even

---

[6] Rice, black beans, beef, cabbage, avocado and plantain

[7] Chilled-marinated sea bass, shrimps and shellfish served with lemon, chopped onion and garlic.

had time to speak. Carlos did not reply. He became mute and motionless; listening to whatever the caller was telling him. After, what to me seemed like a lifetime, Carlos thanked the man and hung up. He remained silent with a bewildered expression on his face. His lips quivered as if they wanted to form words but could not, and my heart sank aching for my other children.

¨For God's sake Carlos, what is going on? ¨ I said as a shook him from the shoulders, unable to face the death of a loved one again, I asked angrily.

He looked at me in utter disbelief and burst out, "Papa, we must pack and leave immediately! Something terrible is going to happen. Just pay the bill! I'll explain everything in the car."

"What about your work?" I asked irritated and not knowing what to make out of the situation.

"Please Papa, do not utter a word and go and pack! I'll explain later" he ordered with urgency and contained desperation, hardly raising his voice.

At half-past seven, having given José a flimsy excuse as to our sudden departure, we were on our way but without a destination.

Carlos explained that the phone call was not from Spain and that the man spoke in a whisper and tried to sound friendly although his voice was shrill and frightening. He claimed to be calling on behalf of someone who wanted to protect us. From what he said, it seemed that Martín Jimenez was planning to have us busted for drugs thus for our own good we were told to leave the Lodge.

As it was dark and the roads were not safe, there was no way we could drive back to San Jose; so, we decided to go to Cahuita, try to find accommodation there, and keep our dinner appointment at Miss Edith's.

We drove in silence. My worst fears realized. However, who was that Martin Jimenez, anyway?

"It's probably just someone's idea of a bad joke. The hotel was probably overbooked, and that freak thought it amusing to get rid of us like that." Carlos broke the silence, hoping to release the tension.

"Damn it!" I exclaimed. "We forgot the Christmas pudding that we've dragged halfway around the bloody world!"

"But I did bring the other bottle of champagne, though!" grunted Carlos laughing.

"Thank goodness for that. "I need a big drink as soon as we get there. Do you think this time they will let us finish the bottle without any upheaval?"

Finally, we reached *Cabinas Atlánticas*, a charming little lodge owned by a Canadian/Dutch couple. The family was already sitting down to dinner, so the husband, Louis, did not bother asking us to fill in the registration forms.

Just before 9 o'clock, we found ourselves sitting down comfortably at Miss Edith's and enjoying a delicious lobster cooked in coconut milk with spices, vegetables and rice, which we washed down with my favourite champagne.

Now that I felt more relaxed; I decided that I was ready

to reveal to my son the secrets of my past.

III

EARLY MEMORIES

I do not remember the house we lived in near Barnstaple in Devonshire, but I do recall that my father rented Dunstrom Castle in Loch Awe (Scotland) for a short period. At the time, it seemed a terrifying dungeon; but in fact, it may be quite a nice place.

My father, Robert Charles Mundy, was fifty-two when I was born. In 1903 he had married a very wealthy lady by the name of Maud Andrew who, a year later, gave him a son called Basil. In 1920, by then a widower, he married my mother, Dorothy Sadler Phillips, the only child of a family that traced its lineage back to the Merovingian dynasty, or so they said. Basil, though only sixteen, had inherited an immense fortune upon the death of his mother, but the minute he came of age and was able to dispose of his wealth, he dilapidated it, leading a dissolute life, travelling extensively, spending millions on women and gambling until, having nothing left, he shot himself. The year was 1933. I was eleven at the time, and hardly knew him. A portrait of Basil at the age of five, painted by Joaquin Sorolla when he lived at my father's home in London, has always been in the family as a constant reminder of a life misspent.

When my mother married, her father decided that on his death the entire fortune would go to the freemasons although she would receive a generous lifetime allowance and the usage of the Sadler Phillips' properties, but her children, if she had any, would not receive a penny. I suppose he was trying to protect me from myself, but fortunately I was not Basil.

My earliest memories are of my prep school, Elstree, in Hertfordshire, and of our house in Henley. The Old House at N°2 New Street was a lovely Elizabethan corner-house painted white with black beams. It is still standing, and I hope it will do so for many more centuries.

Elstree was one of the best and most pompous preparatory schools in England. In those days, an old boy called Sanderson owned it, and later, he passed it on to his son. At the slightest excuse, they would have me, or anybody else they could lay their hands on, beaten across the backside a minimum of six lashes with a strong bamboo cane.

There was the usual collection of boarding school masters, one of whom was the history teacher, Mr. Hardy, whom David Niven calls in his autobiography his 'most hated man'. Niven was at Elstree before me and I only met him some years later in Cannes.

Our home was a happy one, although my upbringing was more formal than strict. Dinner was always a formal occasion, even if we had no guests. The men would wear dinner jackets and my mother would appear in some

Basil Mundy painted by Joaquin Sorolla in 1908

Rodney Meynell Mundy 1934

stunningly beautiful evening gown, most of which were made for her by Elsa Schiaparelli. Doff, my mother, was a born entertainer.

The Mundys descended from Godfrey, 1ˢᵗ Count of Mondaye, a Norman noble who inhabited the Abbey of Fecamp and legend has it was descended from Rollo, the famous Viking. He accompanied William the Conqueror when he invaded England in 1066. In gratitude, the Count of Mondaye had been given lands in Derbyshire where the family prospered. As the title was Norman it has been used discreetly by various of my ancestors in tribute to the founder of our House.

Many members of our family have served the Crown. In 1522 my direct ancestor, John Mundy, was made Lord Mayor of London by Henry VIII and was later knighted for his services in 1529. We have given England, High Sheriffs, a Governor of Jersey, an Admiral of the Fleet, an Undersecretary of State for War and many high-ranking officers in both the Army and the Navy. My family had been Lords of Markeaton in Derbyshire since 1516, and they had resided in the family home, Markeaton Hall, until 1929 when the sole female survivor of an elder branch without issue gave it to a certain Reverend Clark Maxwell who finally donated it to the Corporation in 1929. This upset my father terribly. Unfortunately, after the war, it was allowed to fall into total disrepair and was finally torn down in the sixties. Now, a park honours the family, but only the *Orangerie* and the stables remain of its former grandness.

It was expected that I was to fulfil my duties to Crown and country in the Royal Navy when my turn came. My father was a Major General who had been awarded many medals in the Boer War. A friend of King Alfonso XIII of Spain, he had also been awarded the very prestigious Cross of *Isabel la Católica*. Therefore, when I left Elstree at the age of thirteen, instead of going on to Eton, Harrow or Rugby, they sent me to the Royal Naval College at Dartmouth as a naval cadet to forge myself a career in the Royal Navy. The year was 1936.

Life at Dartmouth was quite exciting. The hard training included many sports. We had one of the best rugby teams that ever existed for boys our age, and we won plenty of games to one or two years older boys, which, at those ages, makes a huge, usually insurmountable, difference. Mark Sudden, one of the greatest Irish scrum halves ever, and a splendid person, coached us. I continued to be in close contact with my good friend Peter Learmond throughout the years. He was in the same ¾ line as me when I played centre ¾, though I often played full back and occasionally forward. The war killed most of the others in the team.

I managed to avoid getting myself beaten at Dartmouth, but poor Peter was always punished for the most ridiculous things. The stupidest of all was for borrowing someone's tracksuit when his own was stolen. For this diabolical sin, he was given twelve official cuts, as they were called, by a huge marine Sergeant Major in front of all cadets and officers. Holding a stick above our heads while trotting or jumping

Rodney Mundy at the Royal Naval College at Dartmouth, 1937

up and down for thirty minutes was a typical punishment for trivial offences. Naturally, I and everyone else were constantly punished in this way.

Whenever time and the officers permitted, we would go roller-skating on the lead roofs of part of the college. However, this led to long queues at the infirmary, as everybody ended up skinning the upper part of their thighs in falls.

Apart from the incessant parades, I remember having to dive every morning, even in winter, after the wake-up call, through the dormitory pool of ice-cold water. The pool was only about three feet deep, so you had to stand in it and then dive through. Our superiors watched us with hawk eyes and made us repeat the exercise several times if we tried to con them. In the end, we would dive in just to save ourselves all the misery.

As it was a long way for my parents to come down from Frensham, Surrey, where we now lived, just to take me out for tea, they had the great idea, one July of renting a small house on the other side of the river Dart, where we were taught sailing.

My mother bought the house in Frensham when my parents left Henley. It had thirteen acres of gardens where my mother built a grass tennis court, which the weather hardly allowed us to use, and thirty-nine acres of fields that provided a little rough shooting: an odd rabbit, partridge or pheasant. There was a stream at the bottom of the property full of water rats and fish, such as small roach. Nearby, mother built a cottage for our cook, a gipsy called Bailey, whom we called Ma Bailey. She was the best cook we ever had. The old house had a lovely entrance hall with a huge fireplace that in winter was always full of burning logs, and a large drawing room leading out onto a vast lawn bordered with flowerbeds. To the left of the drawing-room was a good-sized oak-panelled dining room that led onto a smaller lawn with a large fishpond full of goldfish and a few Muscovy ducks. Opposite the dining room, at the bottom of the garden, was a large oast house in which we built a music room that had excellent acoustics. It was my mother's sole domain where she centred her spirit playing her Bluthner grand piano. She had learnt to play in Dresden becoming a virtuoso, and she had a beautiful mezzo-soprano voice, which her artistic friends had the privilege to enjoy on her frequent musical evenings.

In addition to Ma Bailey, who used one of the first Aga cookers with great success, we had a butler called Wilkin, five maids, and at least five gardeners. My father used to direct operations in the garden and worked on it a lot himself as within his detached and pragmatic being, a sensitive and quite an expert gardener hided. He loved to get his hands dirtied in our exquisite orchard and to monitor closely the progress of the fruit trees growing against the walls of the vegetable garden. I, myself had a penchant for gardening, having often mowed the lawns beside Ma Bailey´s eldest son and tasted the unforgettable peaches we grew.

In July 1937, I had an accident, which completely

changed my lifestyle and, therefore, my future, when I fell off a small cliff at Mill Creek and badly injured the muscles and ligaments in my left arm and leg. As a result, I joined my parents for the summer holidays at their home in the south of France, very close to Monte Carlo. The doctors initially prescribed rest, followed by moderate exercise. I was treated by Dr. Linguelia, an Italian muscle and nerve specialist, who recommended swimming for at least two to three hours a day in addition to rehabilitation exercises.

IV

THE COTE D'AZUR
Between July 1937 and October 1940

Our summerhouse was set on a lovely, terraced land overlooking the bay of Cap Ferrat. My parents loved it, and we always extended our holidays as much as possible. It took me about a year to recover completely, which naturally prevented me from returning to Dartmouth. To tell the truth, I was not very sorry at being unable to continue with my naval training, as the South of France was much more entertaining!

A friend of the family, Jack Bassett whom I called Uncle Jack and whose company my mother adored, joined us. It was not long before another friend, Princess Jane Magaloff, the widow of an impoverished Russian aristocrat, also became part of the family.

When Papa passed away in his sleep, soon after our arrival in the south of France, he was only sixty-eight. My mother, not wanting to return to England, decided, as Papa had been so fond of the Côte d'Azur, to bury him in Nice. She then rented out the house in Surrey to Sir Anthony Eden, who at the time was Under Secretary of Foreign Affairs. After a period of mourning, we continued with our lives. I loved my carefree life. I was nearly sixteen,

Dorothy Mundy, Countess of Mondaye photographed by William Bird in 1923.

Lt. General Robert Charles Mundy, Count of Mondaye

handsome, spoke fluent French and Spanish, my beloved Mama gave me an extremely generous allowance and I felt like a man. That summer, I had my first sexual experience, when a Hungarian countess who doubled me in age seduced me and taught me how to love a woman. Soon I discovered the secrets of seduction and apparently excelled at them.

The South of France was at the time a haven for the rich and famous; royalty mingled with American billionaires and impoverished Russian nobles. Everybody had a good time. I had many friends among the young scions of the Russian nobility, and we received many invitations, as we liked to party hard. Prince Basil Nakashidze, Prince Chervachedze, Prince Igor Trubestkoy, and I were inseparable. We were known as the Four Musketeers! Being slightly older than I was, they taught me many tricks for living on the edge.

Many of these Russian families had lost everything during the Bolshevik Revolution and were now obliged to work in order to support themselves. They worked as taxi-drivers, porters at the top hotels, and waiters in the most fashionable restaurants, displaying always a great sense of humour. I found it highly amusing when former courtiers recognised them and addressed them by their formal titles; it always seemed to happen in the most awkward situations!

Igor Trubestkoy was in his late twenties, very handsome and utterly broke. He had quite a reputation with the women, and in the party circuit, it was rumoured that he was very well endowed. One night, at a private party in a Russian restaurant, an eccentric American millionaire dared him to

Prince Igor Trubetskoy in 1951

Princess Jane Magaloff, Uncle Jack and Dorothy Mundy, Countess of Mondaye show it off and offered him a large sum of money if he did so. Igor got up swiftly from the table, went into the kitchen, and returned, a few minutes later, with his massive erect penis on a silver tray, surrounded by beluga caviar. A perplexing silence took over the room as he casually went around the table, asking us to help ourselves, which we did while trying to keep a straight face. I noticed some would have rather helped themselves to the hot-blooded sausage, but my choice was clear; caviar for me, thank you.

At night, if no other plans came our way, we used to go to the Sporting Club in Monte Carlo and dance to the music of Lecuona and his Cuban Boys. They were undoubtedly the best Latino band that has ever existed. Afterwards, we would often go for a swim and then sleep on the beach until it was time for breakfast.

That summer was my initiation as a socialite. I mingled with people from a broad array of backgrounds, people that had different beliefs, passions, senses of humour, and ways of looking at life. Soon I was to become a great adept at making small talk and reading between the lines.

On one occasion, I went to dine at the Palace in Monte Carlo with Mama, Uncle Jack, and Princess Jane. I think it was to celebrate some anniversary of the Grimaldi´s and Prince Louis II was the host. I was introduced to Crown Prince Rainier, who was just a year younger than I was.

On another occasion, at the Sporting Club, Igor introduced me to the Marquis of San Felice, who was Mussolini's consul in Monte Carlo. He was a man of refined features and of course, a passionate fascist. He, in turn, introduced me to Baron Klaus von Jettenbach who, Basil Nakashidze explained, was one of the wealthiest men in Germany and an avid art collector. Little did I realize then that our paths would cross again.

*

"Rodney, would you like to spend the winter in France? asked my mother unexpectedly while we were having breakfast on the veranda.

I was thrilled!

"What a great idea. I feel so recovered that I can go skiing then." I said with enthusiasm.

"It's too soon for that," she said disapprovingly.

"Don't worry, I will be fine and anyway it is still a few months away."

"Let the boy go, darling. It will do him good," said Uncle Jack as he appeared with Princess Jane by his side, having both just risen from bed.

"Oh, Jack, you are going to spoil him. You are worse than Rodney, she said to him as she kissed him good morning. Jack winked at me with complicity.

Mama did spoil me in many ways but she was such a formidable role model that she knew giving me so much freedom would do me no harm. Uncle Jack was such a support to her and adored her. He took my father's place and though it was never talked about I knew that they were lovers and I was delighted to see her so happy. Delightful

Jane was so different from my mother. She was outrageous, outspoken, and terribly amusing with her husky unrefined accent in contrast to my mother's subdued although extravagant elegance, her discretion and her *savoir faire*. This family set-up did raise a few eyebrows, but mummy found it extremely amusing. I loved them dearly.

I was feeling quite recovered from my injuries and wanted to go skiing; so, as soon as there was enough snow, I took off for Alp d'Huez, taking Igor as my guest. We stayed with friends of his, who owned a chalet, and we had a great time, enjoying the slopes as much as the party atmosphere.

One evening, we met a stunning woman called Princess Niloufer Mourad. She was the daughter of the Sultan of Turkey and had been married to the son of the Nizam of Hyderabad. The Nizam was known for being one of the wealthiest men in the world but a notorious miser. She was in her early forties, and both, Igor and I, found her painfully attractive, especially as she kept us both at a distance. But we became terrific friends and had a lot of fun together.

To my surprise, she asked me to accompany her to Paris. How could I refuse such an enticing offer? Without thinking it once, I left an unhappy Igor behind and set off for the city of lights in the company of one of the most beautiful women in the world. I was over the moon at being the chosen. I was ecstatic with anticipation, but my daydream soon ended when the morning after our arrival, I discovered the reason

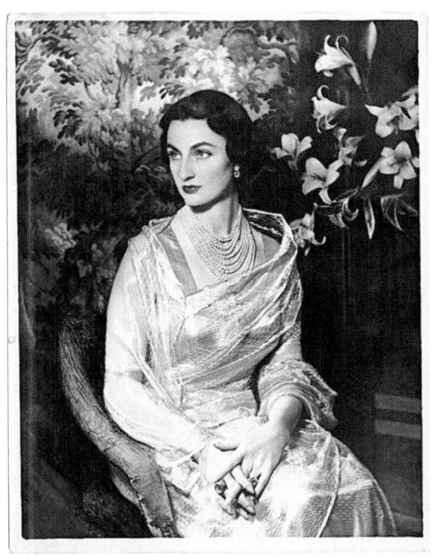

HIH Princess Niloufer Murad of Turkey, Princess of Hyderabad for the trip. Niloufer showed me the most fantastic emerald and diamond necklace. The deep green of the stones was the exact colour of her eyes. I presumed it had been a gift from the Nizam, who had owned a fabulous collection of gems, but I did not ask.

"Rodney, I need you to do me a favour. Please take this to Van Cleef across the street and ask them to value it. It needs to be sold."

I shall never forget the salesclerk's expression when he saw the necklace! It was so large and extravagant that his first impression was that it was a piece of costume jewellery!

We spent about ten days in Paris, which was the time it took the jeweller to arrange the money for the necklace. Princess Niloufer took me to her favourite restaurant, the Tour d'Argent, on the fifth *arrondisement*, which was owned by Claude de Terrail. He would later become an essential member of the resistance and a friend. I was surprised at his brother's not attempting to hide his pro-German sympathies. The Tour was nearly 350 years old and famous for its exquisite duck dishes. Over the years, I became very close to Claude. I dined in his restaurant with my three successive wives, though, naturally, at different periods of my life!

*

The winter passed peacefully, and it was soon summer. Hitler's annexation of Austria and Czechoslovakia hardly seemed to affect us at all, as we lived in a bubble of champagne. In the Cote d´Azur, it was business as usual, and I was ready for another crazy summer. As I had entirely recovered from my injuries, I intended to get back into sports again.   I played tennis every day with King Adolf Gustaf V of Sweden, who was a charming elderly gentleman. He lived close to us, perched like an eagle, in the Château Eza and was often a guest at my mother's *soirees*.

Apart from swimming, which I continued to practise regularly, I also did a lot of water skiing and soon became one of the best water skiers on the coast. I taught many friends, including Lord Beaverbrook, who was not yet Lord B. I guess sports helped me survive through the summer's excesses.

In June, the most talked about news was that the Duke and Duchess of Windsor had taken an apartment at the Hotel de Cap d'Antibes while work was completed under the supervision of Elsie Mendl on the house they had bought, the twelve-acre Château de la Cröe.

Mama's friends spent hours speculating as to what the house would be like, who would receive the Duke and Duchess, and how the British residents would react to their presence. The abdication crisis had been quite traumatic, but it must be said in favour of the ex-king that, at the beginning of his exile, he behaved impeccably in order not to embarrass his brother, the new King George VI.

Mama, delighted to receive an invitation for dinner at Somerset Maughan's house in Cap Ferrat at which the Windsors would be the guests of honour, was terribly excited. She was to finally go alone and appease her curiosity

The Duke and Duchess of Windsor in their home of the Cote d'Azur so, Uncle Jack drove her there at the arranged time.

The next day she appeared brisk and matinal at breakfast and had a broad smile on her face.

"So was your *soiree* Mama?"

"Delightful in the end but tense to start with. When they arrived, Somerset introduced us to her as Her Royal Highness the Duchess of Windsor, and I curtsied despite myself to relieve the charged atmosphere."

"Nothing wrong with that Mama. She is after all the wife of a former king" I said knowing how difficult it must have been for her as she was so strict with protocol matters.

"It was all rather sad, and I felt sorry for them."

"How is she?" I asked.

"She is a very odd woman, probably the oddest I have ever met. She is not very bright but extremely good-willed"

"So, she is not the evil witch, Mama!" I exclaimed.

"The duke is besotted by her, and she does love him very much. Though by marrying the King[8] she did put the monarchy at risk. Now that I have met her, I will never say she is evil again though it is crystal clear to me that she would have never made a good queen." Mama said, accepting that her preconceptions about the Duchess were ill-conceived.

"Why?" Asked Princess Jane?

"She is the American woman *par excellence,* so she speaks in this hideous Southern accent and though wildly good-natured and friendly I just can't imagine her as our queen."

---

[8] King Edward VIII, Duke of Windsor after the abdication

"It's a shame as the duke in his role as monarch would have modernised the monarchy and brought it into touch. After all, Churchill was one of his greatest champions!" Uncle Jack intervened.

"Yes, you might be right, though King George has many more low-key qualities than the duke. He is not only a very decent man, but he also has a sense of public service that the duke by abdicating proved not to have. I think that we are better off as we are now, especially if we consider what is going on with the Germans." Mama concluded.

"You might be right, darling," Uncle Jack assented.

"And how is the duke?" I asked.

"He is less small than I thought and well proportioned. He has his father's[9] eyes, is very elegant and comes across as extremely intelligent, liberal-minded, original and quite capable of leading a conversation or taking part in one. He has completely charmed me!" Mama replied.

"And is she as elegant as they say?" Princess Jane enquired, unable to conceal her excited curiosity.

"She is formidable to look at, and she was beautifully dressed."

"What did she wear Doff?"

"A lovely burgundy Balenciaga with crinoline."

I looked at Uncle Jack and without exchanging a word between us, we got up, said our farewells and left Mama and

---

[9] King George V

H.M King Zahir Shah of Afghanistan

HM King Peter II of Yugoslavia

Princess Jane to their conversation.

Our home was the venue of many garden parties, teas, and formal dinners. Among our regular guests were King Peter II of Yugoslavia and the Agha Khan III. I saw His Majesty many years later in London where he lived at Claridge's after going into exile. The Aga Khan who had been President of the League of Nations used to come with the beautiful Yvette Blanche Labrousee, who had been crowned Miss France in 1930. In 1944, she married him; thus, becoming the Begum of the Ismaelites. King Zahir Shah of Afghanistan also was a regular that summer. Whenever he could escape from his responsibilities in Kabul, he enjoyed the South of France. History has been very unjust to him because he was an enlightened monarch that brought his backward country into the 20th century. Since he was deposed in 1973 the country is in a state of constant civil war and is still today suffering the terrible consequences.

I clearly remember Lord Alfred Douglas, or Bosie as he was known to his friends. He had been Oscar Wilde's lover, which had caused a massive scandal in Victorian society. When I met him, he was in his late sixties, and I always had the impression, by the way, he looked at me and praised me, that he fancied me. Although he adored my mother, and he would recite his poems to her and her friends, he often quarrelled with her because of Churchill. Mamma was very fond of him as a politician. Still, Bosie disliked him intensely and was always telling her what an awful man he was. Churchill sued Lord Douglas for libel on more than one

Nicolae Titulesco

occasion though he, naturally, had at stake more important things than worrying about what Bosie might think or say about him.

Another fascinating person who was a regular visitor was Nicolae Titulescu. He used to sit with his charming family around our pool and hold court in French for the other Rumanian guests that my mother always invited whenever he came. It amazed me how upper-class Rumanians always spoke in French to each other, and I even wondered if they actually knew their own language. Titulescu was a statesman whose desire for peace, stability, and good neighbourly relations was out of step with the rise of fascism throughout the continent. As Rumania moved closer to Germany, Titulescu's close ties to France became a political liability and his King, Carol II, forced him to retire and leave Bucharest.

One day after lunch, Titulescu wrote in my mother's scrapbook a phrase that has always marked me, *'To avoid war, one must not be afraid to wage it.'* It was a pointed remark for those days. We had many political discussions and talked about the role of the League of Nations of which he had been president. He foresaw the disaster and devastation that was about to befall Europe.

By summer 1939, the war was in the air, and people seemed very worried. Rumours abounded as to who had Nazi sympathies, and at my mother's parties, the talk was of nothing else. I had discovered the good life and was determined to indulge in it for as long as my mother continued giving me the money or history allowed me to do so.

On September 1st, 1939, German troops invaded Poland,
after which Great Britain and France declared war on Germany. Our lives were soon to change dramatically.

As we could still receive money from England and I was too young to go to war, we decided it was better to stay put and wait for the war to finish.

Despite the overall atmosphere of gloom during the winter of 39/40, we were all full of hope. We expected our troops to be victorious against the Germans but soon realized that we were no match for the well-trained and disciplined German war machine.

We had heard that when German troops were advancing towards Paris, the Duke of Windsor had sent the Duchess to Biarritz. He had then abandoned his post at the N° 1 Military Mission at Nogent-sur-Marne, where he was liaison officer of the French and British armies. We heard that he had closed the house on 24 Boulevard Suchet and had followed the Duchess south to La Chröe. Mother was quite upset about the whole situation. What on earth were they doing in a country that was about to lose the war against the Germans? What if they were made prisoners? However, the Windsors seemed entirely oblivious to this possibility. They finally came to their senses and left for Spain on the 19th of June, and we all felt quite relieved. At least they were in a neutral country and relatively safe until the King decided where they should go.

*

On June 14th, 1940, Paris fell to the Germans, and on the 22nd France was forced to sign the infamous Armistice by which the country was divided. One half under the direct control of the Nazis and the other under Petain and his Vichy-based government.

We soon heard rumours about what the new fascist government had in mind for citizens of unfriendly countries. We were all to be rounded up and sent to prisoner-of-war camps in the centre of France until the end of the war. Socialists, communists, and people of political affiliations other than the far-right policies of the new regime had a grim future planned for them. We soon lost all hope as now only Britain stood against Hitler.

After the Armistice, our lives changed drastically, and no one came to the house. So, it was quite a surprise when one morning the servants announced the visit of Enrico Giglioli, whom we called Harry. He was the Italian Consul in Cannes and had been a regular at Mama's parties. He was in a cheerful mood and could not hide his delight at the prospect of a fascist Europe.

"*Comtessa*," he said to my mother, "you and your family are safe in the new order. I shall speak to the authorities to make sure you are not disturbed so that you can live here peacefully until we win the war."

She was quite fond of him because, like most well-bred Italians, he had good manners, was always impeccably dressed and was a charmer. Still, she had always avoided discussing politics with him. Now she was prepared for a confrontation.

"Harry, your new order will not win this war. It is lunacy! I do not wish to be rude, but I must ask you to leave this house immediately and to please never return at least until we win the war. Unfortunately, despite how fond we are of you in this house, we are enemies now."

The Italian Consul kissed my mother's hand and left without uttering another word. We never saw Enrico again.

The atmosphere was gloomy. Nobody could be trusted anymore, and we were apprehensive about our immediate future with neither money nor friends. General de Gaulle had formed a government in exile called *France Libre*, and soon resistance cells were created throughout France.

We never knew if it had anything to do with the incident with Enrico Giglioli or not. Still, a couple of days later, the police came to the house and gave us fifteen minutes in which to pack and abandon our home. We were taken to the Hotel de la Barbacan, which was run by a friendly French family whom we assumed were pro the new fascist government. We shared the hotel with SS officers. It was all somewhat awkward as I soon found out that the cook was the leader of the local *maquis* and held meetings in the cellar while we and the SS were upstairs! The *Milice Français*, which was the equivalent of the Gestapo, kept a close eye on us too. Danger loomed everywhere; the friendly cook told me people were disappearing after the militia had taken them in for questioning. We felt very uneasy when our passports were suddenly confiscated, but things were about to get even worst.

Very early, one morning, the militia came to the hotel and dragged us out of our rooms. Mama became very agitated; she was furious. She was wearing her nightgown, and she considered it an unforgivable humiliation to be seen like that by all. She was a very dignified woman and loathed any form of bad manners. To her, this was the ultimate insult, and she was outraged. The captain slapped her across the face, and she fell to the floor. Princess Jane and I jumped on him and, had it not been for the rapid intervention of the *patron*, we would almost certainly have been shot on the spot.

We were forced to dress immediately and pack our belongings. Then, we were taken in a lorry full of foreigners, guarded by five Gestapo officers and members of the SS, to an internment camp in Foix.

It was a very welcome surprise to come across a good friend of mine on the journey. He was an Australian called Fred McEvoy.

Foix was a prisoner-of-war camp for foreigners that had many Spanish inmates, exiles from the Civil War and now persona undesirables under the Vichy regime. We were under the watchful eye of Petain's acolytes. We were their 'guests', as they were fond of calling us. We were reasonably well treated, but there was not much to do, and I became extremely restless at such inactivity. My mother, Uncle Jack, Princess Jane, and I all shared a room with bunk beds and an outside toilet. Facilities were very Spartan in comparison with the luxuries to which we were accustomed. Still, at least we were all together and safe.

Fred and I were soon busily hatching all sorts of plans to escape from the camp. We held lengthy conversations outdoors, at which he confided he had plenty of money to bribe a guard. We spent some time figuring out which of them would be the ideal candidate. We finally decided to approach a rather shy and friendly one called Jean-Marc, who seemed quite uncomfortable with his job. We could not have chosen better. Jean-Marc not only agreed to help us but also turned out to be a member of the resistance. He would not accept any money, only enough to arrange all the details of the escape and to pay the guide who would lead us through the Pyrenees into Spain.

"I can arrange for you to leave France for Spain through the mountains via Andorra. A friend of mine knows a Spanish guide who was a former captain in the Red Army. He received five death sentences and is the most wanted man in both France and Spain." The next crossing was to be on my birthday, October 27th, 1942, in just three days.

Our family farewell was a terribly sad affair. For the first time in my life, I was aware that I might never see my mother again and that my life was in dire danger. She tried to convince me to stay, giving me all sorts of reasons why I should not leave, but there was nothing she could say that would make me change my mind.

Before sunrise, on the eve of my eighteenth birthday, Fred and I escaped from the camp with the help of Jean-Marc. My only belongings were a gold watch, a silver cigarette case that my father had given me, and an astrakhan fur coat. We walked through the countryside for a couple of hours and arrived at a marketplace where several members of the resistance met with us. It, then, took us two weeks to reach what we thought would be safety in Spain. The most wanted man was called Mario, and he went about his business while we followed him, without a word. I told him that there was no need to murder us on the way, as upon arrival, he would get the coat and watch as payment for his services. The other members of the expedition were a few Jewish families escaping from the Nuremberg Rules that deprived them of the most basic human rights.

The Pyrenees were heavily patrolled, and we were forced to travel at night in freezing temperatures and with hardly any food to put into our mouths.

We hid for three days in Mario's home in the Principality of Andorra, which was neutral territory, before finally reaching the safety of Spain. The reason for this break was that I had started the trip wearing a pair of boots, and my feet became so sore that Mario decided I needed to nurse them and rest. I continued the rest of the march wearing a pair of espadrilles.

V

SHATTERED DREAMS

As soon as we entered Spain illegally and without documents, the group was divided.

My good friend Fred McEvoy and I went to the home of the notary of Gosol, where due to exhaustion we slept for a couple of days. Fred was an Australian that I had met when he was runner up to a water-skiing race that I had one from Cannes to Monte Carlo. Fred was close to thirty and was very popular with the wealthy widows. He had confessed to me how thrilled they were to give him large sums of money in exchange for his attention. I completely understood the reasons for his success as not only he was very handsome and reminded me of Errol Flynn, but he was extraordinarily enchanting and could seduce anyone. He came from old money, so he only worked for pleasure. He had tried to persuade me to join his lucrative trade as he had more widows that he could satisfy. I declined his offer as in those days, not only I had plenty of money, but I had more than enough female admirers.

We had not fully recovered when we had to meet the British Consul in Barcelona, Mr Scheuel. The plan was to board a small fishing boat at the harbour and be taken to a British destroyer out at sea that would take us to the safety of Gibraltar. It would be New Year's Eve so the year could not start in a better way!

Once onboard, I realised that something was awfully wrong. Suddenly the motor stopped, and the fisherman caused such a riot that they attracted the attention of the police who reached us and came on board. Later, we found out that thc British Consul was, in fact, an agent of the Germans and sold out those he helped to escape to Franco's police, that collaborated with the Gestapo.

As Fred and I had no documents, I tried to bribe the officer that I thought was in charge who instead of accepting the bribe started yelling at me. Both Fred and I understood that we were in serious trouble. I signalled to Fred, and we both dived into the cold Mediterranean Sea with the hope of being able to swim to the coast on that moonless night, but the sea was too rough.

I heard the crazed firing of guns. The guards were randomly shooting into the night, trusting that sooner than later, they would hit the target. We were in serious trouble.

The sea did not let me swim in a straight line, nor did it make me advance much. I was frightened and knew that I had very little chance to get ashore alive. "*Me rindo*, I surrender.." I started to yell.

Within seconds, the police patrol boat was upon me, blinding me with an intense spotlight as they dragged me on board. Fred was shivering in a corner.

We spent the night in a cell, accused of entering the country illegally, attempting to bribe an officer, trying to resist arrest, and of being spies. A few days later, we found ourselves in Barcelona's notorious Modelo Prison with our heads shaved and sentenced without a trial to life imprisonment.

Our future was not in our hands, it depended on the outcome of the war, or so we thought at the time.

I was just twenty-one and the idea of spending a lifetime in such a hellhole was more than I could bear. I missed my mother and wondered whether I would not have done better listening to her. Our cell was filthy, smelly, and lice-infested with just a hole in the corner for a W.C. There was not enough space for all of us to lie down at the same time, and we slept on the concrete floor without a mattress.

There were nine of us. One of our cellmates was a Frenchman called Jean Pierre Melville, who later became a very famous film director. The others included a communist priest and some common criminals. I argued with the priest about theology as he tried unsuccessfully to convert me to Catholicism. Mealtimes were an exercise on active visualization. We were only given a small piece of dry brown bread and a bowl of dirty water with a tiny morsel of half-rotten meat floating in it. Following the example of Jesus in the Canaan wedding, I tried to transmute, in my imagination, of course, without success the filthy soup into a tasty broth. But, and perhaps thanks to the priest who continuously prayed for us all, the guards were avid for a bit of extra money and bought us whatever we could afford. Fred and Jean Pierre indulged in chocolates while I, not knowing how long we would be there, bought an onion a day, which I ate

Confirmation of the entry to the Modelo Prison dated 5th January 1943

DEPARTAMENTO MARITIMO
DE
CARTAGENA

CAÑONERO "CANALEJAS"

JUZGADO DE INSTRUCCION

58312

Tengo el honor de informar a
Vd., que el detenido RODNEY MUNDY,
desde el dia de su ingreso en esa
Cárcel Modelo, se encuentra procesa-
do y en prisión preventiva, como re-
sultas de procedimiento que se le
instruye.

Dios guarde a Vd. muchos años.

A bordo, Barcelona 15 Enero 1943

EL TENIENTE CORONEL AUDITOR JUEZ INSTRUCTOR

P.A

José Luis Diaz Herrera.

PRISION CELULAR
DE
BARCELONA

18 ENE 1943

REGISTRO Entrada n.° 1640
Salida n.°

Sr. Director de la Carcel Modelo de Barcelona.

3

Letter informing the naval authorities that Rodney Mundy was in custody dated 18th January. The British Embassy was in negotiations for his liberation.

like an apple, and I am sure that it kept me healthier than the others.

Luckily, it was not hot. The cell was full of insect holes, and if it had been summer, we would have been eaten alive. We believed no one knew where we were, which only added to our desperation.

Once a week, a doctor in a dirty white overall would make his rounds. The guards would order us to pull our trousers down, and the doctor would inject us, using the same dirty needle, with some unknown substance. Despite this or because of it, we were continuously sick. The stench in the cell was unbearable. We were not allowed to wash, which made matters even worst. Fred, Jean Pierre, and I became close friends, and this 'camaraderie' made our ordeal more bearable.

I spent hours recollecting the events that had landed me in that pigsty. Maybe Mama had been right all along, and I should have stayed with them in the camp. I missed her and the marvellous life I had once known. The sameness of the long and aimless days in prison was suddenly broken on the morning of the 23rd of January. The guard handed our clothes back to us and informed us that we had a visitor. It was the British Consul in Cartagena, Mr Leverkus who was also temporarily in charge of the British Consulate in Barcelona. He explained to our delight that Mr Scheuel had left his post in dishonour, having been involved in duplicitous activities and duly discharged. Mr Leverkus had a strong German accent that caused us certain misgivings.

Departamento Maritimo
de
Cartagena
Cañonero "CANALEJAS"

Juzgado de Instruccion

Ruego a Vd. entregue al Cabo de
la dotacion del "Canalejas" porta-
dor de la presente orden a los de-
tenidos a disposicion de este Juzgado, RODNEY MUNDY y ANDRES MONTES
que deberán traer todos sus efec-
tos por haber dispuesto el Excmo.
Sr. Capitan General del Departamento
su traslado a Cartagena a bordo de
este buque.

Dios guarde a Vd. muchos años
A bordo Barcelona 23 de enero de 1943

El T. de N. SECRETARIO,

Daniel Yusty

Sr. Director de la Carcel Modelo.

4

The letter requesting the transfer of prisoners dated 23rd January 1943

Still, noticing our dismay, he quickly explained that although he had been the German Consul until Hitler's rise to power, he had been able to switch nationality due to his mother being English.

He was an amiable fellow that could not offer us immediate relief. However, he promised that soon we would be transferred to the Naval Prison in Cartagena, which we would find much more bearable, and that he would speak to Sir Samuel Hoare, the British Ambassador in Madrid, and see what they could do to help us.

As promised, two weeks later, we moved to our new abode. Cartagena was a prominent Spanish naval base, and the prison was the responsibility of the Spanish Navy. Upon our arrival, we were disinfected, washed, and given a clean change of clothes.

Fred, Jean Pierre and I were in high spirits; compared to the Modelo Prison this was a five-star hotel. We were four to a cell, which had two bunk beds with sheets: an absolute luxury. We were allowed to exercise in the patio, the food tasted delicious, and we had access to cigars, cigarettes, and other delicacies. Our wardens treated us with courtesy, and we soon developed a friendly relationship. The three months spent in Barcelona were a nightmare I wanted to forget.

Our new cellmate was a Jew from Alsace called Fred Kempler. Nature had not endowed him with physical beauty, yet he had an enchanting smile and vibrant twinkling eyes. He was a sturdy little fellow who, being no more than 5´7´´ tall, had become an SS officer, achieving an amazing and incredible feat for a Jew especially as his features were distinctly Jewish. He had managed to get hold of a plan of the gun deployment along the Brittany coast and to escape via the same route that we had taken, but once in Spain, the police arrested him for not having any papers. He was tough, wiry, and an expert in weapons, including knives.

Kempler had asked me to tell the British authorities he had some vital information that he would give the British Ambassador if he secured his release, gave him British papers, and arranged for him to go to England. Therefore, the first day Mr Leverkus came to see us, he arranged to meet Kempler, who would not tell anything he had not told me before. The Consul promised he would speak to the Ambassador but explained there was not much they could do because he was a Frenchman.

Mr Leverkus visited us quite regularly. He gave us fruit and sweets and kept us up to date on how the war was going. He informed us that Winston Churchill, the British Prime Minister, had secured the friendship of US President Roosevelt, who was hesitant to enter the war but had ordered the American Secret Service to work in close collaboration with the British. Britain was under constant threat of a German invasion and London was being bombed on a regular basis. The situation was desperate, and I felt utterly frustrated, being locked up and unable to help.

Six months after our arrival, Mr. Leverkus finally bought us the news we had been waiting so anxiously for. The British Embassy had secured Fred's and my release, and we would be leaving for Madrid the next day. Unfortunately, Fred Kempler and Jean Pierre were to remain behind. I never saw Jean Pierre again, although I did see most of his films.

The day prior to our departure, Mr. Leverkus bought us some clean clothes for the trip. Fred and I travelled on a sleeper train from Cartagena to Madrid. The Civil Guards, looking for communists, anarchists, and all those without papers, constantly stopped the train and violently dragged them off it. Fortunately, we were carrying provisional passports; but, after our ordeal, the trip seemed endless, as we could not be sure, we would make it to Madrid.

VI

A NEW LIFE

As arranged, Captain Hillgarth, the Naval Attaché at the British Embassy, was at the station waiting for us. He was a tall thin handsome man with bushy eyebrows, a wide nose, and straight thin lips that made him look humourless. He was not the typical Englishman. Because of his dark looks, he could easily have been mistaken for a Spaniard. He was wearing an impeccably tailored suit that looked as if made to measure in Saville Row. With him was Alan Lubbock, the Military Attaché. We were asked to say our farewells.

"Won't we be going to England together?" Fred asked surprised.

"No. You will be driven to the airport now and Rodney will be taken to the Embassy," Lubbock replied

"That probably means that they have good news for you Rodney. News about your mother." Fred said reassuringly.

The farewells became quite emotional as we hugged. We had been through so much together.

After the war, he returned to the South of France where he resumed his life as a gigolo. We would meet again in the early fifties and sail on the Black Swan together. Fred left with Alan Lubbock. An old, polished Ford with diplomatic plates was waiting for Captain Hillgarth and we were driven

Captain Alan Hillgarth

by a middle-aged Englishman with a Northern accent to the Hotel Nacional, opposite the station.

"All Embassy drivers are English as we can't trust the Spaniards. They are all spies! By the way, I bought a suit for you. I hope it fits."

"Oh thanks. I don't have any clothes with me." I said gratefully.

"You'll have to go shopping then. Madrid is now very conservative, and jackets must be always worn. Please take a quick bath and change as the Ambassador is waiting for you."

On the way to the Embassy, I tried to engage the captain in conversation, but he hardly spoke. Alan Hillgarth seemed not to be very generous with his words or his smiles. The expression on his face barely changed. He spoke in a low-pitched voice and looked older than he was, as he admitted being under forty. For some reason, there was something in him that I immediately liked.

Madrid looked grim. The buildings were dilapidated and in need of paint. Most of the people I saw on the streets looked thin and tired and were shabbily dressed. The Embassy was located on *Calle Fernando el Santo*, where I was to meet Samuel Hoare, the Ambassador. As we turned the corner, I saw the Union Jack and I somehow had a feeling of relief. I was certain they would have news on my mother and that I would soon be sent back to England to help in the war effort. A pair of armed *Guardia Civiles*, in their green uniforms and wearing their bicorn shiny hats stood guard.

Sir Samuel Hoare, British Ambassador to Spain

They did not look to friendly.

Once inside the Embassy I followed Captain Hillgarth to the Ambassador's office. Samuel Hoare was sitting behind a large mahogany desk under a portrait of the King. He was a cultured, intelligent man who was a prominent member of the Conservative party. He had been Foreign Secretary and First Lord of the Admiralty with Baldwin and Chamberlain, and Churchill had only recently appointed him Ambassador to Madrid with the special mission to keep Spain out of the war. I later found out that his relationship with the Prime Minister was not as good as it seemed like the ambassador was resentful at not having been appointed Viceroy of India.

As we entered the spacious room, he stood and shook my hand firmly as Alan introduced us. He smiled broadly. A small man, with thin white hair and expressive blue eyes, he was wearing a morning coat.

The three of us sat comfortably in his study. I asked about my mother, but there was no news. I felt very disappointed. A maidservant came in carrying a tray with tea. The Ambassador proceeded to explain the plans England had for me.

"You're a fine young man, and your family has served our country for generations. Now it is your turn young man," he started saying.

"When do I return to the navy Sir?" I asked as I was eager to go back.

"We have other plans for you, Rodney. You are young, intelligent, speak fluent Spanish and have the right upbringing to infiltrate Spanish high society. I have heard that you have many social skills and we have decided that you are perfect for the job."

"What job? What am I supposed to do?" I asked incredulously.

"Promote pro-British sentiments," he said adding after a long pause, "these are very dangerous times. We need you to stay in Madrid and obtain as much information as possible. It is vital for us to know who our friends and who our enemy's friends are. From time to time, we will feed you bits of information that you will nonchalantly reveal to certain people. Go out and enjoy yourself. Madrid is a great city. I will give a dinner party in early October, at which you will meet the key people. At this time of year, all the wives and children of the most important families are in the north on holiday. They leave in July and return at the end of September. The husbands stay behind in Madrid with their *queridas*[10] and only join their families at weekends and for a few weeks in August. So now, may I suggest that you get to know the city and discover all it has to offer? Captain Hillgarth will be your liaison officer, and he will give you some money. Of course, we will pay your hotel bills and your expenses. You must inform him of everything you see and hear. Rodney do not trust anybody. The Germans have spies everywhere."

The Madrid heat was dry and unbearable, but it was so

---

[10] Lovers

wonderful to be free that I did not complain.

The devastation of the city shocked me. During the civil war, it had been besieged for three years, and it had obviously paid a hefty price for being Spain's capital. The suffering that the people had endured, was obvious everywhere. Women with patched and mended shawls mostly dressed in black as a sign of having lost a loved one and expressionless beaten men roamed around the city. There were many skinny bare foot children dressed in rags begging in the streets or playing in the gutters. Most buildings were riddled with bullet holes if not destroyed, a reminder of the horrors of the civil war. Outside of the better areas, heaps of stones overgrown with weeds stood as mute witnesses to many fallen bombs. Public transport consisted of the underground, trams, and some ancient taxis that, like the few private cars, ran on charcoal and weaved their way around mule-drawn carts and bicycles that crisscrossed the city, carrying all sorts of produce, whilst the nobility still moved around in their beautiful horse-drawn carriages. Posters of Franco with the symbol of the Falange[11], the yokes and arrows were plastered everywhere. Even the Nazi swastika flew beside the Spanish flag in a few buildings!

I soon discovered that, unlike France or England, there was no middle class at all. The gap between classes was wide. The aristocracy was divided into two groups: the Grandees

---

[11] National Socialist Party that backed General Franco

or *Grandes de España*, which included all dukes and few other titles that had been granted this distinction by the different monarchs, and the rest of the nobility. The former ones had the privilege, under the fallen monarchy, of being members of the Council of Grandees, an advisory body to the Crown. They even could request an audience with the Sovereign at any time, as they were considered cousins by the King! They also had the right to a diplomatic passport which Franco duly supplied. This was because most of them had supported him during the Civil War against communism but now some of them mocked him in private.

The summer passed very quickly. I visited the Prado Museum, which still had many empty spaces of the paintings that had been taken down during the war for safekeeping and had still not been hanged. It was very quiet- hardly any visitors and it had an abandoned feeling about it. I admired Goya's frescos at San Antonio de la Florida. I also explored outside Madrid and visited the impressive Escorial and the Segovia Aqueduct. But most of all I met with my liaison officer, as I had much to learn.

In one of my first meetings with Alan Hillgarth, who was wearing his naval uniform, he explained that Winston Churchill had recently reorganized the Secret Service and set up the Secret Intelligence Service better known as MI6. Alan's unofficial job in Madrid was to be in charge of MI6 and MI9 operations in Spain. The latter consisted of rescuing refugees and prisoners of war and getting them to safety. Churchill, himself, had personally offered him the job and had called him to London. In 1933, Hillgarth had been appointed British Vice Consul in Mallorca, and it was there where the two men met for the first time. During the Civil War, Hillgarth had demonstrated the political skills that had led him to be offered the post in Madrid.

One day at the end of September, after one of our meetings, I walked past the German school in Madrid and was shocked to see a large group of German youths, in Nazi uniforms, marching down the street and singing fascist songs. Next morning when I went to see Hillgarth, Lubbock was there, and they put me in the loop that Franco had taken a pro-axis non-belligerence stance, which meant the Gestapo moved about freely and the German war vessels and submarines docked for supplies at Spanish ports along the country's western coast, Morocco and the Canary Islands. Landing strips had also been made available to German planes, and the Generalissimo helped Germany with strategic war materials, particularly the tungsten that was vital for armour-piercing shells and armour plating. He also permitted the installation of German observation posts, radar installations, and radio interception stations. The reason for this was that Franco had received a lot of support from Hitler and Mussolini during the Civil War and he felt indebted to them; that was the reason why he had sent a unit of over 18,000 soldiers, known as the Blue Division, to fight alongside the Germans in Russia.

"This neutrality is just a joke. Imagine, every week the Gestapo gives the Ministry of the Interior a list of

Hitler and General Franco at the train station in Hendaye on the 23rd October 1943

Ramon Serrano-Suñer and General Franco

undesirables!" Alan Lubbock interrupted. "You can just only imagine what happens to them!"

"The Prime Minister was very worried when Franco met Hitler in Hendaye last October. The possibility that he would finally be persuaded to join the war never had been closer. However, he has yet not made up his mind. Franco is a very shrewd man and knows rebuilding Spain is his main priority and the country is in no position to start a new war. We know that the conditions he demanded from Hitler for his participation were fortunately too much for him to accept, at least for the moment. But things can change if he feels that the Germans have the upper hand in the war so you can imagine how worrying the whole situation is. Of course, it does not help our cause that the newspapers and the radio are widely pro-German."

I had never reflected on the political situation of the moment; I was, after all, quite young. What I had been told and asked to do made quite an impact on me. This was in fact my first real responsibility. One must be inside of intrigue before you can appreciate the thrill of it.

Historians now speculate as to whether Franco understood his conditions would be unacceptable or whether he was just being greedy. Yet the possibility of Spain's joining the war on the German side had been very real during the first part of the conflict and, consequently, Madrid and Lisbon, being neutral, had become operation centres for the intelligence services of the main players. It had been Churchill's idea to set up a network of civilian spies without the knowledge of the Spanish authorities.

*

Alan Hillgarth put me into the picture as to the schemers and plotters in Madrid, explaining in detail, while he showed me photographs of the various people. There had even been a plan the Germans had hatched to kidnap the Duke and Duchess of Windsor. I was stunned by what I learned.

The former king and his American wife had arrived in Spain on July 25th, 1940, in their Buick, followed by an immense amount of luggage. On their arrival, Samuel Hoare informed them that Churchill wished them to return immediately to England.

Madrid was at the time full of German agents. The German Embassy was the largest in the world and the Ambassador, Baron von Stohrer, and his wife not only were guests in the houses of the most prominent Spanish families but also had direct access to Franco and his wife, Doña Carmen, wielding unparalleled influence while Samuel Hoare was rarely invited to the Pardo Palace, the centre of power. They also worked in close collaboration with Franco's brother-in-law, Ramón Serrano Suñer, Spain's Interior Minister. Hoare knew that Madrid could prove too much of a temptation for the Windsors who could easily fall prey to all the flattery and adulation. They had been received everywhere as if the duke were still king, and the duchess was treated like his queen, even by some of the remaining members of the former Spanish Royal family, such as the

The Duke and Duchess of Windsor in Berlin with Hitler 1937

Infante D. Alfonso de Orleans, who was a general in Franco's Air Force. Miguel Primo de Rivera, Marquis of Estella and son of the founder of the Falange and Doña Sol, sister of the Duke of Alba visited their hotel suite, and it was rumoured gave the fascist salute! A very real danger existed of them being lured into the arms of the Germans with the promise of being restored to the throne. After all, the duke's admiration for Hitler was no secret, nor was the duchess' rancour of Britain at what she felt their mistreatment after the abdication.

While Captain Hillgarth was telling me all this, I realized how extremely concerned he was. He barely was able to conceal his indignation, but being a true Englishman, he managed to control his feelings. I was struck by what a highly disciplined man he was; a discipline he had undoubtedly learnt in the Royal Navy.

"During their nine days in Madrid and under the close scrutiny of the ambassador, " he went on explaining, " they visited the city, went to a bullfight, were invited to a flamenco evening by the Count and Countess of Herentals, and were wined and dined by the most prominent fascists.

Mr. Hoare's efforts to persuade them to return to England did not bear any fruit. Alas, the duke demanded to know exactly what post he would be appointed to and was adamant that the duchess be addressed officially as Her Royal Highness! "

"I would have thought that being a duchess, for an absolute nobody like her, would have been sufficient honour!" I interrupted though my mother did say she thought that His Majesty should have allowed her to use the title!

"In hindsight, however," he continued saying undisturbed by my inappropriate comment, "I now believe that His Majesty should have been more generous in this affair. It would have been in our interest to grant her the damned title she so covets, and thus to have lured them both to return home. It would certainly have saved everybody a lot of aggravation. I think that both queens have much influence on the king, and they did not want the duchess anywhere near him. They wished at all costs to prevent the duke's presence from overshadowing that of His Majesty, but in my opinion, the medicine has been worse than the disease."

"So, what happened?" I asked impatiently.

"They were finally persuaded to leave Madrid and in early July they moved to Estoril where they stayed at a villa owned by Ricardo Espiritu Santo, one of the wealthiest men in Portugal and a close friend of Sir Walford Selby, our ambassador there, who had arranged it all. It was in Estoril that the duke received the news from England that they were welcome to return but there would be no royal treatment for the duchess. The decision was final. The Prime Minister, fed up with the duke, sent to Portugal a common friend, Sir Walter Mockton, to offer him the Governorship of the Bahamas and to inform him that British Intelligence had uncovered signs of a Nazi plot to beginning to realize that they found themselves between a rock and a hard place: on one hand, we were pressuring them to take the post in the Bahamas as soon as possible; and on the other, the Germans and their friends were sending envoys to convince them to return to Spain.

We found out later that on July 11th, the German Foreign Minister, Von Ribbentrop, had outlined a plan in a telegram to Baron von Stohrer. The plan was to have the Count and Countess of Herentals and other Spanish friends of the duke invite them for a fortnight's visit to Spain so as not to raise their or the British authorities´ suspicions. Once in Spain, they were to be persuaded to remain there, even if it meant that the Spanish authorities had to arrest them. Under German influence, the duke would be made to see that the Germans wanted peace and it was the Prime Minister who stood in the way. The Germans wanted to force peace on us at whatever cost and were prepared to offer the duke the throne allowing him to make the duchess his queen."

I was flabbergasted. I sat in silence and looked at Alan Hillgarth in disbelief.

"The duke would have found this plan very appealing, but it is still unknown whether he himself had any part in it. It was no secret how attractive a return to Spain seemed to him, nor that he loathed the idea of being sent to a remote outpost of the Empire such as the Bahamas. Baron Oswald von Hoyningen-Huene, the German Ambassador in Lisbon, was a regular at the dinner parties they gave in the Espiritu Santo villa."

I could not believe what I was being told. The fact that the former king could bring himself to sit at his table the Ambassador of a country at which his own country was at war, struck me as incomprehensible!

"Fortunately for us, the duke had left both their passports at the Embassy to obtain return visas for Spain and France, and Sir Walford Selby, had not returned them. It was at this point that Von Ribbentrop, aware of the impasse, arranged for senior agent Walter Schellenberg to go to Lisbon and organize a secret operation to kidnap them and take them to Spain. He was working directly under Himmler's orders."

"But how could they carry out such a plan?" I asked in bewilderment.

"Portuguese friends within the aristocracy were to invite them to a shooting expedition at a mountain estate close to Spain. The border police had been bribed to look the other way while the duke and duchess entered Spain. They were to be escorted to Madrid under Spanish military protection as guests of the Spanish Government. The Germans were to keep their intervention secret and have the couple under surveillance. Fortunately, the whole plot collapsed when, after much hesitation, the duke finally accepted the post in the Bahamas. Frantic last-minute efforts were made and the Spanish Interior Minister, Serrano Suñer, sent the Marquis of Estella to try to persuade them to change their minds on the very eve of their departure for Nassau. They were told that our government planned to have them murdered. Obviously, he was unable to show them any proof, as it was a complete fabrication of the German Intelligence.

To our relief, In the end, they set sail for their new post on August 17th, though, unbelievably, keeping Von Ribbentrop under the mistaken impression that they were still open to other possibilities. You can imagine, Rodney, how uneasy we have all been with this entire affair and I am sure by now you realize how valuable all the information you will gather will be for us."

I had to admit that I fully shared the Naval Attaché's indignation, as the whole incident had put Britain's war effort in jeopardy. How could the Duke of Windsor possibly believe that Hitler could reinstate him on the British throne with Queen Wallis at his side? Had he gone mad? I wondered.

VII

NEST OF SPIES

The dinner at the Embassy went very well and the Ambassador and his wife, Lady Maud, a large and unglamorous but charming woman, introduced me to all their Spanish friends. I have learnt to love Madrid and felt quite at ease amidst the very polite *madrileños*. The autumn temperature was pleasant, and the intense blue of Madrid's clear and crispy sky bewitched me then as much as it does today.

That October I was swamped accepting invitations to different parties, where my host generally introduced me to the whole family, knowing within weeks tout Madrid. I went to partridge shoots in the countryside, which were quite an elaborate affair. Nonetheless, rural life in Spain was primitive, to say the least. Most *fincas*[12] had no electricity or heating, and barely any plumbing. To make matters worse, the roads leading to them were quite dreadful. The landscape of the countryside was empty, broken by a few peasants riding their donkeys. They all looked rather famished and gaunt. I have never been a good shot, but I went through the motions and got on splendidly well with my hosts.

---

[12] Country Estates

On most evenings, I would start the night with a drink at the bar of the Palace Hotel, where a Hungarian pianist Jorge Jalpen played. He was a highly accomplished musician who excelled at the classics.

I soon got used to dining at eleven, which I found extremely civilized. Afterwards, I would go with my new friends to Villa Rosa, the fashionable nightclub, where one could also have dinner.

I took eagerly to my new job and was soon in full waltz with Madrid society. I think the combination of my age and my cosmopolitan education opened me all doors. I befriended not only with people my generation but also their parents who loved to talk and gossip with a foreigner.

The first thing I learnt was to be very discreet. The Gestapo had many informers amongst Spanish civilians, so I limited myself to listening, observing, and making small talk. I got used to being watched and followed, so I had to be extremely cautious.

The smart thing to do in the afternoons was to go for tea to a tea-room named Embassy, situated on the very central *Paseo de la Castellana* and owned by a delightful Irish lady called Margaret Taylor and known to all as Margarita. Embassy was in a remarkable location. Only a small Lutheran church stood between its front door and the entrance to the German embassy, which was festooned with swastika flags. The German embassy was headquarters for Abwehr, the Nazis' intelligence unit, which had about 1,000 spies in Madrid alone.

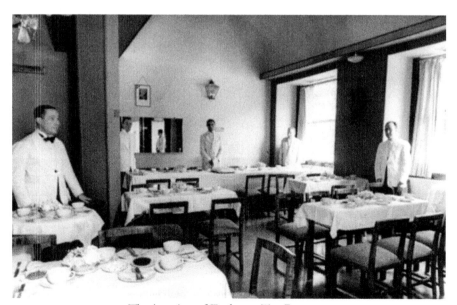

The interior of Embassy Tea Room

MI9 had the task to rescue prisoners of war and help Jews and gentiles escape from the Nazis, being Spain a natural evasion route unit, which had about 1,000 spies in Madrid alone. I soon learnt that Embassy had become the most active escapee rescue centre in Spain. Although the Spanish government accepted their entrance, their evacuation to Portugal and Gibraltar had to be clandestine as the Gestapo was well informed of most activities, and the rescue of Jews through Spain would be unacceptable. It was a fantastic feat and a paradox that such a frivolous place was the centre for such humanitarian activities.

The mixture of Embassy's clients was incredible. Mingling with the old-time aristocracy were many Germans from the embassy on *Paseo de la Castellana* 5, the English crowd with their Spanish friends, and diehard *falangistas*[13]

Prince Max von Hohenlohe was always passing messages to us, to persuade the Ambassador to push for peace, which he naturally refused to do. I once bumped into Princess Elsa Cantacuccene, accompanied by none other than Countess Ciano, daughter of the Duce. This explosive cocktail of people explains the highly charged atmosphere of Embassy that was in those days quite a remarkable place. Margaret Taylor was the sole captain of the ship.

I remember one afternoon having tea with friends among who was Pepe Ruiz Gimenez, whom we called Opus Night, and his brother Joaquín, known as Opus Day, and who went

---

[13] Members of the National Socialist Party

on to become Spanish Ambassador to the Vatican during the fifties. They were both highly intelligent members of Opus Dei, a Catholic sect that is still very influential in Spain today. Sitting at a large table, opposite us, was Alan Lubbock with Michael and Elisabeth Creswell, the Babington-Smiths, David Thompson, and a Spanish couple whom I had met at a dinner party at the British Embassy.

I knew they were discussing the best ways to save the many Jews and other refugees who had reached Spain without any papers. The presence of the most prominent members of society sipping tea and nibbling on cucumber sandwiches was an excellent cover for the clandestine activities that went on there.

I was not involved in any way with MI9 but was aware of their work. Michael Creswell was the head of the organization in Spain, and he did a splendid job. To aid him in his difficult task, Creswell recruited a hundred and sixty-eight Spanish civilians with conservative views. Leftists were out of the question because the Spanish police had them all under constant surveillance.

Every week I reported to Captain Hillgarth, of whom I was becoming quite fond. We often discussed leisurely many subjects. He spoke to me about his life: starting from Osborne Naval College, which he had entered at the tender age of eight, the Riff Rebellion in North Africa in which he had fought in the twenties, his time as a gold prospector in Bolivia and his success as an adventure novelist. He gave me some of his novels to read that I thoroughly enjoyed especially 'The War Maker', set in Spanish Morocco and which he autographed for me. It is one of the treasures of my library! Alan was a highly accomplished man that treated people in such a way that made them feel completely at ease. His sense of humour was very British, dry and ironic; so that at times I was unsure as to whether he was joking or deadly serious. Our meetings were often interrupted by calls from the Prime Minister, and soon I became aware that he was receiving direct instructions from Downing Street. He found the information I passed on to him very useful, or so he said.

As the Ambassador had thought, no one considered me a threat. I was able to move easily in all circles and also befriend many German sympathizers who were very sympathetic and charming to me. I was enjoying myself very much and lived very well on the generous allowance the embassy gave me. One thing that fascinated me about Madrid society was how they loved mingling with the gipsies, whom they invited to their homes to dance, sing and party.

The gipsy matador, *Gitanillo de Triana*, whom I went to see at the Ventas bullring during the San Isidro festivities, though illiterate, knew life equivalent to that of any philosopher. I sometimes went with him, Lola Flores, Manolo Caracol, and Imperio Argentina, who had an overwhelming personality, to the flamenco *tablaos* that only gipsies and artists frequented. I was learning a lot about Spanish culture, and as the days passed, I appreciated it more and more.

Chicote was a bar on the *Gran Vía* where men went to

meet the most beautiful women in the city. In the basement, the owner, Pedro Chicote, had a drink museum full of unique bottles from all over the world. He also ran a black-market operation. In those days, penicillin was in high demand and very difficult to obtain, so those families that could afford it bought it there at exorbitant prices; payment in works of art and jewels was accepted. I have to say, I found this situation quite unacceptable, but it must be understood that Spain had just emerged from a terrible war that had left the country devastated and in ruins.

One evening in Chicote, Dionisio Sanchez, who worked for MI6, introduced me to one of the most sophisticated and elegant women I have ever met. Her name was Felisin. She was in her mid-twenties. She looked irresistible in her Balenciaga dress, which emphasized her long delicate neck. That same evening, I went to her apartment, and we spent an unforgettable night together. The attraction was mutual, and we continued our rendezvous regularly until I left Madrid.

She never charged me a peseta, and I treated her like a lady and a close friend, taking her out to dinner, showering her with presents, and dancing together at Villa Rosa. She was a mine of information, as she had a wide variety of clients. Captain Hillgarth was delighted with the information that I got from her.

Until I had arrived in Spain, I was not familiar with its recent history. I had heard my mother say that it had been awfully sad when King Alfonso XIII had gone into exile as he was such a charming gentleman, but we never discussed the reasons. So once in Madrid, I was given a crash course on the events of the last years that led to the bloody Civil War that cost Spain over a million lives.

In April of 1931, the leftist republican parties won a majority at local elections and King Alfonso fearing that the only way to prevent the country from becoming a republic was the use of force, decided in a dramatic and generous decision to go into exile until the Spanish people would call him back. He aimed to prevent a blood bath. This decision, although honourable, was disastrous for Spain. During the early days of the brief second Republican experiment, the country enjoyed for the first time in its history a short period of tolerance and freedom. Unfortunately, the liberal-socialist and conservative governments were unsuccessful in governing, and in early 1936 a radical left-wing coalition won the elections. Isolated, the Republic turned to Moscow, and Spain became a Soviet satellite with the rise to power of the communist party who even sent Spain's gold reserves to Russia. Anarchy took over. The army finally rose and fought a bitter and fierce three-year war aided by Hitler and Mussolini, which ended with the victory of Franco's army in the Civil War and many shattered dreams.

The Civil War had wrecked Spain, the infrastructure during the conflict. There were two Madrids—the sad Madrid of most of the population who could hardly make ends meet. The Madrid of people who went hungry suffered the bitter winter cold and had no access to medicines or

H.M King Alfonso XIII of Spain. His Majesty died in Rome on the 28th of February 1941.

King Alfonso XIII wife, Queen Victoria Eugenie, was a granddaughter of
Queen Victoria and went to live her exile in Laussane (Switzerland)

education. Of people who were victims of the bad harvests and the scarce food rations. A city where packs of wild dogs attacked the starving population at night in the dark alleys. A real nightmare not much better than the terrible war that they had recently endured.

In contrast, there was the Madrid of the privileged few to which I had been accepted with open arms. They bought everything in the black market and enjoyed life as best they could. The regime too was divided into two camps. On one side stood the fascists of the Falange party, the only legalized political party, who was besotted by Hitler and Mussolini. They wanted to turn Spain into a National Socialist state and who were trying with all their might to win the struggle for the Generalissimo's ear and convince him to enter the war on the Axis' side. On the other side stood the Monarchist, traditional conservatives who had supported Franco during the war but admired Britain and its class structure and were waiting eagerly for the return of King Alfonso XIII. They despised the fascist, whom they found vulgar and unsophisticated, although most of them were not too keen on democracy. They were adamant that Spain should stay neutral, worried that entering the war would consolidate the Falange's power and would prevent the King from returning from exile. Spanish society was now rigidly ultra-conservative and governed by strict Catholic principles. There was little room for reconciliation as Franco cleaned the country of what he considered all undesirables. The strict Catholic policies meant that for a young man of my age, the only way to satisfy a healthy sex drive was to be fortunate enough to know someone like Felisín or one of her friends. My friends' daughters or sisters were entirely out of bounds, although I must admit I flirted very innocently with some of them! A double moral standard governed Spanish society. Prostitution was illegal, but men in high places protected certain women and were able to carry on their business undisturbed. As these men gave them money and financed their homes, they felt they had the right to have sex with them whenever they had the urge. In this way, beautiful women from poor families became lovers of prominent men in society. As their lovers, they were taken to places where the men would never take their wives, and they led comfortable lives. Most of the wives were aware of this arrangement but ignored it as just an accepted fact of life in Madrid's high society.

One day, I was having lunch with Pepe and Joaquin Ruiz-Gimenezat Edelweiss, a German restaurant on *Calle Jovellanos*, which has not changed in the slightest since those days. It was the favourite restaurant of the German residents and their friends, as the food was genuine German staple. It was and still is excellent: herrings, *sauerkraut* and many other delicacies.

As we had lunch, a tall, well-dressed man approached our table, and I was finally introduced to the Count of Herentals. The Ruiz-Gimenez brothers later explained that the family had originated from Spanish Flanders, with the first Count receiving his title from Phillip II. The current Count owned a beautiful palace in Madrid and a country estate in Toledo, where he and the countess entertained lavishly. They had two sons like me in age.

"My wife and I are giving a small dinner in honour of Baron Klaus von Jettenbbach, who is a good friend and our guest for a few days. I would be delighted if you could come," he said.

My friends, having a prior engagement, declined the invitation, but I accepted readily. I was confident it would be a fascinating evening and I was not to be disappointed.

*

The home of the Count and Countess of Herentals was a small palace on the *Paseo de la Castellana*. A relatively large park with ancient trees surrounded it. Unfortunately, so many of those palaces have since been destroyed to make way for large, characterless modern buildings.

I received invitations to many Madrid homes. Most of the times, I found the interior decoration quite dreary; I have always disliked heavy Castilian furniture, and I hated to be surrounded by so many religious paintings. As winter was approaching, most of the homes I visited were always cold and damp, as coal was heavily rationed. Thus, I was not prepared for the exquisite taste of the Herentals' home or for their display of luxury.

Magnificent paintings and tapestries hung from the walls, while Bohemian chandeliers full of candles gave the house a sedate atmosphere from another era. Jorge Jalpen provided entertainment. He played exquisitely on a grand piano, pieces by Mozart, Wagner, and other German composers.

The countess was petite but had a strong personality not overshadowed by that of her husband. She wore an exquisite evening dress and a stunning diamond necklace with a matching bracelet that glittered in the candlelight. Her vibrant eyes were almond-shaped, and their colour complemented her beautiful olive complexion. She was a charming host who promptly introduced me to the other guests.

"Rodney, let me introduce you to our guest of honour, Baron Klaus von Jettenbach, who owns a magnificent collection of paintings, probably one of the best in the world."

"You exaggerate, my dear," he said as we shook hands.

"We were introduced once before, in Monte Carlo, by the Marquis of San Felice," I said.

The Baron seemed to remember me. At that moment, Jose Luis de Arrese, a top Falange[14] leader, arrived and a big fuss was made of him by the other guests. In an amazing twist of fate, I would marry his niece in 1955. I knew from Alan Hillgarth that he was a very influential man in the regime, and a few years later, he became the housing minister.

I had been served a scotch when a beautiful woman

---

[14] Member of the Spanish Nationalist Party

approached me from across the room. She must have been in her early thirties. Her fabulous red hair fell loose over her shoulders. She was wearing a sleeveless black gown with fine gold and diamond choker, which had a diamond brooch in the shape of a swastika. Her pale skin, covered in freckles, and her delicate feminine appearance belied the strength of her character, as I was soon to discover. She had a broad smile lacking in warmth. I felt that she seemed very much in control

"My name is Gisella von Krieger, Rodney," she introduced herself in perfect English with a heavy German accent.

"Have we met before?" I asked politely.

"I saw you in the South of France, but we have never been formally introduced although we do have some friends in common."

"And who are they, may I ask?

"Harry Giglioli and the Marquis of San Felice."

"They are friends no more. Both are my enemies now, and so are you, it seems." I said provocatively.

She laughed seductively and took a sip of champagne.

"I have always found you very attractive. Besides, you are quite daring for someone your age. Do you like older women?"

"I like all types of women, even those who are the enemy! But what is such a beautiful woman like you doing in Madrid?

"I am a spy," she said jokingly. "Ah, I see that you don't

believe me?" she asked provocatively. I found her effortless sense of humour very sexy, and she knew it. She was in control.

¨I am in fact an art consultant and a close friend of Klaus. I am staying at the home of the German Ambassador and shall be in Madrid for a few weeks. You must meet them; they are a very nice enemy couple."

Gisella introduced me to Baron Eberhard von Stroher and his wife who, I knew from the reports at the embassy, were very close to the centre of power in Madrid. I had seen them having lunch at Edelweiss, but we had not met yet. They were a formidable fascist couple, always trying to recruit people to embrace Nazi ideals. They hosted luncheons and dinners to which most of the ministers and their wives were invited. They went for lunch with Mrs Franco at the Palacio del Pardo regularly, no doubt to ensure that she used her powerful influence over her husband in the right direction. They had been very active in the Windsor plot revealed to me earlier by Alan Hillgarth.

We exchanged some pleasantries, and then Gisella took me by the arm and led me to a corner where we chatted happily until a rather unpleasant-looking man in an SS Captain's uniform interrupted.

"This is Captain Hans Vogel," Gisella introduced him to me as she frowned.

The captain kissed her hand. "What a lovely surprise, Gisella. What brings you here?" He said, raising his eyebrows.

"Hans, you are interrupting us. And you know very well what I am doing here, so if you don't mind…..."

I could sense some tension between them. Captain Vogel moved on without uttering another word, and Gisella muttered something in German to herself that was not pleasant.

My situation suddenly downed on me. I was only going on nineteen, and yet there I was in a foreign country, working for my government, and surrounded by incredibly charming people, most of whom were, almost certainly, extremely dangerous. I thought about my mother, Uncle Jack and Princess Magaloff. I wondered if they were still alive, and I felt a pang of loneliness.

"Rodney, what is bothering you?" she asked with a kind of alluring sweetness in her voice.

At that moment, the Count approached and whisked Gisella away to introduce her to some of the other guests. We were about twenty people in all, and I knew several of them. I could see that most were Nazi sympathizers and that they felt very much at ease because they knew each other well.

I was sitting alone, observing everything, when the countess came up and introduced me to a distinguished Hungarian of medium height. He was about forty and had a broad smile.

"This is my dear friend, Laszlo Szekeres. He is a magnificent painter. You must come to the opening of his exhibition next week."

"I will be delighted to do so," I replied.

Laszlo was a refined man who wore an impeccably tailored suit. Surely a gentleman, I thought.

"Saville Row?" I asked.

No. Cutuli. He is a local tailor. He has nothing to envy Saville Row though. I'll take you to meet him if you want."

"I'd be delighted."

We had a drink together and soon discovered we felt a great affinity for each other. We had a friend in common, Prince George Govecki, a journalist whose nom de plume was Armand Arronsart and who was a great-grandson of the poet Misckiewicz. We both had stayed at his estate near Vilno in Poland.[15]

"It's a small world," he said.

"Tell me," I asked in a matter-of-fact tone, "what do you know about our friend the Baron?"

"Well, Rodney, his origins are obscure. It is an old title, and his family was quite prominent under the Kaiser. He is very influential and is now very wealthy. Over the last few years, he has managed to acquire an outstanding art collection: Brac, Picasso, Kandinsky, Manet, Ingres, Corot, Courbet, Leger, Tintoretto, El Greco, Degas, Monet, Renoir. You name them, and he has them. He is a close friend of Göering, and they both share an insatiable appetite for art. Most of his best paintings were apparently given to him for safekeeping by Jewish acquaintances, first in Germany and

---

[15] Now in Lithuania

later in Poland and France. He has shared them with his master, who permits and encourages the spoil if he gets the first choice. The clown in Berlin admires his patriotism!" he added sarcastically.

"He has no intention of giving the paintings back to their owners once the war is over?" I asked naïvely.

"My dear chap, those poor Jews are all probably dead by now!"

Over dinner, Baron Stohrer tried to convince us that Britain would soon lose the war and that it would be in Britain's best interest to seek peace with Germany. He went on and on about Hitler's plans for Europe and even tried to persuade me that we English were blind for not seeing the greatness of his master plan. I kept my eyes and ears wide open while I made polite conversation.

When the coffee was served, Gisella von Krieger joined me again.

"Are you enjoying yourself?"

"I am very much so."

"Well, Rodney. The best is still to come.

That night she took me to the von Stohrer's residence. I knew I was entering a snake pit but could not refuse the invitation, and the challenge excited me in more ways than one.

Her body was that of a goddess with small but firm breasts. Freckles covered every single inch of her entire lustful body. Her big green eyes were full of desire for my body that she grabbed with hunger, tearing off my clothes and kissing me passionately. There was no feeling between us, only unrestricted carnal desire.

"I want to tie you up and blindfold you," she said suddenly but firmly. I shuddered with excitement, probably because I was walking on thin ice.

She took a silk scarf out of a drawer, and I dutifully let her cover my eyes. Then, with another scarf, she tied my wrists in front of my body. I felt her nails softly scratch my chest slowly down to my navel. She kissed me, and I kissed her back. Her tongue was caressing my gums. She moved her juicy lips to my ears, kissed them and blew the air of passion into them. It felt so, so good! Getting behind me she started licking with her warm tongue the back of my neck. She continued down my spine. I gasped with pleasure when I felt her tongue on my hole as she kissed it. Then, she turned me around forcefully and took me in her mouth. I was so hard with excitement that I was on the verge of crossing the gates of bliss.

"You like it, Rodney, don't you?" she whispered in my ear.

"Yes, I do very much," I said with a gasp. I was about to reach an orgasm, and she felt it too because she let go of my hard member. Gisela pushed me on the bed violently and then she mounted me. She rode me wildly, and after a period of ecstasy, we simultaneously reached the point of no return.

I must admit it was a night I would never forget.

*

Up to now, the news from the front had not been very encouraging, as the Germans appeared to be unstoppable. After the Japanese attack on Pearl Harbour, the sceptic Americans finally joined the war on the side of the Allies, and we all became more optimistic. Nazi propaganda was everywhere, and the Spanish press did very little to report British successes.

That December was bitterly cold, and it snowed on and off continuously. The power cuts occurred regularly. I went to the cinema on several occasions with the intent of watching the No-do, the government news broadcast. The scenes of bombed London devastated me. According to the broadcaster, it was only a question of time before Britain lost the war. The fascist propaganda was formidable. A bishop blessed the opening of a factory in Bilbao; a battalion of Falange Youth wearing their uniforms paraded in front of a beaming Caudillo and his wife; the ever-present dictator and a delighted Doña Carmen entering the Cathedral in Burgos under a canopy followed by Bishops and Cardinals for a *Te Deum* and so on. Franco had saved Spain from the claws of communism and had become the father of the nation, its saviour.

Hitler had scrapped the plan to invade Britain after realizing the huge cost involved. Even so, the Luftwaffe had bombed and destroyed many British cities between

H.R.H Prince Juan of Borbon and Battenberg and his son Prince Juan Carlos (Prince of Asturias). For the Royalists, Don Juan was King Juan III. For the democrats the only hope of bringing democracy to Spain with a Constitutional Monarchy.

September and November yet had not succeeded in breaking our fighting spirit. Much to Germany's surprise, and despite our isolation and painful exposure to the
Luftwaffe, we did not surrender. Germany then decided to attack the last potential ally on whom Churchill could count, and he invaded Russia on June 22nd, 1941. Little did he realize that this would be the beginning of the end of the Third Reich. For an invasion of such magnitude, it had begun too late in the year, and, ignoring the lessons of history, Hitler made the same mistake as Napoleon had done before him.

My life continued much the same. I still had no news from my mother, but I tried to convince myself that no information whatsoever was good news. I had no choice but to go on with my r daily routine. Most mornings I played golf in *Puerta de Hierro*, which is still a very sophisticated sports club just outside Madrid; then lunch at L'Hardy, Botín or some other fashionable restaurant followed by a siesta in the early afternoon. Nearly most afternoons, I would go to Embassy for tea, to the Palace for a few drinks, and then after dinner, to the favourite nightspots. Chipen, on *Calle Peligros,* was a noisy restaurant very much *a la mode*, where I ate regularly. Once a week, I would meet Alan Hillgarth at his office. He had become something of a father figure to me.

I became good friends with Laszlo Szekeres and naturally attended his exhibition, which was a huge success. He was a good horseman, and I accompanied him to the Alberto

Aguilera stables, where he rented a horse. He introduced me to Beltran Osorio, Marquis of Cuellar, the son and heir to the Duke of Alburquerque, who was an excellent rider and later became world-famous at the turf. The Alburquerques They lived on an enormous estate in Algete, outside Madrid. I also met Cayetana Fitz James Stuart, the Duchess of Montoro, heir to the Duke of Berwick and Alba, who was also a very keen rider. I had the pleasure to be invited to their home for tea and contemplate their exquisite art collection. Cayetana upon her father's death would become the most titled woman in the world!

Most of these people dreamed nostalgically of the restoration of the monarchy. King Alfonso XIII had died in February in a hotel in Rome, and his son, Don Juan, was now the rightful King.

Laszlo and I went out together on many nights, and sometimes we would take Felisin and her friends to dine at Horcher, one of the capital's most sophisticated restaurants. People would whisper as we walked in. Some of the men did not feel very comfortable with our presence. Still, Felisin was so graceful and elegant that there was never an awkward moment when we introduced her to the wives of men whom she knew very intimately. Both Laszlo and I thought it was all extremely amusing. We enjoyed the provocation and got away with it. Laszlo was very generous and, in his company, the champagne, a rare and expensive item in those austere days, flowed freely.

I could not stop feeling somewhat guilty. Each time I

moved around Madrid, the signs of poverty and misery were everywhere. The shop windows were half empty, beggars huddled together trying to keep warm in doorways, and the barefoot wild faced children with their bloated stomachs broke my heart. Madrid was half-starved, the fascist economic policies of self-sufficiency and the chaotic and very corrupt distribution system did not help make matters easier for the needy. The small elite to which I belonged went about life as if all was alien to them.

One Monday morning, I received a call from Alan Hillgarth and he invited me for lunch at the Ritz Hotel.

"I will pick you up at 2.30 at your hotel," he said. It was the first time we were meeting outside of the Embassy.

At the agreed time, a large black Packard stopped at the entrance of the Hotel Nacional. In the car with the Naval Attaché was Alan Lubock. Located at *the Plaza de la Lealtad* opposite the Palace Hotel where I used to go regularly, the imposing hotel was a favourite haunt with the Germans and Italians.

The dining room was elegant with many fascist officers in uniform accompanied by a few well-dressed women. Alan was wearing his too and with all his medals for that matter!

"A little provocation is good!" he lowered his voice to a whisper as we were shown to our table by the *maître d.*

Sitting at a table close to ours I recognised Hans Thomsen sitting with an elegantly dressed woman whom I assumed was his wife.

"Is he as dangerous as he looks?" I asked.

"More! Both Alans exclaimed in unison.

"Why does the German National party have a leader in Madrid?"

"Thomsen must make sure that the German community here is totally loyal to the party. Himmler signed a pact with the Spanish government in 1938 by which any German suspected of not being loyal to the Reich could be arrested and deported to Germany without trial. Needless to say,, since the Civil War all German residents here at least pretend to be loyal party members or else!" Alan Hilgarth explained.

"Rodney, we are outnumbered here, there are also very few Spanish. The Ambassador likes that we come here now and then. He will be joining us in a moment with Lady Maud. Before they arrive, Alan has some news for you."

"Yes Rodney," said Alan Lubock, I have just returned with Lalo Martinez-Alonso from the camp in Miranda del Ebro. The situation is quite dangerous there. There are more than three thousand prisoners, yet the facilities are for only five hundred."

"This is a camp for prisoners of war with no papers," Hillgarth explained to me, "and our Embassy and that of the Americans oversee the general well-being of the prisoners. We try to have them released, and then we help them leave the country as fast as possible."

"Who is this Lalo?" I inquired.

"He's a Spanish doctor and a close friend. He is very active in MI9 and is doing a great job helping us get people out of the country. I'm sure you'll meet him soon."

"What does this have to do with me?" I asked.

"Rodney, you will be glad to know we have finally, after so many negotiations, secured the release of your friend Alfred Kempler. He is quite ill though and will stay at Dr Martinez-Alonso's home until he's well enough to travel." Alan Lubbock said sternly and suddenly coughed to announce the arrival of the Ambassador and his wife.

*

That December 1941, while the Americans were mobilizing for war, Alan Lubbock came by my hotel on the 23rd. I would finally be seeing Fred, and I was so excited.

"It would be nice if we could meet for tea today. Let's say at seven at Embassy,"

At the agreed time, I arrived at 12 *Paseo de la Castellana*. Alan was sitting with the lovely Margaret Taylor. I joined them at the table.

"He can't wait to see you, Rodney!" she said softly.

"Right now, he's upstairs, as he will be spending a couple of nights at my house. It is probably better if you join me for dinner tomorrow. It is Christmas Eve, after all, I am Irish, you are British and on your own. Our friendship will not be cause for suspicion."

The following morning, I went to buy some presents for Margaret and her young daughter, Consuelo, and naturally for good old Fred whom I considered a hero.

It was my first Christmas in Madrid. There were not many lights in the streets, except for a few lighted shops. Spain was

Margaret Taylor

slowly rising from its ashes, and the official attitude was one of complete austerity. It was tranquil in the streets, and it was raining solidly. A pair of *Guardia Civiles*[16] huddled under their green capes. I had arranged a taxi to pick me up at the hotel. On the way, we passed a gasogene stuck in the middle of the street and a desperate soaked man trying to start the engine. I felt sorry for him. At about eight, I arrived at Margaret's house. The moment he saw me, Fred threw his arms around me, and we hugged while he cried like a child.

"Fred! It is so good to see you. Finally, you are on your way to freedom." I said happily.

"Let's all sit down and have a glass of champagne to celebrate this most auspicious reunion," said Margaret who had been watching us with a broad smile.

We followed her into the sitting room. The house, decorated in a very English style was elegant yet subdued, with no concessions to extravagance. There were several floral motifs, and it felt cosy and homely. Consuelo, Margarita's lovely little girl, came to wish us goodnight before her nanny whisked her off to bed.

Dinner was a delightful affair. There was a warm sense of family, and traditional English food was delicious. Fred recounted how he had been released from Cartagena and taken to Miranda del Ebro where he fell ill with TB which was rampant in Spain. Apparently, Michael Creswell stumbled on him lying in the camp's hospital during one of

[16] Civil Guards

his routine visits to the camp. The British immediately took hold of the excellent opportunity and had him released to them on medical grounds. Fortunately, the Gestapo never discovered who he was and what information he possessed.

"I'll be quite glad to leave this country. I haven't been treated too well," Fred said, forcing a smile. Miranda del Ebro was a nightmare. The fact that we did not know when we were going to be deported, or shot did not make things any easier. I lived in a constant state of fear. However, I am leaving at last, Rodney, after dinner."

"Well, my friend, you'll soon be a free man."

"The Spanish press is manipulating public opinion by saying we are freemasons and responsible for the Civil War. They blame us for Spain's economic problems and use the same rhetoric against us as the Nazis do. I have been told that Serrano Suñer has ordered all the ministries to comply with Gestapo policies! It is absurd! The government is using the same anti-Jewish rhetoric as in the time of Queen Isabella, the Catholic!"

"This lunacy will soon be over, now that the Americans are joining in the war," I said hesitantly trying to boost his morale.

Fred went on as if he needed to get things off his chest. "The Spanish Ministry of Foreign Affairs has even made it a crime to sell to European Jews passage on Spanish vessels leaving from Portugal. They want us all dead. Wiped out!" he added bitterly.

"A bright future lies ahead of you," said Margaret

reassuringly.

She served a delicious Christmas pudding with homemade brandy butter, and to our delight, Fred drew the lucky sixpence. This was a good omen indeed.

At exactly midnight, a car with diplomatic plates pulled up in front of Margaret's home. The rain had shortly ceased. Making sure there was nobody on the streets, and with the utmost caution, we bundled Fred into the car. Then I heard Margaret whispering, "God bless you!" We both knew he would still face many dangers before arriving at the border, as the Civil Guard had many roadblocks.

Despite the bitterly cold night and as the skies were now clear, I walked back to my hotel. I could not stop thinking about Margaret and the group of Spaniards who were helping so altruistically in rescue operations that were saving thousands of lives. These were true anonymous heroes.

The following day I had an unexpected call from Alan asking me to go to the Embassy. I was in for a surprise. I took a bath and soon afterwards was in his office. Captain Hillgart was sitting behind his desk and stood up to greet me. King George stared at me from the portrait behind him.

"Merry Christmas, Rodney!"

"Do you have any news about my mother?" I asked, hopefully. They had obviously not summoned me to wish me a merry Christmas.

"No, I'm afraid I don't. I called you because we have a delicate mission for you. We are delighted with your work and…"

"What mission?" I interrupted with eagerness.

"You are to return to London immediately and then you will be flown to Cairo."

"Egypt?" I exclaimed in utter surprise.

Alan said nothing but offered me a John Players, the cigarettes that I smoked ever after until I quit when I was reaching forty. I accepted it, and he took one too. We both took a deep puff, and a cloud of smoke filled the room.

"Your mission is to befriend a young Spaniard who we believe is working for the Germans. His name is Francisco de Beaumont. Sir Miles Lampson, the Ambassador in Cairo, will brief you as soon as you arrive. The war in the desert is not going well for us. Rommel, who we call the Desert Fox, is a very able commander with great tactical awareness and a natural flair for mobile warfare. We cannot afford to lose the Suez Canal to the enemy, and we must do our utmost to stop any intelligence information from reaching him."

"Why is he called the Desert Fox?"

"Because he is as cunning as a fox, and he constantly improvises and uses any trick to outsmart us. Unfortunately, he is being successful on many occasions,"

VIII

TITILLATING CAIRO
Late December 1941

I left Madrid on Boxing Day without having the chance to say goodbye to anybody. I had arranged to meet Felisin as I was certain she would be terribly worried, though Alan had promised that Sam Hoare would make excuses for my sudden disappearance.

Four days after arriving in London, I took the Imperial Airways flight to Cairo where an Embassy car was waiting for me. A young Foreign Office chap was there to collect me at the airport. His name was James, but I do not recall his surname. He was in his mid-twenties, pleasant looking and rather pompous.

Everything seemed fascinating; the colours, the sounds and smells were as if from another world. We drove through the bazaar area where the men were wearing *djellabas* and I could hear them speaking in Arabic, a language that was completely foreign to me. The streets were full of camels and donkeys used for transport.

"This area is called the Mouski," James said breaking the silence.

"This is where the ancient mosques are."

"It's amazingly interesting! I must come and visit," I said.

"I wouldn't recommend that. We are not particularly popular with the Egyptians."

"How is that?" I asked with genuine curiosity.

"The wogs[17] think the Germans will liberate them from British oppression."

I wouldn't say I liked his tone of disrespect, which I soon discovered was quite generalized among the British and based on a total misconception, so I let him know my opinion that to be respected one had to respect.

The scenery soon changed dramatically. The donkeys and camels gave way to Rolls Royce and Bentleys, and the streets took on the appearance of a sophisticated city like Paris. The men wore elegant linen suits, and I saw many chic women in front of *Circurel* and *Le Salon Vert*, which, according to James, were the top department stores. We passed through Suleiman Pasha Square, which he said was the city's glamorous commercial centre. Here everybody was speaking French and appeared entirely oblivious to what was going on at the front.

"There are some really fancy brothels near the hotel. We can have a night out if you feel up to it," James said, smiling.

The car stopped at the entrance to the Shepherd Hotel, which faced the Ezbekkiah Gardens, Cairo's *Tuilleries*. James escorted me to reception and then, before leaving me to go up to my room, showed me around what would be my new

---

[17] The term stood for Working on Government Service but it was used in a derogatory way to mean Wily Oriental Gentlemen

home for an unknown period. The Karnak Ballroom and the Moorish Hall were quite outstanding.

"Maybe we can have a drink together at the Long Bar this evening unless Sir Miles has other plans for you," James suggested cheerfully, "I shall wait here for you while you freshen up, and then we shall go to the Embassy as soon as you are ready."

Sir Miles Lampson was much taller than I was. At around six foot five, he was a towering figure with a majestic bearing. He rose from his chair to greet me in his office while saying:

"Well, well, who do we have here? Alan and Samuel Hoare have highly recommended you, young man. They seem to believe you are perfect for this mission, are you not?"

"What would you have me do, Sir?"

"You are about the same age as the boy."

"The boy! What boy? You mean Francisco de Beaumont?" I asked, confused.

"No, no, no. Farouk, the bloody king." Being a royalist, I was not too fond of his disrespectful tone.

Captain Hillgarth told me that his people very much love His Majesty," I said, trying tactfully to put him in his place.

"He is! Very much loved by ignorant people who consider the Germans are their saviours. Bloody idiots!" I could feel the Ambassador was irritated, but his arrogance made me feel uncomfortable. "The German propaganda could feel the Ambassador was irritated, but his arrogance made me feel uncomfortable. "The German propaganda

Sir Miles Lapson at 6'5 was a towering figure with a majestic bearing machine has led them to believe that Hitler was a Moslem born in Egypt. Fools! They do not realize that if the Germans take Egypt, the first thing they will do is depose their beloved king and replace him on the throne with his fascist uncle." He paused and then asked as an afterthought," Did you know, Rodney, that they call Hitler, Mohammed Haider? We believe your new friend Francisco de Beaumont has a lot to do with all this rubbish propaganda. We also believe he passes very sensitive information to Rommel. We suspect he must be working for the Germans."

"But if you are so certain, why don't you bag him?"

Sir Miles took a few seconds to reply.

"We need proof dear chap and that is where you come in. You see, Francisco de Beaumont is close to the king. He is also under the protection of some of our friends and some of the emerging Arab sheikhs, whom he has befriended, protect him. He currently lives in Dubai but is constantly on the move between Cairo, Teheran, and Bagdad. In Bagdad he is now close to Prince Abdallah, the Regent. It is all rather complicated, but we believe his scheming is undermining our war efforts. It's challenging to know what he's up to, and he is even a good friend of the Duke of Aosta, who as you might know is the Italian Viceroy of Ethiopia. Nice decent chap, the duke! Pity he's on the wrong side!"

"I'd like to hear more about de Beaumont, Sir," I said.

"Here read these papers! But to put you in the picture, he is twenty-five years old, and his family descends from

H.M King Farouk I of Egypt

Francois du Beaumont, who arrived in Madrid in the cortege of King Joseph I, Napoleon's brother. This charming and debonair character married into the Spanish aristocracy. The family stayed on after the Bourbon restoration. Francisco's father died soon after he was born, and his young mother then married a German count and went to live in Bavaria with her husband and her only son. Our man is fluent in German, French and English, and evidently, Spanish. He is a charmer and moves like a fish in a pond in the upper circles of society. He is the darling of the Egyptian aristocracy. He is known to have no scruples and can be very dangerous. As you can see, we need proof of his activities."

"So, what's the plan of action?" I asked eagerly.

"Your mission is to befriend him. Your cover is that of a young and ambitious war correspondent. It would help if you made him believe that he can get some interesting information out of you, when in fact, hopefully, it will be the other way round. We need to know what he is up to before we decide what to do with him. It should not be a difficult job for you, young man. He is now in town, so you must meet him and enjoy the city's decadent nightlife. If you are as good as Alan says, you will have no problem succeeding in this mission.

"And how will I do that?

"I am expecting a lovely lady very shortly," he continued. "Her name is Irene Guile. She is from Alexandria and comes from a very prominent Jewish trading family from Venice. The King is infatuated with her beauty and sophistication.

As she is as worried about the Germans as we are, she is aiding us in ensuring the king does not lean towards the Axis. She is highly popular and will find a way of introducing you to our man."

A knock on the door interrupted our conversation, and James walked in, accompanied by a stunning woman. Just one look into her eyes, and I could understand how she had won the monarch's heart. She was not only beautiful but had that kind of allure that makes some women extremely special. She offered me her hand, and I kissed it.

"This is the charming Rodney, Sir Miles?" she asked the Ambassador.

"Yes, my dear, and now we depend on you to introduce him into the right circles if you know what I mean."

She smiled at me.

"Tomorrow I shall send my car to pick you up at the hotel at eight. We will be going to a very special soiree at Princess Shivekiar's palace. You will never forget this New Year's Eve party.

Princess Shivekiar's palace stood just a few blocks from the Shepherd's Hotel. The wealthy princess had been married to her impoverished and loathed cousin Fuad before he ascended the throne. King Farouk was very fond of his stepmother, as she organised for him the wildest parties, put women in his path, and encouraged him to gamble. It was the princess' way of wreaking revenge on the Fuad. She had the reputation of being somewhat Machiavellian, and many

The Machiavellian Princess Shivekiar with King Farouk and other guests at the New Year Party people questioned the king's good judgement when he had restored her to full palace rights.

I was ill-prepared for the dreamlike setting that awaited me at the palace. It felt like if I had stepped into the thousand- and one-night's tale. The palace glittered in the night with thousands of lights. There were coloured tents placed around the park where the party took place. An army of exotically dressed servants served gallons of pink champagne of an exquisite vintage while three different and magnificent orchestras played the latest tunes. Irene had not yet arrived, so I wandered around the party and noticed some very sophisticated and ravishing women were eyeing me. Being the new face in town had its advantages. I felt good in my white dinner jacket. The party seemed an exercise in glamorous excess, the like of which I had never seen before.

Suddenly the music came to a halt, the chitchat ceased, and the band struck up the Egyptian national anthem. The king had arrived with the ravishing Irene Guile by his side. Many of the guests stood on their chairs to get a better look at the couple, whom they watched in admiration.

Irene looked like a queen. She was wearing a long ivory-coloured robe embroidered in geometric patterns. The fantastic dress could very well have been a creation of Elsa Schiaparelli, my mother's favourite couturiers.

"They are lovely, aren't they?" I turned and found myself looking at an attractive and elegant woman that was behind me. She smiled flirtatiously. "My name is Helen Mosseri. I am a friend of Irene's, and she has asked me to look out for you. You must be Rodney." She had an intense gaze and exuded charm. She was rather tantalizing. I kissed her hand.

"You speak remarkably good English, though I detect a slight Greek accent," I replied.

"Yes, I am Greek. my family are the Polymires. Mosseri is the name of my late husband."

"I am so sorry. May I be bold and say that you are delightful!"

"Yes, you may, and I may say you are a handsome young man! You will be very successful in Cairo if you stay with us long enough. Come! Let me introduce you to His Majesty." We walked over towards the king and Irene. They both looked at us. Irene's smile was captivating.

"Your Majesty," she said, "may I introduce you to Rodney Mundy, a very likeable Englishman?" The King seemed to be in an excellent mood. He smiled broadly, and we shook hands as I bowed my head. All eyes were now on us.

"You could not have a better introduction card than Irene and Helen," the King chirped, putting his arm around me with such unexpected familiarity that though I felt delighted was rather out of place. Irene winked at me, while Helen kissed her on the cheeks. The King and I walked forward in this way. No doubt everybody was wondering who I was. His Majesty suddenly burped. I was aghast, not knowing how to react. He laughed. The two beautiful ladies giggled with embarrassment. I later found out that he used to do this on purpose to annoy people. It was his way of testing people by their reactions. King Farouk was about my age, and he was a handsome man in possession of worldly charm.

"Some Englishmen don't please me too much. Your ambassador, for instance, particularly irritates me," he said, changing the tone.

"I am sorry to hear that, Your Majesty", I replied, slightly embarrassed at his indiscretion.

"Helen, darling, why don't you introduce Rodney to some of our friends?" Irene asked aiming to change the subject.

I took my leave of the King and strolled around the party arm in arm with Helen, who introduced me to the *crème de la crème* of Egyptian society. First, she introduced me to our host, Princess Shivekiar, a small and frail older woman who looked like a crow and had a remarkable personality. One could feel she was undoubtedly a plotter and a schemer by observing her as she talked to her guests. I also met her son, Prince Wahid, - whom Helen said was allegedly having an affair with Queen Farida, the King's wife! -, Victor Smaika, the famous playboy and friend of Barbara Hutton, and some of the most prominent Jews like the Lambrossis, Victor Harari, the Cattawis, Baron George de Menasce, and finally I was introduced me to my prey, Francisco de Beaumont.

We hit it off immediately. Francisco was well-bred, articulate, highly sophisticated, and cheerful, so I did not have to try to like him, as he was very likeable. I knew that I had to be cautious because he was, after all, supposed to be the enemy. Helen, obviously well indoctrinated by Irene, left us together to dine on the magnificent selection of French, Italian and Russian dishes served in the different tents. We spoke in Spanish, which pleased him, and he asked me a lot about Madrid where he had not been since his childhood. I explained that I was a war correspondent, and from him, I learnt that he was a pearl dealer that spent quite a lot of time in Dubai where he was a close friend of the ruling Sheikh.

"You must come and stay with me. Dubai is a fascinating place!" I agreed to go when and if my work allowed me to do so, knowing all too well that it would not happen.

"Would you like a cigarette?" I asked, searching in the inside pocket of my dinner jacket.

"What have you lost?" he asked, seeing my confused expression.

"I must have misplaced my cigarette case. I am certain I put in my pocket. It's quite upsetting as it was a present from my father!" I replied as I frowned startled.

He started to laugh and could not stop.

"You have just been a victim of the king's longhand."

"You must be joking!" I exclaimed in astonishment as I frowned again.

"Farouk thinks it's a joke! He is very good at it. They say he received lessons from a master thief he had pardoned from the Turah prison."

"You are teasing me," I said bewildered.

"No. It's absolutely true!"

Years later, in 1954, I bought back the cigarette case at

an auction at Sotheby's. The army had organized it after the king's overthrow, with articles from his private collection.

Just before the midnight chimes, we refilled our glasses with champagne to toast the New Year while an extravaganza of fireworks lit up the Cairo night. The contrast between Cairo and Madrid could not have been greater.

I decided to get to know Cairo and get my bearings of the city. James took me to play golf at the Gezira Sporting Club. There he introduced me to Jacqueline Lampson, Sir Miles' charming young wife. She was the daughter of Sir Aldo Castellani, doctor to the Italian troops, which was no doubt a bit difficult for Sir Miles to digest. I fact, it was common gossip that Sir Miles concerned by the number of Italian advisors that the king had in his payroll[18] asked him to get rid of them and the king's reply was: "When you get rid of yours, I will get rid of mine!".

One thing that bothered me was that the native Egyptians and the Turkish aristocracy, were excluded from the club, and this was a disappointment as I looked forward to mingling with them.

On the evening of January 1st, I invited James over for dinner at the hotel, and afterwards, he took me gambling at the Royal Automobile Club. It was surprisingly unstuffy and rather fun and was allegedly the king's favourite gambling

---

[18] Mussolini had invaded Ethiopia and annexed the country on May 7th, 1936

den. After I had lost at the roulette, James decided to take me to visit the red-light district, which was known as the Fish Market. It was the seediest place I had ever seen. Heavily made-up young girls, catered to the many Commonwealth and British soldiers stationed in the city. We witnessed several brawls between drunken soldiers and locals. Violence here was the order of the day, and the murder of both whores and soldiers was not uncommon. James, considering these brothels beneath our station, decided to spare me the unpleasantness of visiting any of them. Instead, we toured the fancier ones that were popular with the officers and were run by European Madams with *filles de joies* from many different nations. Cairo was undoubtedly a city of pleasure and very unlike Madrid. Despite the many temptations, I indulged in no sex that night, but a few too many drinks.

I slept well and woke up late. After a hearty English breakfast, I visited Ismail Pasha Square near the banks of the Nile and then went to the Egyptian Museum, where I was awestruck by the treasures of the ancient Egyptian rulers. I also visited the Cathedral of All Saints, not far from the Kasr El Nil Barracks, home of the British Army, before wandering through the Garden City where the embassies and residences of the rich were located.

I could see that modern and ancient Cairo did not mingle, which, I soon discovered, was a sour point with the man on the street, who resented the British troops' overbearing presence and obscene disregard for the King. Although a neutral country, Egypt felt like part of the British Empire.

No wonder the locals believed their admired king was the only person who could liberate them from us. I realized for the first time that our old imperialistic attitude was hurting our cause. Venturing bravely into the Khan el-Khalilli bazaar, I bought a cotton *djellabah,* and by putting it on, I amused the locals, which only goes to show that making a small effort of integration helps people accept you. I did not feel threatened at all at any time. Entirely, on the contrary, I managed to speak to some of the locals who although friendly towards me were quite blunt about their feelings. They got the message across to me as best they could that we were no better than imperialist pigs—an animal not much liked by the followers of the prophet. What could be expected from people that came from a land were pigs are lawful food?

Later in the afternoon, I ventured to the historical Cairo: The Al Azhar and Sultan Hassan Mosques, the Ben Ezra Synagogue, the Coptic churches, and the medieval gates of Bab Zuwayla. Time passed in a flash and as night fell, I heard the wailing of the muezzin over the city when I decided to take a taxi back to The Shepheard's. I created quite a commotion when I entered wearing my djellaba!

The following day I could not resist visiting the Cairo of antiquity: the Pyramids and the Sphynx. A dream to any traveller and which left me totally and utterly in awe. I could not help asking me how could have such an ancient civilization build such architectonical marvels?

That evening, on the 3rd of January, at the appointed

time, Francisco met me at the Long Bar for a drink. His insolent indifference struck me though he was in a cheerful mood and most friendly towards me. After a couple of whiskeys, he took me to dinner at the *Auberge des Pyramids,* which was one of the most popular nightclubs with Cairo's *jeunesse dorée* and well known for its excellent food. While we were waiting for our meal, sipping cold Chablis, the orchestra played 'I get a kick out of you'.

"The king is here," said Francisco, suddenly.

Everyone stood up as King Farouk was escorted to his table, accompanied by a once again ravishing Irene and a large entourage of friends that included the lovely Helen Mosseri. In those days he was really a king taken out of a picture book: handsome, charming, wealthy and with a practical good humour.

After dinner, a waiter asked us to accompany him to the king's table. The group was in a jolly mood. Farouk sipped orangeade while the rest of us drank champagne. We talked about cars, his passion. He seemed rather immature for his age and quite desperate to fit in and be part of the gang. He was smoking a large cigar, much to Irene's irritation, and he laughed as he shot bread pellets at anyone who seemed too pompous for his liking; I must admit there were many of them around. I thought the whole thing quite hilarious, as the king cracked endless jokes and puns at everyone's expense, including his own. I noticed that he was very fond of Francisco, with whom he confided several times during the evening.

"I am leaving for Aswan tomorrow," Farouk said, "you should come too Francisco and bring Rodney with you. We will be there for a few weeks."

"Unfortunately, I cannot go Your Majesty, as I must return to Dubai in a few days. But, Rodney, you should go," Francisco said, nothing I'd enjoy more, but I have just arrived, and my boss in London would not be too happy…." I addressed the king apologetically. The truth is that I could not think of a more appealing plan as Helen would undoubtedly be there as well.

"I will accept Your Majesty's invitation at any other time with pleasure," I said.

"What a pity! We shall be going now." Farouk got up, and soon after he had left with his group, we left the club. However, for Francisco and me, the night was only just beginning.

The Opera Casino owned by Madam Badia was in Giza. Francisco said it was Cairo's famous headquarter for the *beau monde*. Everyone acknowledged him as we entered, and we had one of the best tables in the house, close to the stage where a lovely belly dancer in high heels performed her fine and sensual art. She moved her pelvis rhythmically as she looked at the crowded floor of the club flirtatiously. I feasted my eyes on her magnificent body, and her sensual movements turned me on. She performed like a classical ballerina with a mixture of rhythms from Latin American, which made her dancing very original. Francisco touched me on the elbow and laughed.

"She is lovely. Her name is Samia Gamal. But wait until you see Tahiya Carioca!"

Tahiya came on next, and Francisco was right. She was even more alluring swirling around the stage, raising her thin arms and covering for brief intriguing moments, her eyes with her perfectly manicured hands. She was one of the sexiest creatures I had ever seen. She smiled as she shook her breasts, jerked her hips, and rolled her belly in an indescribable way that had all the men in the audience thinking of only one thing: possessing her. Waves of excitement rippled through my body as I fantasized making love to her. She danced until she seemed close to ecstasy. The crowd cheered her on as the music reached its climax and she kept thrusting her pelvis in perfect rhythm and then, suddenly the stage lights went out. The roar of applause was deafening.

"Enjoying yourself?" asked Francisco with a grin, "I can see you need a woman tonight.

I'm going to take you to meet a friend of mine who will take care of your needs."

The gaiety of the Cairo night was terrific and quite unbelievable when you stopped to think that a savage war was taking place. Only the uniforms at the clubs indicated that a conflict of some sort might be taking place somewhere far away.

Much as I tried to engage Francisco in a discussion on current events, h place and like the city itself, it was full of intrigue as at night most people in Cairo sought relief in revelry. The showgirls were performing anti-Nazi vaudeville skits, which were very popular although offensive to many, as most Egyptians considered the Germans their liberators from British shackles.

"This place is full of spies!" Francisco said after our second glass of champagne, "even those Hungarian showgirls are spies." I jumped at the opportunity that the conversation offered.

"Whom do they work for?" I asked.

"For the Germans, of course," he said cheerfully, "and those women sitting over there are the Endozzi sisters, who work at the Italian Embassy."

"Are they spies too?" I asked in disbelief at my new friend's sudden revelations.

"They work the Italian population in Cairo and Alexandria and inform their government about who is pro-Axis and who is not." I smiled inwardly at the similarity between their work and mine. I felt that Francisco was probably expecting me to lower my guard and tell him something that could be useful to him, but as he seemed relaxed and chatty, I tried to get some more information from
him.

"Tell me, why do the Egyptians call Hitler, Mohamed Haider? I find it quite extraordinary!"

"It's a German master plan! Somehow, they have managed to make them believe that he has Muslim origins."

The arrival of a remarkably voluptuous and sexy young

woman interrupted our conversation. I estimated her to be in her late twenties. Of medium height, her long, thick black hair fell loosely over her shoulders. Before introducing her, Francisco told me she was the niece of a well-known Egyptian actress called Aziza Amir.

"Rodney, please meet my good friend Hekmet Tadros. She is the most famous exponent of the *danse de ventre in* Egypt!" Francisco said, as he pulled a chair over and invited her to sit down. Pouring her a glass of champagne, he whispered in my ear, "she'll be yours tonight."

She was certainly very attractive and immediately showed signs of having a strong personality.

Without really acknowledging me, she addressed Francisco with a touch of sarcasm, "what a pity your friend is British, as he is rather good looking." She then put her hand on my knee and moved it slowly upwards.

"What is a young man like you doing without a uniform?" she asked me.

"I am a journalist."

"Well, tell your readers that we want our country back. If you promise to do so, I will make you a very happy man." She teased me as her hand continued upwards until it nearly reached my crotch. By now, I was extremely excited and had an erection. She had her hand on me and she smiled at my uneasiness.

"Not bad at all. You are a big boy."

I blushed but tried to regain my composure.

"We live in dangerous times and, like it or not, the

survival of Egypt goes hand in hand with the defeat of the Germans," I said with conviction. Francisco, who had been surreptitiously watching me and paying attention to every one of my words, laughed, aware of my difficulties.

"Hekmet has a lovely dahabiya on the Nile. We should go and have a nightcap at her place." I agreed, and the two of us followed him out of the nightclub. While we were waiting for his driver, a tall handsome blonde bloke appeared, accompanied by none other than Gisella von Krieger.

After our night together, Gisella lost interest in me and we only met at a few social functions. I presume she collected men like trophies much as many men of my generation collected women, but each time I saw her, I could not help becoming sexually aroused.

"Why, darling, how lovely to see you!" she cried, kissing Francisco on both cheeks and feigning surprise.

"Let me introduce you to my friends, Gisella von Krieger and Paul Roberts. Gisella works for an important art collector and Paul... well, he's an American and is enjoying this great city." Hekmet kissed Paul, so I gathered they knew each other quite well.

"What a happy coincidence, Gisella!" I said as I kissed her hand.

"What brings you to Cairo?"

"You two know each other?" Francisco interjected.

"Yes, Francisco, Rodney and I know each other from Madrid."

Something about the casualness of the encounter made me believe it was not by chance but rather a setup. I gathered the friendship between Gisella, and Francisco meant they both were working on the same side, but I could not place Paul Roberts. Was he just a victim squeezed for any useful information he might have had?

"We'd better move on. Why don't you join us for a drink on Hekmet's houseboat?" Francisco suggested.

"What a good idea. Ideal!" Paul exclaimed. "Close to home. I am Hekmet's neighbour," he added.

Hekmet's *dahabiya* was moored by the bank of the Nile, which was like a papyrus-lined oasis. Creeping hyacinth and guava trees virtually blocked out Cairo's crowds and noise. I could not believe I was looking at the longest river that flowed into the Mediterranean.

The sky was studded with stars, and it was all quite romantic. I was already a bit tipsy but was still sober enough to know that I was in dangerous if charming company.

Hekmet led us over the gangplank, across the deck, and down the stairs to her cosy private world.

"Make yourselves comfortable," she said, disappearing behind a curtain. "Francisco, be a darling and fetch some champagne from the fridge. You know where the glasses are."

The room was luxurious and exuded oriental charm. Persian carpets with exquisite patterns covered the floor. We took our shoes off and sat down on large cushions. The champagne cork flew up and hit the chandelier. I was feeling rather horny and felt a bit disappointed that there were five of us in the room.

Hekmet came back into the room wearing a satin nightgown that revealed the shape of her small nipples. She sat down next to me and without a word, kissed me on the lips. I helped her out of her gown, entirely oblivious of the others, as I sucked her brown nipples, making her groan with pleasure.

Then out of the corner of my eye, I saw Paul and Francisco. They were naked, kissing, and playing with each other. I had never seen another man erect, not even in my boarding school days, and the sight, made me feel slightly uncomfortable. Gisella approached them, and falling on her knees, she caressed both their erections, touching them with her lips and tongue.

I was aghast. Hekmet tried to recapture my attention, but I felt uptight. I downed my champagne in one gulp and poured myself another glass, which I also drank, hoping to overcome my prejudices. I was in unfamiliar territory.

"Relax, Rodney, relax." Hekmet said before kissing me again. Her skin was soft all over and she had no pubic hair. She excited me and I l was not prepared to let her go. She undressed me and imitated Gisella. The pleasure was extraordinary, and I was losing myself in it. Then I realized that I was feeling dizzy. My head started spinning. I was losing my mind. Where was I? I tried to struggle but was unable to do so. I could hear voices, but I could not command my body. I felt that I had entered a dark tunnel with no light at the end. I could sense that Gisella was over me now or maybe it was Paul or Francisco. They were all kissing each other and then kissing me, their hands all over my body. I finally had to surrender, as I had no strength or willpower left. I managed to open my eyes, briefly regaining my bearings and glimpsed Paul going through my clothes, still naked and erect.

"Nothing!" I heard him say and then I drowned in the sea of forbidden pleasure.

*

The sunlight coming through the hatch hit my face. I had a terrible headache and could hardly move. My clothes lay in a pile beside me on the floor. A naked man's body also lay close to me. He was sleeping, and I could feel his breathing close to my face. There did not seem to be anybody else in the room. I could hear a low rumble of voices in the distance. The Nile was alive.

Memories of the night before started pouring in. I felt my head was about to explode. I saw images of the King, Irene, Helen. I could hear the music and saw the sensual dancing. Then there were the faces of Francisco, Gisella, Hekmet and Paul and I listened to their laughter. I felt I had to get out. What had I done?

"They must have drugged me," I thought as I tried to justify my irresponsible behaviour.

I started to dress hurriedly. There was no sign of the

others. I looked behind the curtain and saw Hekmet fast asleep on her bed. Gisella and Francisco had already gone. In utmost silence I tiptoed around the room and searched the pockets of the jacket and trousers that lay in a pile on the floor and that obviously belonged to Paul. I found only a note written in German. It looked like a list. Who was Paul? I wondered. I had to get back to the hotel and speak to Sir Miles. I walked towards the exit, and just as I was about to leave, I heard Paul's voice.

"Don't move. Where do you think you are going?"

I turned around and saw that he was pointing a gun at me. Something in his attitude revealed that I had it all very wrong.

"Who are you? Why are you searching for my clothes?

"Take it easy. I am a friend! Our countries are fighting on the same side." I tried to remain calm. I was rather confused, and I could not think clearly. My words seemed not to change his attitude. I tried to hide the list, but he already knew I had it.

"You sneaky bastard! So Gisella was right. You do work for British intelligence."

"Paul, you are an American! You are one of us." I exclaimed again.

He laughed.

"You are quite wrong dear chap. It is unfortunate that you know too much for your own good Rodney. Place that note back where you found it." I did as I was told moving very cautiously as behind the superficial calmness he was rather upset.

"A pity. We could have had a good time. But I can't let you leave now."

"What do you mean?" I was trying to figure out what was going on. My head throbbed. I hoped Hekmet would wake up, but she probably had drunk too much and was oblivious as to what was going on.

"Come on Paul, put the gun down. Don't joke with me." I tried to remain calm, but I heard the click of the gun.

"Don't move or I'll shoot! He hissed. Was he being about to shoot or was he going to keep me there until Francisco returned and they figured out how to get rid of me? There cover had been blown and they could surely not let me go. I could not take the chance, so I decided to take a gamble.

"You bloody pervert! That's what you are. What did you do to me last night?" I shouted. Driven by the force of my fear, I leapt towards him. The sheer surprise and the impact of my body against his made him fall backwards.

He screamed as he hit the floor. I heard gunshots. Warm blood poured over my stomach. I saw the stunned face of Hekmet out of the corner of my eye …… and then I had no doubt that I was dying as I entered a tunnel of total darkness.

IX

ABDUCTION IN THE DESSERT

I woke up in a spacious room tastefully decorated with antiques. I admired the portrait of an attractive woman that was hanging on one of the walls. I was clueless as to my whereabouts. I felt a sudden pain in my stomach and noticed a stain of dry blood on the bandage.

"That is my mother." The voice sounded familiar.
I turned and saw Francisco standing in the doorway, smiling.

I was flummoxed. "Where am I?"

"Don't worry, Rodney. You're safe." He walked over to the bed and sat down, placing his hand gently on the sheet covering my knee.

"What are you doing? Please do not touch me! Where am I?" My uneasiness betrayed me.

"You are lucky to be alive. You suffered an accident."

"An accident?" I asked in bewilderment, "I don't remember...."

"You really don't remember?

"But what happened?"

"You were shot, and I saved your life."

"Why did you do that?"

"Because I like you. Do you not remember what happened the other night? It was quite a party........."

Images suddenly started pouring in, but I was baffled. "You are just a bunch of decadent perverts!" I blurted out angrily

"Well, you seemed to enjoy yourself very much indeed. Orgies are as old as mankind!" Francisco's sarcasm upset me.

"You drugged me!" I retorted angrily realizing what had happened.

"That's beside the point. Hekmet was right. You are a big boy!"

I felt disgusted. "Where are we?" I asked trying to be emotionless.

"We are at my home in Dubai. You did after all accept my invitation. You have been out for a few days!" He grinned. I was under his thumb, and he knew it. He was in total control and obviously enjoying himself.

"What date is it?"

"January 15th, 1942," he replied calmly.

I fell silent while I recollected my thoughts. Madrid, Cairo. So many things had happened since I had crossed the Pyrenees. I wondered if my mother was still alive. I hated the war and all it has done to my lovely life.

"Does anybody know where I am or what happened to me?" I asked, trying to look more relaxed though I was sure my face reflected my strained worry.

"No, Rodney. You are a missing person. You have vanished and they probably have stopped looking for you, thinking you are dead by now. Many people disappear in Cairo's Fish Market; it can be a dangerous city. Now, you and I need to chat. Tell me what you were doing in Cairo. know you are not a journalist. You see, Gisella and I are close friends."

So, he knew. Gisella obviously knew him.

"You are right. I am not a professional journalist but as the British Ambassador in Madrid is a family friend; he found this job for me. Madrid was too dull, and I wanted to leave. Given the situation in Europe, Samuel Hoare, who is like a second father to me, decided that Cairo was the right place for me to go to. Journalism was only an excuse!" I tried to sound as convincing as possible, hoping he would believe me.

"Don't give me that crap! I know what you are! Nevertheless, now that you are here, I do not give a damn! You are no threat to us, and you cannot harm our interests. Don't look so bloody worried, you are safe with me." Francisco stood up and came closer. He put his hand on my head and passed his long fingers softly through my hair.

"You are a handsome man, Rodney, and when you recover, you owe me one." He lowered himself, kissed me on the cheek and left.

I knew I had to escape. However, I felt weak, was in enemy hands, and in a foreign country where I did not know a soul. I remembered Sir Miles at the embassy in Cairo had mentioned that Francisco lived in Dubai. I had asked a few questions about the country. Together with its larger neighbours, it had become vital to our government, due to its strategic importance on the route between East and West.

Since the mid-nineteenth century when they had signed a treaty with us, these states had been known as the Trucial Sheikhdoms, and we had agreed to protect their coasts from any aggression by sea and to help them fight any attack by land. In exchange for our protection, their rulers had agreed not to dispose of any territory, except to us, nor to enter any relationship with other countries without London's consent. In other words, they were satellite friendly states; so I only needed to get out of the house and reach the political agent or the British Army barracks. But how could I achieve this, being wounded, in pain, and virtually a prisoner? I was sure Francisco would return to get his dues sooner than later.

Just as I was thinking about ways to escape, a young Bedouin girl, not older than fifteen, entered the room with a tray. She had amazing dark eyes accentuated with *khol*[19] and wore her silver jewellery with pride. When I saw the food, I realized how hungry and how weak I was. I managed to sit up in bed, and the girl observed me as I feasted on lentils with chard and lemon, broiled lamb, tabbouleh[20], pita bread, and a plate of dates.

"Do you speak English?" I asked her.

"A little," she replied to my surprise.

"I need your help. Do you understand?"

---

[19] Natural black eye liner used by Arab men and women

[20] A refreshing parsley salad with lemon juice

"Yes," she said

"Bring me some women's clothes, please. Will you help me get out of the house?"

"Very dangerous. Dangerous Sir!"

"Please!" I pleaded. She was my only ticket to freedom, my only chance. She took the empty tray and left the room. I felt gloomy, as I realised, she would not help me.

Thoughts of Francisco turning me into some sort of sex slave crossed my mind. As I was already officially dead, I had no chance of anyone coming to my rescue. He could quickly rid himself of me whenever he pleased, and in my current state, I was not much of a match.

I did not have any more visitors until that evening. An elderly overweight woman brought me my dinner, cleaned my wound, and changed my bandages. Intricate designs stained the palms of her hands; she did not speak a word of English and was not particularly friendly. I was terribly disappointed. By now, I had given up any hope of the Bedouin girl ever returning to help me. I started thinking of England, my childhood, and eventually, I fell asleep.

Someone shook me, and I woke up. By the light of the flickering candle, I was able to recognise who it was. To my relief, it was not Francisco but the Bedouin girl. She put her fingers to my lips and helped me put on a dark dress. She then placed a *burka* over my head so that it covered my face. As I stood up, I realized how weak I was. I could barely keep upright; the wound was still tender and hurt. Taking my hand, she led me in nearly total darkness down a corridor and then down some stairs. The house did not seem very large, as it was not long before I could smell the scent of flowers in an interior courtyard.

When we reached the main door, a man was waiting for us, and the girl turned back and left. Walking was agony for me, and the man had to support me by the arm as we progressed silently. We walked through narrow alleys, and past houses built close together. The night temperature was very pleasant. A North wind blew freely, and the generous light of the full moon made it easier to move. We walked through a maze of streets until it seemed we were on the outskirts of town. Finally, we reached a large tent made of animal skin and hair shared by both men and beasts. Inside, a group of men sat around a fire, together with a few camels.

"*Salaam Allah khoum,*" said the man as we entered.

"*Salaam,*" they responded in unison.

Pushed into a corner of the stable, he forced me to sit down. After a few words in Arabic, a man who seemed to be in charge gave my guide some coins, and he left. I thought it was odd, but at last, I was safe and on my way to freedom. I assumed they would hand me over to the British as soon as the city awoke. I felt tired but happy to have survived the ordeal.

The men spoke among themselves, laughing as they sipped their tea, but I could not understand what they said. Through the window of my *burka,* I could see they were all young, sturdy, and heavily armed with weapons I had never seen before: double-edged blades with hilts of horn inlaid in what seemed silver[21] and axes with steel heads[22]. They looked quite lethal. They were six in all, had thick black beards, and wore traditional dress[23].

I only had to minutely glance through my burka to see that the chief had a sinister appearance. He stood up and walked towards me. He lifted his white *khandura,* revealing that he was wearing nothing underneath. He laughed and said something to the other men that sounded obscene. He had a big stomach, a nasty looking erection, and the expression on his ugly face was one of lust. Something was very wrong. Two of the other men walked towards me and dragged me to my feet. I was shaking. They started tearing my burka off, and I knew I was in grave danger and utterly terrified. They must have misled me to believe that I was a white woman. A bunch of dangerous ruffians had sold me to them.

This time I would not be able to escape.

The two men pulled my burka off while their leader stroked his penis in anticipation. When he saw my unshaven face, he jerked back as if struck by lightning and shouted to the others. He was livid. I could see the horror and disappointment on his face at having been so deceived. He grabbed a shovel and walloped me across my chest, and I fell to the ground. The other men started cursing and kicking me

---

[21] Khanjars

[22] Yirz

[23] Kandurah

all over, and my wound opened, blood gushing out once again.

*

I opened my eyes, and the first thing I saw was the smiling face of a middle-aged nurse. I was not sure where I was, if I had fallen into enemy hands or if I was in friendly surroundings; but at least, I was alive and had survived the ordeal.

"Welcome back. What is your name? Do you speak English?" she asked softly.

"Thank God! You are English! My name is Rodney Mundy," I blurted out with relief. "Where am I?"

"You are at the British Garrison Hospital in Dubai," she said kindly, "What happened to you, Rodney? You were fortunate that our boys found you in time. You were haemorrhaging very badly."

She must have seen how worried I was because she took my hand in hers. She seemed a compassionate woman, and it felt good to let her take care of me. I tried to assemble my thoughts but could not.

"I need to talk to someone, someone in charge…an officer perhaps, I should call Madrid…...the embassy. They must be informed immediately." I incoherently rumbled as I tried to remove the drip from my arm.

"That is enough, Rodney. Relax, be a good boy! The nurse ordered while injecting me a tranquillizer. When you get better, I will get someone from the political agency to come and see you.

Several days had passed, although I was not sure as to how many when I received a visit from an officer by the name of Smith. I was already feeling more robust, thanks to Mary's care and the frequent visits from the doctor. I had received three-gun wounds in the stomach, not one as I had previously believed, but, miraculously, the bullets had not touched any of my vital organs.

I told Smith my story, leaving out some of the more sordid details that I preferred not to remember.

"I say, dear chap, that's quite a story. I shall inform Cairo immediately and the Political Resident. As soon as the doctor says that you are well enough to leave hospital, I will come and pick you up, " he said cheerfully.

"What news do you have from Cairo, Major Smith?" I sighed.

The Major hesitated before answering, "nothing very encouraging. The pro-German student demonstrations seem to be at fever pitch. The Prime Minister resigned, and Sir Miles, wanting to make sure that his successor was our choice and not King Farouk's, is behind the Abdine Palace coup. We surrounded the Palace with our troops and forced the king to accept a pro-British Prime Minister, which has left the Egyptian Army in a highly volatile state with many officers wishing to avenge their national honour. These are challenging times for us, dear chap!"

I could well understand the frustration of the Egyptians,

but with the Germans on our doorstep, the decisions that Sir Miles had to take must have been tough indeed.

"Major, what are you going to do about Francisco de Beaumont?"

"I shall, of course, inform Cairo of your findings, but I am afraid that even if he is a German spy, as you seem to believe, there is not much we can do about it over here. He is well-liked by the Sheikh, and he is one of the most successful pearl merchants in town.

I wanted Francisco locked up, and the Major's somewhat patronising tone angered me. I was wondering if my loathing was personal, but I blurted out anyway, "it is not a question of what I believe, Major Smith. He is a German spy for God's sake, and he is very dangerous!"

*

A week later, Smith drove me from the hospital to the home of a British gold trader, who had a thriving business in Dubai as the Sheik had abolished all import and export tariffs.

Alistair Sinclair came from a prominent Scottish family. He was an unmarried adventurer who was very proud to descend from the Merovingians which made us sort of cousins as Mama was also proud of her Merovingian ancestors! His house was in the Shindhaga area on the Western Bank, a narrow strip of land that separated the sea from the creek and was the town's smallest area but its central residential district. The living quarters consisted of three wind towers laid around a courtyard with the doors, the lattice screens, and the balustrades made of teak.

Alistair and I liked each other from the start. His eyes were brim-full of alert intelligence. We spent many an evening talking about the good old days over a few whiskeys; amidst the flickering light of candles as in those days, they did not have electricity.

I soon found out that not only we were neighbours of the ruler, Sheikh Saeed bin Maktoum, but also that the Scotsman was a close friend of his, often consulted for advice on a variety of subjects.

Because we, British, considered the Trucial States as having merely strategic importance for the route to India, we were not involved in their internal affairs as we were in Egypt. Dubai was just a port of call for our ships on their way to India, and during the war we increased our presence there and installed defence measures, fearing the Germans might go after the oil in Persia and Iraq.

Although a small old-world town, Dubai certainly had a cosmopolitan atmosphere and an air of tolerance. Unlike Cairo, it was not sophisticated, yet it was quite fascinating, with a large Indian population that mingled not only with us, British, but also with the Persians, Baluchis, and Arabs from different parts of the Middle East. The centre of town was Deira, where the 'souk' comprised over three hundred and fifty stalls. The area was a maze of narrow covered passageways, where one could get lost easily. Many of the artisans had no shops but simply worked on a vacant piece of ground as close as possible to their clients.

Donkeys and camels provided the primary transportation on land, and crossing the creek involved an arduous journey around its end or a ride on a small wooden boat. The old fort dominated the town. The watchtowers and the *barajils* or wind towers - the most distinctive architectural element of the houses designed to deflect the wind downwards to cool the rooms below, fascinated me.

Alistair had instructed one of his trusted servants to take me all around town. The muezzins wailed all over the city several times a day calling the pious to prayer. On Friday we went to the Grand Mosque. It was undoubtedly an imposing and elegant building, with its minarets and fifty-two domes. As I looked towards Mecca and did like all the worshipers, I felt a sense of belonging that thrilled me. This alien culture fascinated me, and I was very impressed by the Arab women, their elegance, and flamboyance, which they carried off with great modesty.

On the 21st of February, while Alistair and I were having breakfast, the servant announced the visit of Major Smith. He seemed in high spirits and did not allow anything, not even a cup of tea, to delay him from delivering his message.

"I have good news for you, dear chap. In four days, you will   fly back to London from Sharjah and will then proceed back to Madrid. I'm told they are eagerly awaiting your return there."

"And what are you going to do about Beaumont?" I enquired.

"Still waiting for orders from Cairo, I'm afraid. Don't worry we will eventually take care of him." I was upset at hearing such uncompromising words.

Once the major had left, Alistair, the adventurer, gave me a wonderful surprise. "Tomorrow," he said, "I have been invited by His Highness to hunt *houbara*[24] with falcons. His young sons, Sheikhs Rashid and Khalifa, will be there and I think you will enjoy meeting them."

"I'd love to go," I said excitedly, "and before I leave I would very much like to go out one night on a pearl-fishing expedition. Can you arrange that?"

"I most certainly can."

*

Sheikh Saeed's hunting camp was on the outskirts of town. Alistair introduced me to him and to his two sons. They both seemed focused and intelligent, and I found Rashid to be a visionary. His vision of what Dubai could become overcame all timidity and broke all limits.

The Sheikh was an uncomplicated man, and one could easily see that he relished the simple pleasures of life, his favourite pastime being falconry.

Soon after our arrival Francisco de Beaumont appeared. The Sheikh and his family greeted him warmly, and it was

---

[24] A large bird of the Bustard family

evident that they enjoyed a close friendship. The minute he saw me, he walked towards us.

"Good morning, Alistair. I see you are taking good care of my friend Rodney." He was full of scorn, and no doubt annoyed at my having outsmarted him and upset his plans. His eyes flicked.

"Rodney, I would like to have a word with you in private," he said to me in Spanish.

Sensing the atmosphere, Alistair discreetly moved on to speak to some of his other friends.

"Why did you leave like a thief in the middle of the night? I told you, you were safe with me." He sounded quite desperate.

"Rodney, I'm in love with you! Can't you understand that?"

"No, I can't," I said coldly. His confession took me entirely by surprise. I was horrified.

"You must be out of your bloody mind! I am not a homosexual. And even if I were, you are my bloody enemy!"

He grabbed me by the arm rather violently.

"Please, Rodney, please!" He pleaded desperately.

"Leave me alone.!" I pushed him off, calling the attention of several guests who looked at us with curiosity.

Realising that we were being watched, Francisco regained his composure immediately, and whispering in my ear, he threatened me, "watch out! You will pay for this! Even if it takes me a whole lifetime, one day you'll regret it!" Then he just walked away.

"What was all that about?" Asked Alistair as he approached me.

"You'd rather not know," I said.

The hunt was about to start. The guests had all finally arrived, and the splendid Arab horses, from the ruling family's stables, were ready for us to mount. I was not much of a rider, but I did my best and concentrated on not falling off my horse, which helped me put the incident with Francisco at the back of my mind. There was something in his eyes when he threatened me that made me believe revenge would be the main motor of his life, but somehow, I felt pity for him.

"Falconry is a very noble art. The falconer is a figure of authority, and as he controls his falcon so does he control his territory," Alistair explained from atop his beautiful grey stallion.

We all placed ourselves around Sheikh Saeed as the hunt was about to commence. The chief falconer, who was responsible for the bird's daily training, handed the Sheikh his bird. The falcon had on its head, covering its eyes, an *al burgu*, a hood of decorated leather, which the Sheikh removed slowly.

"*Yalla!*" he shouted. In a split second, the falcon flapped its wings with majestic grace and launched itself powerfully into the sky. We all looked up as an exciting chase took place among the birds. The Sheikh broke into a gallop, and we all followed while he tore across the desert, watching his falcon hunt the *houbara*, which on several occasions managed to escape by a hair's breadth. The chase continued until the prey, no doubt exhausted, began to slow down, at which moment the falcon swooped down and pulled it to the ground. The Sheikh's presence on the spot within seconds of the falcon's pouncing on the houbara ensured that the animal would be killed according to Islamic custom.

"That was amazing!" I said to Alistair, as we tried to recover our breath after galloping several miles.

"It teaches endurance, skill, and patience. All of which are the virtues that make a good ruler."

"And is he?" I enquired with genuine curiosity.

"Exceptional, I would say. And his son Sheikh Rashid has all the potential to be one too."

"I have to say I was quite impressed by the brief conversation I had with him when we arrived. Thanks for bringing me, Alistair. The sight of the falcon soaring upward from the Sheik's hand was breath-taking, and I shall always treasure the memory of such an unforgettable experience."

"It's my pleasure, dear friend. Wait until you taste the delicious meat of the houbara that will be served when the hunt is over. I am glad that you have had the opportunity to experience the inborn Eastern sense of sacredness in the relationship between host and guest."

*

Pearls were the region's main export and many of the merchants had made veritable fortunes with them. They were considered the Sheikhdom's aristocracy, and most were from the Bai Yas tribe to which the Al Maktoums belonged. Although the primary pearl-fishing season only lasted from May to September, some boats went out to sea all year round, and it was on one of these that Alistair had arranged for me to sail. Francisco de Beaumont was one of the few Europeans to have his own fleet of boats and, like the other merchants, he provided the capital and the equipment in return for a majority share of the profit obtained from the sale of the pearls. For centuries, the best pearls had come from these seas, but now there were genuine worries that the much cheaper cultivated pearls from Japan would affect the market very negatively. Naturally, the ongoing war did nothing to help business.

Despite this, the crew on the boat that I sailed on were extremely cheerful and friendly, although, as they spoke no English, we could barely understand each other. We set sail early in the morning, not before having a large breakfast, as no food or drink would be consumed until sunset. Until we were well clear from the harbour, heavy oars, each manned by two oarsmen, propelled the boat, and they invited me to be one of them. The crew looked healthy, strong, and showed unusually fine muscles, overall. They sang the pearl-fishers' song as we rowed.

The divers wore pegs or clips on their nostrils, protective leather sheaths on their fingers, and big toes to enable them to separate the shells from the rocks. Each one of them descended on a rope with a heavy stone attached to the end, and when they reached the bottom, I helped the men on board haul up the ropes. All the divers had a string bag slung around their necks, which they would fill with shells. The bags were attached to ropes held by the men on board, the pullers. When the divers were ready, they pulled on the ropes to signal us to draw them up. The men went underwater for well over a minute per dive. They repeated this procedure throughout the day, with the divers going down quite deep more than thirty times, having in between descents very short rests. After each dive, they heaped the shells on deck.

At sunset when the day's work was over, we opened the shells under the vigilant eye of the captain, putting the pearls away in his sea chest and throwing the shells back into the sea. Alistair later explained that the divers believed that oysters fed on empty shells and that drops of rain caught by the oysters became pearls at night.

After a long day's work, we ate the meal of rice, dates, and fish that with such hunger that we seemed we had not eaten in months. The men thought I was rather strange when they saw me eating the oysters I had reserved for my meal, but using body language, I managed to convince them to try some, and to my surprise, they seemed to find them as delicious as I did. What a pity I did not have a lemon or some chilled white wine with me!

As night fell, we returned with the high tide. The sound of the sailors chanting, and the splash of the oars carried across the still water to the town. The sky was full of stars such as can only be seen in the desert. It had been a wonderful experience, in which the men made me feel welcome. It probably was the first time a white man had joined them on a fishing expedition.

X

BACK IN SPAIN

I was back in Spain in early March 1942. Alan collected me at the airport and dropped me at my hotel. He was happy to see me and could not wait to hear all the details of my ordeal. Unfortunately, he had no news from my mother. I promised I would visit him in his office the next afternoon. The first thing I did when I found myself alone in my room was to call Felisin, who was so happy to know I was well and eager to see me. I needed an embrace, of feeling the closeness of a woman. She had been distraught by my sudden departure, and not even Alan's reassurances had calmed her down; she was delighted to hear my voice.

"How about having lunch tomorrow?" I spoke. "Where would you like to go? It's Thursday, so how about Lhardy?"

On Thursdays, this very well-known restaurant that still exists, served their famous *cocido madrileño*[25], a delicious stew of chickpeas, chicken, ham, leeks, carrots and cabbage. The meal has its own rules: first, you have the soup with vermicelli, then the vegetables and chickpeas, and finally the meat. The dining room was always noisy and full of familiar faces.

I picked Felisin up at 2:30 sharp. It was a lovely sunny

---

[25] Traditional Winter stew from Madrid

day, although still fresh. She had sounded very eager to tell me something that seemed to be bothering her. I had never seen Felisin during the daytime, and although there is a saying that at night all the cats seem grey, she did not disappoint me. She was wearing a burgundy two-piece suit and a mink collar. Around her long, gracious neck, she wore a delicate string of pearls. Her hair was up in a bun, under an elegant little hat, and she wore just the right amount of makeup. She had so much allure that she would have made an excellent wife for a member of the nobility had it not been for her profession and her coming from the wrong social background, which in Spain, in those days, was an unforgivable sin. Felisin never ceased to surprise me with her elegant manners and candid charm, and had she ever visited the South of France or Paris; she would have conquered the highest levels of society.

I kissed her hand and, as we walked to the restaurant, told her briefly about my trip to Cairo; so that she would not need to make me any questions.

"Rodney, I know you are not a student, and that you are up to something, but I'd prefer not to know about it. A woman like me needs her sixth sense to survive; besides a young man would not be here during the war. You know I am very fond of you. You are the first man who has ever made me feel that I am worth more. You have always treated me so well and with such respect …"

"You are better than a duchess to me, my dear," I interrupted, taking her delicate porcelain hand and raising it to my lips.

"I need to tell you something, but I don't know if I should.

"You know you can trust me. Are you pregnant, my darling?" I asked prepared to take the responsibility of fatherhood even if the child was not mine.

"No. It is not that. Don't worry." She took my hand and smiled reassuringly.

"There's a plot to murder Franco and to restore the monarchy," she whispered in my ear.

"What? Who told you this?" I asked in bewilderment.

"I can reveal the sin to you but not the sinner. You should know that."

"Tell me more," I urged.

"They know about it," she said mysteriously.

"Who knows, Felisin?"

"The *Falangistas*."

"And what are they going to do about it?"

"According to what I know, wait. Just wait."

After lunch, much to my regret, I had to walk Felisin home and take a taxi to the embassy. Sex had to wait as Alan was expecting me. Speculation is the enemy of peace of mind.

I could not believe that only a day after my arrival, I was embroiled in another dangerous plot.

"Rodney, take a seat and make yourself comfortable. I can't wait to hear everything."

"Alan, I'm afraid Cairo will have to wait. I have just been

informed of some extraordinary news. Felisin has heard from one of her well-placed clients in the government that they've uncovered a plot to murder Franco and restore the monarchy," I said excitedly.

Captain Hillgarth did not react. His jaw dropped. From the fearless man that I was used to seeing, I saw a very worried one. He was in some dilemma, and I felt a lot of tension in the room. He lit a John Players and offered me one. He took a deep puff then clearing his throat he finally spoke.

"Listen, Rodney. Your work in Madrid and Cairo has been excellent, the information you bring us is handy, and I have precise instructions from the ambassador not to involve you in any risky operations nor inform you of our specific activities. Because of your age, he wants to protect you as this is getting more and more dangerous, and I agree with him. However, under the present circumstances, it is probably better if I explain to you the situation. You are a man now, and I will take full responsibility for what I am about to say."

I listened attentively and in silence.

"In April last year, we devised a plan to convince the more moderate members of the army to support the restoration of the monarchy, if and when the timing was right. A few months earlier, Himmler had visited Madrid and held important meetings with Serrano Suñer and Franco; so we got to work. You may be aware that thanks to the influence of generals like Aranda, Beigbeder, Kindelan, Varela, Ponte, and Solchaga we have succeeded in getting General Valentín Galarza, a royalist who is totally opposed to Nazism as Minister of the Interior."

"How did you arrange that?" I interrupted.

"That's our job! To prevent at all costs that Spain enters the war."

"And the plan?" I enquired with genuine interest.

"We shelved the plan momentarily, but since the Americans entered the war, Berlin renewed its pressure on Franco to join the Axis; therefore, we have started working again¨

"How did you manage to be so persuasive?" I interrupted.

"We had over twelve million dollars at our disposal for this project and, though they are mostly good patriots, none of these generals are insensitive to money. These are difficult times for everyone. We are sponsoring any voices in the government that can argue for Spain staying out of the war. So now, with the collaboration of the American Office of Secret Services (OSS), the operation is once again in full swing, we call it Operation Relator.   Part of the army is prepared to rise if, and only if, we feel that Franco plans to join the war. The plan is for the British Navy to invade the Canary Islands and establish a Free Spanish Government headed by Prince Don Juan as King, with Pedro Sainz Rodriguez as Prime Minister. We feel this could occur at any moment. Have you heard what Franco said yesterday to his troops in Seville? He promised the

Germans a million men to defend Berlin whenever they were needed! The prospect of Hitler and the *Caudillo* in eternal friendship is quite appalling as you might well imagine."

"This is a huge fish, indeed!"

"Too big and too dangerous. Do not breathe a word about this to anybody. We must warn the Americans that it is probable that Franco knows about Operation Relator. We must do nothing at least for the time being. I feel sorry for Don Juan, as he will be bitterly disappointed!"

*

That night I felt very restless. I had too many things on my mind. I was dead worried about my mother, Uncle Jack and Princess Jane. I could not believe that by now the Embassy could not at least confirm that they were still in Foix; I started fearing the worst and feeling somewhat angry with Alan and the lot. I needed a stiff drink, so I went to Pasapoga, a glittering nightclub where married men took their lovers. I was sitting at the bar with Laszlo, when we saw Gisella walk in, accompanied by Hans Vogel, the SS Captain she had led me to believe she despised. He was wearing a swastika armband on his dinner jacket. What was she doing back in Madrid? I wondered. Did she have anything to do with what was going on? She saw us and walked straight towards us.

"Hello, Rodney. What a small world! You seem to be everywhere."

"And so do you," I replied coldly, the memories of Hekmet's houseboat all too fresh.

"You remember my friend, Captain Vogel?" We shook hands without exchanging words. I looked him straight in the eyes and did not like what I saw. Neither did Laszlo.

"You look ravishing, my dear. Travelling suits you," I said sarcastically.

"And so do you, darling. I have heard you had just vanished from Cairo. I am glad you have not left us altogether...at least yet!" she mused in her usual provocative manner.

"Well, you should know my dear." I could not hide my irritation.

"Of course, we do seem to move in the same circles!" She winked as she passed her finger over her juicy red lips. She was wearing a long red velvet dress open on one side. Her shoulders were bare, and the diamond swastika brooch was pinned strategically on her bosom. She had remarkably long legs, and she excited me despite me.

"So, what brings you to Madrid this time?" I asked.

"Art makes me travel extensively. I am now looking at some Spanish paintings that Marshal Göring is interested in buying." Despite her aloofness she could not conceal her surprise to see me there though nothing in her voice or demeanour denoted that she held Paul's views about my activities. I wondered how Francisco had explained our sudden disappearance.

"Ta-ta, see you!" she said, turning around with a brisk,

sexy thrust of her hip, letting her long leg out, in full view.

Laszlo looked worried but remained silent for a while, before muttering, "I don't like this."

"What don't you like, my friend? "I asked.

I was becoming quite good at getting people to confide in me. I felt that we all needed to talk. Unable to trust anybody, we tended to keep our fears, worries, and most intimate thoughts to ourselves.

"Rodney, I know I can trust you. Listen to me carefully. I am an undercover agent, and I work for the OSS. There are just a handful of us here in Madrid." He said with an exquisite benignancy. His confession took me entirely by surprise, and he must have seen my look of bewilderment. I said nothing.

"You need to know that Gisella is a very dangerous woman." He went on, "she is Himmler"s right hand and her presence here in Madrid indicates that something is about to happen. Did you know that Vogel is the head of the SS in Spain? Those two used to be lovers."

"Gisella told me she hated the chap," I replied nonchalantly, before I added presently by way of an afterthought, "I wasn't aware of any of that, but Laszlo why do you tell me these things?"

"Rodney, you know why. We fight on the same side."

Could I trust Laszlo, I wondered? I felt confident I could, but one could not be too careful. I was not about to reveal my activities to him even though he seemed to know. I felt he had been unnecessarily careless in speaking to me so openly although, I suppose, it is only human nature to want to share your worries with others.

"You see, Rodney, I'm in charge of preparing a coup against Franco and setting up a democratic government that will support the Allies."

I could not believe my ears! My friend Laszlo was the man in charge of the entire operation! We remained there for hours, while he filled me in on all the details of Operation Relator, parts of which I already knew.

Laszlo's revelations had come as a huge surprise. As far as I was concerned, if anyone in Madrid was not a spy, it was he. This only goes to show how complicated our work was and how good he was at it. I never told the embassy that I knew who the agent was, as I felt it would not help matters but would probably only make Laszlo more vulnerable. He was a friend who in a moment of weakness, had felt the need to talk, and I left it at that.

The following morning, I felt I needed to think things over quietly, so I decided to take a stroll in the Retiro Park, the meeting place for the respectable women in Madrid. Because of the good weather, many nannies were pushing prams carrying the newborn babies of the elite. Quite a few pretty
looking younger women with their mothers giggled and whispered as I passed. I smiled at them, and they blushed. I wanted to investigate further. I felt an enormous curiosity as to how the events would develop, and I knew I would be leaving soon. I decided that the first thing I was going to do

was to go to Felisin's flat. I felt a strong sexual desire as I thought of her. After some glorious lovemaking, I told her I was a journalist in search of a good story, and she appeared to believe me. She promised to let me know if she heard anything that could help me write my story.

I intended to spend the next few days visiting the places that the Germans most frequented. I arranged to lunch at Edelweiss opposite the Zarzuela Theatre, and to allay any suspicions I invited Gonzaga and Pelayo, sons of the Count of Herentals. By now, I knew that the Count was Himmler's man in Madrid, so I thought this quite a clever move on my part.

The Herentals boys were very handsome and well-bred. They had their father's large blue eyes, but whereas his were despotic, theirs were full of warmth. One lad was my age, and the other was twenty-one. They spoke fluent German, French and English, which was very rare in Spain in those days. They were both unwillingly studying university careers imposed on them by their autocratic father, whom they disliked while living under the constant protection of their mother. In the Count's presence, they were not allowed to express their feelings, and they lived in constant fear of his rages and tantrums. I felt quite sorry for them. We had a shared love of women and sports, and I enjoyed their company. Initially, we avoided discussing politics, but as we grew to know each other better, they began to confide in me. They hated the Germans, maybe as an act of rebellion against their father; so now and then they would give me crucial information. The Herental's palace was the centre of German espionage in Madrid.

On that day, Edelweiss was unusually busy, and there was a surprising number of men in German uniforms.

"What have you been up to?" I asked as we enjoyed our first glass of Riesling.

"You, tell us. We hear that you are having an affair with Felisin".

Gonzaga, the eldest, was the more outspoken of the two, while Pelayo was the artist and a trifle shy. I had seen some of the paintings he did without his father's knowledge and could see he had great talent. To boost his morale, I had bought two of them, which are still in my possession. For the Count of Herentals all artists were *maricones*,[26] which traumatized poor Pelayo. The two brothers were very close and felt quite at ease in my company, as they thought they could be themselves, and I encouraged them to do so.

"You Spanish like your gossip!" I said laughing, "she's a friend," I added casually.

"But are you having sex with her?" Gonzaga asked excitedly.

"I wouldn't lie to you. The answer is yes, and she is quite amazing!" The conversation went off in that direction for a while, and they talked about their sexual fantasies as we had a good laugh together.

"It's very odd to see so many Germans in uniform, don't

---

[26] A derogative term for Gay

you think?" I asked.

"You're right," said Pelayo.

"Do you want to know something, Rodney?" asked Gonzaga

"I'd be delighted."

"I'll tell you a secret if you promise to introduce Pelayo and me to Felisin. We want to have sex with her."

"Together?" I asked, feigning surprise, and we all laughed at the thought.

"Ok. You have a deal. It better be good, though, Gonzaga",

"Yesterday, my father had a meeting with Gisella von Krieger and Captain Vogel. The German Ambassador and some officers also came to the house."

"Did I ever tell you that I had sex with her, too?" I interrupted, intending to get them to relax even more and lower their guard, and thus tell me everything they knew. I told them all about my sexual experience with Gisella in Madrid, which had them both mesmerized.

"Sorry, Gonzaga. Go on." I said after I finished narrating my sexual encounter.

"I overheard everything they discussed yesterday, and you are in for a shock, my friend." The waiter who brought the main course interrupted him. We waited, sipping the wine, and then he blurted out, "The Germans are plotting to kill Franco!" I tried to conceal my surprise at what he was saying.

Gonzaga was unable to tell me the details of the plot. Still, it appeared that Hitler had lost his patience with Franco and wanted him to commit firmly, once and for all, to what I later learnt was called Operation Felix. The plan was for the German Army to march from France through Spain, conquer Gibraltar and advance on North Africa.

I took the story straight to Allan, and it was news to him too.

"I'm afraid you know too much for your good, Rodney."

"But, Alan, don't you think it's a paradox that both our enemies and we want to get rid of Franco?"

"Well, our objectives are very different. Franco is a very skilful political tactician who is balancing the factions that make up the regime, and I presume that the Germans are fed up with the dithering and want to have him replaced by someone like General Muñoz-Grandes who would go along with their plans. If they do so, it would put our own plans in jeopardy."

"What plans?" I asked with interest.

"The plan to land allied troops in North Africa."

I sat there and listened while he told me of plans that would change the course of history, and I felt immensely proud to be helping the cause of justice and freedom.

"We, on the other hand, want to restore the monarchy, which is after all the traditional form of government in this country. We don't want to back a fascist dictator. With Prince Juan as King, we would invite the political parties to return to Spain and hold democratic elections."

"They are very different objectives, and it amazes me that

they both involve eliminating Franco. Do you think he has any inkling about this plot?" I inquired.

"I've no idea son, but if the *Falangistas* know as your informant has told you, what is certain is that everybody must be very busy right now. Franco still believes in an Axis victory. I will inform the Prime Minister and the OSS immediately. Rodney, it would probably be advisable to consider sending you back to England as soon as it is feasibly possible. I think staying here would make you very vulnerable. I will talk to the Ambassador about it. In the meantime, as always, be very careful and keep your eyes wide open."

Everywhere I went, I could feel the tension in the air, and I do not know if it was my imagination running away with me or whether it was genuine. The atmosphere was gloomy. Every morning when I woke up, I expected to hear the news of a 'coup' against the dictator. I just hoped it would be 'our coup'. However, the days passed, and nothing happened.

I had heard nothing further about my departure and had not asked. Captains Lubbock and Hillgarth were both very busy those days. I tried to keep a low profile and make myself as useful as I could while continuing with my routine.

One evening I invited Felisin to the *Teatro Real* for a production of Puccini's Madame Butterfly. She had never been there and was terribly excited at the prospect. I knew our presence would raise more than one eyebrow, but that amused me very much. Before the performance, everybody stood up as the orchestra played the National Anthem, and most of the audience raised their arms in the fascist salute. Felisin looked stunning. She had such a sense of style and was so elegant that she made most women in the audience look plain. The evening was a success and ended with a splendid night of lovemaking.

About two weeks later, I met Laszlo for tea at Embassy. I could see that he was in a state of shock when he walked in.

"They've k.. killed him," he stammered.

"Who are you talking about?"

"I've just had a very brief encounter with my contact in the Spanish army on the Puente de Segovia. He was my go-between with General Aranda. We barely exchanged a glance when I passed him an envelope. I had started walking towards the *Plaza de Oriente* when I heard a scream and saw him fall to from the bridge. I am sure they must know who I am now. I'll be next!" I could see the fear in my friend's eyes.

"Calm down, Laszlo. Did you see anybody push him?"

"No"

"He could have jumped. If he knew they were on to him, jumping might have been a better option than being interrogated by Franco's police. We are at war, and we are all in danger," I said. "Let's not panic. Go to your Embassy, inform them, and then go home. I will see you soon." I tried to reassure him, but it did not help. I realized that what I was saying was utter nonsense.

✳

Easter came, and the city went completely dead. Franco's ultra-conservative government went into mourning for the suffering and death of Christ, and all flags flew at half-mast. Everything closed even restaurants and cafes. The radio stations played martial music. I had never seen anything like it in my life.

During Holy Week, the most famous churches in the city paraded their statues of Christ and the Virgin, which competed in extravagance and luxury. Their velvet and silk robes, embroidered in gold and silver were encrusted with precious stones. The statues were paraded through the city on heavy floats supported on the shoulders of about twenty men. Each float was covered with hundreds of lit candles. The processions moved slowly to the sound of a slow regular drumbeat. Behind the statues, men paraded orderly, wearing purple robes with hoods that resembled those of the Ku-Klux-Klan and carrying long tapers. Now and then the floats would stop for the bearers to rest, and someone selected for the occasion would sing a beautiful *saeta* in honour of Christ or the Virgin. When the song was over, the bearers would lift the float again and carry on, watched by thousands of awed *madrileños*. The women traditionally wore black, with their hair caught up in a *peineta*[27] and *mantilla*[28]. The religious devotion of the masses was very moving, even to an agnostic like me.

---

[27] High Combs

[28] Lace handmade head scarves

On the evening of Glory Saturday, many cinemas and theatres opened with a new show, and the city came back to life, as Spain prepared to celebrate Christ's Resurrection.

During the Easter holidays, I did not see Lazlo, but I knew he had gone to Seville to enjoy their famous Holy Week.

On Easter Monday, which was no longer a holiday, I was summoned to the British Embassy for a meeting with the Ambassador, whom I had hardly seen since my arrival, except for a few brief encounters.

It was a warm spring day, and as I had some time, I decided to walk part of the way before taking a taxi. I saw a family dressed in rags hunting in the rubbish bins for scraps of food around the corner from the hotel. A pair of *Guardia Civiles* approached them and using force made them leave. It was heart breaking, but that is how post-war Madrid was. The bureaucracy was utterly corrupt, and rations did not get to the people that needed them more: so many contrasts between the privileged few and the rest.

When I arrived, he was waiting in his large study with Alan Hillgarth. They both rose from their chairs to greet me.

"Well, Rodney," he said without a preamble, "I've been following your progress, and I'm very proud of you. Captain Hillgarth has told me that you have surpassed our highest expectations. The information you have gathered over the past few months has been beneficial and has saved many lives. However, you could be in danger if you stay in Madrid

any longer. We have decided that the time has come for you to leave Spain. We would like you to consider joining The Firm as soon as you return to England. If you agree, you will be sent to Fort Monckton to receive proper
training, and by January you can start active service in London."

"I would like to stay here a bit longer, Sir. I know everybody now, and I think I can still be useful."

Samuel Hoare looked at Alan Hillgarth and smiled, "I'm afraid that is completely out of the question. The embassy is under a lot of pressure. We have pro-Nazi protestors outside daily now, and six of our men have been murdered in the last month alone. Only yesterday, a large group of Falange youths voiced their anti-British sentiment in front of the embassy! *Gibraltar Español,* they screamed. It was rather nerve-racking, and the *Civiles* just stood and watched. I am afraid that I cannot allow it. You must go."

I was disappointed, but I understood that I had to leave.

"I will gladly join MI6 and serve my country then Sir. When am I to leave?"

"Soon. Alan will let you know."

I went straight to see Felisin. I had become used to her lovemaking and missed her caresses and the warmth of her body. Each time we were in each other's arms, she surprised me with something new and taught me many of her most intimate secrets. It is to Felisin that all credit is due to my success with women later on in my life.

"Felisin, I will be leaving Madrid very soon. My work here

is over." I said as we lay naked in bed.

"Have you finished writing your articles?" she asked.

"Yes. I am returning to England. I also want to find out where my mother is. I hope she's still alive."

I kissed her. She was a delightful creature. Her cosy little flat, not far from the *Barrio de las Letras*, was home in Madrid. She had her head on my shoulder and I stroke her hair. I told her about my life in the South of France and how I had escaped through the mountains ending up in a Spanish jail. She laughed and kissed me tenderly.

"Let's celebrate life! Let's drink a toast to our paths having crossed!"

She got out of bed, and the satin sheets fell to the floor. Her body would have made the delights of Leonardo. She knew I was watching her, and she swayed her hips in a way she knew made me crazy. She returned with a chilled bottle of champagne and two glasses.

"What a luxury, my love!"

"You won't believe who gave me this, Rodney", she said, handing me the bottle to uncork.

"Last night at Chicote I met this German officer called Hans Vogel. Do you know him?"

I filled the glasses, and we toasted and drank.

"He's a dangerous man," I replied after the toast.

"He invited me to spend some time with me, and suggested we go to his flat. He gave me a lot of money upfront; so I was expecting something kinky, you know what strange sexual tastes these Germans have. Anyway, I went along …after all, that's my job".

"Did he hurt you?"

"No, Rodney. To my surprise, he wasn't interested in having sex with me at all."

"So, what was he after?"

"Information! He gave me twenty thousand pesetas and has offered me one hundred thousand if I got him what he is after."

"And what is that. Do you, have it?"

"No, I don't, but I will certainly do my best to get it for him."

"What does he want to know?" I insisted.

Felisin hesitated for a moment and then turned serious. "You remember the story I told you about a plot to kill Franco and reinstate the king?"

"Yes, I do. It was just a rumour."

"No, it wasn't. Vogel told me they aborted the plan because Franco had found out about it. Right now, someone has a huge amount of money that was supposed to be used to finance the plot, and the Germans are after it."

God, she knew too much for her own good. I wondered how I could protect her. I needed to warn her, but how?

"Felisin, promise me that even if you find something out, you won't say a word to Vogel, or anyone else for that matter," I said gravely.

"Why? That money would change my life. It would allow me to stop working!"

"You know that I do care for you, and believe me that

money would be your ticket to the grave. Promise me. Please promise me that you will forget it completely." I pleaded.

"Ok, beautiful. I promise!" She kissed me and turned over me. Her sensual body covered mine. I embraced her, and this time we made love hurriedly but with a passion that I had never felt before. Then after a sublime orgasm, I rushed out of her apartment. My head was spinning as I contemplated my choices. I would have to see Laszlo immediately and, naturally, inform the Embassy. Once the Germans knew he had the money, he would be dead, and they were bound to know eventually. I now knew that his contact had been murdered by the Gestapo or by Franco's secret police. I thought it probably had been a Gestapo job, in which case Laszlo's life was certainly at risk. It all now began to make sense to me. I had just managed to listen on the BBC radio station that the Nazi offensive in Russia was not going well and was an enormous drain on the resources of the Third Reich. The Falange newspaper Arriba, of course, reported the opposite as was to be expected. The Spanish National Socialist Party still hoped for a German victory and a fascist Europe.

I figured that such a vast sum of money would enable the Germans to carry out their plans in Spain, including murdering Franco and replacing him with Muñoz Grandes or Serrano Suñer and the Falange would undoubtedly go along with the project. The situation was extremely delicate.

As soon as I arrived at my hotel, I called the embassy, but was told that Captain Hillgarth would not be in until the next day. I urged the secretary to let him know I called as soon as possible. There was no way I could reach him, but through the embassy and time was of vital importance; accordingly, I decided to go to Laszlo's apartment to tell him everything I knew. I had not seen him since our night out at Pasapoga, and I assumed he had returned from Seville by now. I hoped he had.

I took a taxi to Calle Garcia de Paredes where he lived in a modernist building from the turn of the century. Many bourgeois families lived in those types of buildings as most of the aristocratic families still lived in palaces. As I walked in, the *portera*[29] was mopping the marble floors. "*Buenas tardes, Señor*".

"Buenas tardes, Remedios. Is *Señor* Szekeres in?"

"Yes, *Señor* Mundy. He has some visitors. Two foreigners and an exquisite lady. Lovely red hair she has."

I had not time for the usual small talk and gossip. My heart was pounding as I took the elevator up to the fifth floor. I hoped I had not arrived too late. As the lift rose, I heard a door slam and people dashing down the stairs. I could not see who they were through the lift's stained glass windows: nevertheless, I did not doubt as to the identity of the visitors.

When I got out of the lift, I saw that Laszlo's door had been forced open. I walked into his apartment, calling out to him.

---

[29] Caretaker. In those days these women knew everything that happened in their buildings and were famous for their love of gossip

I found a ransacked flat. Things lay broken and scattered all over the floor. The intruders had cut open the sofas in the living room and the mattress in the bedroom, allowing the feathers to take over the rooms. They had been very thorough in their search. Bloodstains covered Laszlo's favourite armchair, and a piece of rope on the floor indicated that he had been tied up and probably tortured. Had they found what they had come for? If the Gestapo were now in possession of the money, the German could carry out very soon the coup to replace Franco.

"Laszlo! Laszlo! Where are you?" I called out.

I tried to remain calm, but I was shaking. It was one thing to pass on information to my superiors, but quite another to be in the midst of what probably was the murder of my friend.

The sliding doors leading on to the balcony were wide open, and the curtains billowed in the spring breeze. I went onto the balcony and looked down. There it was, my friend's body lying on the pavement in a pool of blood, surrounded by passers-by and the police. I realized I was in serious trouble, and not knowing what to do, I walked back into the living room where I saw something glittering on the floor. It was Gisella von Krieger's diamond swastika. I picked it up and hid it in my underwear.

Within minutes, the police stormed into the apartment, followed by a hysterical Remedios.

"Poor *Señor* Szekeres! I know you did not kill him, *Señor* Mundy. You were his friend. It must have been those German visitors who ran out of the building, overturning my bucket onto the floor I have just cleaned."

"Be quiet, *Señora*", the police Captain snapped at the *portera* ."Go and wait downstairs. We will need you to answer a few questions later".

When Remedios left, still blabbering on, the captain switched his attention to me and had me searched.

"Your papers," he demanded in a firm voice.

I was in trouble. To be caught without papers in Spain meant immediate arrest and questioning, and I had left my passport at the hotel when I had rushed out.

"I am a British citizen. I am staying at the Hotel Nacional, and my papers are in my room. I am a friend of the British Ambassador, and I would appreciate it if you got in touch with the Embassy." I said firmly, hoping they would not automatically arrest me.

"*Señor*, you are under arrest on suspicion of the murder of *Señor* Szekeres."

I was handcuffed and rough-handled out of the apartment by two sturdy police officers in their grey uniforms. Their facial expressions were most unfriendly.

"But you heard what *Señora* Remedios said," I interjected sharply. "When I arrived, I heard people running down the stairs. She will confirm what I say." I protested.

"You can explain everything to the *Comisario*."
I was taken to the cells in the basement of the Interior Ministry in the Puerta del Sol. The same place where the communist had their torture chambers after they had taken

198

over the republic.

As I feared, I spent over a week in solitary confinement in the eerie basement of the police headquarters. The police did not allow me to call the British Embassy and the thought that the Germans might have got the money and succeed in the coup while I was wasting away, was agony. Though I was not tortured, hearing the screams coming from other cells was terrifying, and I had no doubt my life was in jeopardy.

The *Comisario* was a very unpleasant man with an inclination for cruelty. Though rather frail, he wielded high power in his little kingdom. He sported a neatly trimmed narrow moustache and wore an old brown suit, which showed signs of having been mended several times by a submissive wife. He struck me as being someone who had a price; however, after my experience in Barcelona, I dared not bribe him as I could only make matters worse for myself.

I was hardly given any food or water and interrogated ceaselessly. Why had I killed Szekeres? What was I looking for? Was I a spy? Was he a spy?

I stuck to my story that I was writing an article about the 'new' Spain for an English magazine. I also insisted that the British Ambassador and his wife knew me well. "We don't like *ingleses* in this country", he said, frustrated at the lack of information I was giving him. "*El Caudillo*[30] says the Germans will win this war, and they will".

One morning the door of my cell opened, and *Comisario*

---

[30] As many Spaniards called General Franco

García walked in as usual. I presumed he would subject me to another round of pointless questioning.

"You have a friend who wants to speak to you," he said with a stupid grin.

I was relieved, believing it was someone from the Embassy, but my heart sank when I saw that my visitor was none other than Hans Vogel, wearing an SS captain's uniform. All hope of ever seeing my mother again vanished instantly. I was petrified. The *Comisario* clapped me in a pair of handcuffs and left, locking the cell door behind him.

"Where is the money?" Vogel asked without any preamble while he paced the cell impatiently. I was relieved to know they had not found it yet.

"What money?" I asked innocently.

"Don't try to fool me! I don't have the patience for games."

"The money that Lazlo had." He said savagely.

"I don't know what you are talking about. Laszlo was my friend. We used to go out together and have fun. He was just an eccentric and wealthy artist. What do you want from me? My arrest is illegal. I have done nothing. I don't know anything about any money."

Ignoring my pleas, he took an electric prod out of his pocket and put it to my face.

"Are you going to tell me, or do you want me to stick this up your arse?"

"I don't know anything," I insisted. At that, he forced the prod into my mouth. I suddenly felt as if my head was about to explode, and I started vomiting. Blood spurted from my nose and ears. Now I knew what caused the constant screaming I heard throughout my confinement. I felt as if I were fainting. He started to unbutton my trousers, but I was too weak and dizzy even to react. What he was about to do was too ghastly for words. I knew I would not survive another electric shock.

My screams must have alerted *Comisario* García because he burst into the cell.

"What the hell do you think you're doing? You cannot torture our prisoners! You have no jurisdiction here! You are not in Berlin! I warned you!" He shook his head, sorrowfully.

The *Comisario* was furious and ordered a police officer to drag Captain Vogel out despite his protests and threats.

"You're going to regret this! Our countries have a pact! I shall inform the Minister! I shall have you fired!" The police officer undid the handcuffs and gave me some water to drink. I felt dreadful.

"When are you going to let me out of here?" I asked the *Comisario*.

"You will be leaving tomorrow. Your embassy has just secured your release," he replied with a stern face.

"Tomorrow morning you will be driven to Gibraltar and put on a boat in convoy bound for England," Captain Hillgarth told me with a strained worried expression on his face. "You should consider yourself lucky. Tonight, you will be the Ambassador's guest at the Residence but please for your good do not mention to anyone that you are leaving."

"I must go then and collect my things at the hotel and pack."

"I'm afraid that will not be possible, Rodney. The Gestapo has already been there, and there is nothing left except for these two paintings." He pointed at the two oils I had bought from Pelayo Herentals.

"They haven't found the money yet?"

"Yes, they have."

"Oh, my God! That is terrible! Poor Laszlo! He paid with his life, trying to prevent the money from falling into German hands, and all for nothing."

"What was left of the money has not fallen into German hands, but into Franco's. Franco just got lucky!"

"There'll be no coup against him, then?"

"No. He has already moved against all the royalist generals and has had them purged. Sainz Rodriguez, whom Don Juan had chosen as Prime Minister of his Resistance Government, has been ordered into exile to the island of Fuerteventura. Eugenio Vegas has also been ordered out of the country and has joined the Prince in Lausanne. I am afraid to say that, quite unintentionally, we have damaged any chances that the Prince had of regaining the throne. From what we know of Franco and his wife, they probably despise him now, and they are people who never forget".

"Alan….."

"Yes, Rodney."

"I need to ask you a big favour. Promise me that you will protect Felisin. I know this is something that I should not be asking. However, I must. Can you get her out of the country, please? Send her to England. If necessary, I will marry her."

"That is out of the question. And would she want to leave?" Alan asked gravely. "You love her, don't you? What you are asking is most honourable, but I cannot let you marry a prostitute. The Ambassador will never allow it. It is impossible. I am sorry."

"I don't know, but I would feel terrible if something happened to her. Please promise..." I pleaded.

"What you are asking is extremely difficult, but I promise I will look into it and do what I can to get her out of the country."

XI

HOME

As usual, I left Madrid without having had the chance to say goodbye to any of my friends, not even Felisin whose love I longed for. I promised myself that if Alan did not manage to get her to England, I would return after the war to look for her and give her the life she deserved.

The trip to Gibraltar was uneventful, but the one to England was a terrifying ordeal as the food convoy was bombed several times by German Stukas.

As planned, I arrived in London and went straight to Fort Monckton, where I received intense training for over four months before joining 'The Firm'. I found the training tough as I was not too good with discipline and order although I worked hard at it. We were woken at dawn and were kept very busy until we collapsed into bed at about eight in the evening.

I had not been able to save any money from my stay in Madrid and was virtually broke. Nobody had any news of my mother who was officially still at the displaced persons' camp in Foix. I longed to see her.

August 1942 saw the start of what was to be known as the Battleof Stalingrad. This fierce battle took a devastating death toll of both the Red Army and the Nazis, and by the end of January, the Russians had defeated the hitherto invincible Germans.

After my intense training, I returned to London in October but was wholly unprepared for the devastation I found there. The city had suffered dramatically during the blitz, and nothing had been spared, not even Buckingham Palace or the Houses of Parliament. Thousands of Londoners lost their lives, and many more were now homeless. Everything was rationed, except for fish, but at least there was enough food to go around for everybody. The shortages and the suffering created a sense of purpose and resistance against the common enemy that seemed challenging to erase.

Of course, extreme situations create seedy characters, and a new breed of men appeared in those difficult days. Known as the spivs, they controlled the black market and as a result, became quite prosperous and went to many of London's nightspots to show off their newly acquired wealth. They were flamboyant characters, most of them young men discharged from the front on medical grounds.

My work in London was like what I had done in Madrid. Our government had interned Sir Oswald Mosley, his wife Diana, and other fascist sympathizers. Mosley had many followers, as he preached a unique form of fascism. Its central policies rested on the concept of a united British Empire, which appealed to those older members of society that had served that Empire. Mosley was a brilliant politician who had always advocated peace and negotiations with Hitler as a way of solving the problems affecting Europe since the Treaty of Versailles at the end of the First World War. He had followers within the British establishment, who provided funds in secret, and my job was to find out who those people were. By now, I was exceptionally well suited for the job.

I took a small apartment in South Kensington and started going out and enjoying London's social life.

News from Spain were quite encouraging. In September, Franco substituted Serrano Suñer by Francisco Gomez-Jordana and he soon declared the neutrality of Spain. Operation Torch was finally launched in November after the American and British governments assured Franco that Spain's sovereignty would be respected. The disembarking in North Africa was successful, and there was hope the tide would change in our favour.

One evening, as I was having a drink at the bar of The Renaissance Club, I noticed a beautiful woman sitting by herself. I, of course, was not in uniform, which was rare for a young man in those days. I approached her and looked straight into her eyes.

"My name is Rodney Mundy. And yours?"

"Phryne Alabaster," she replied with a laugh and offered to buy me a drink, which I found rather odd but attributed to her just reaffirming her independence.

That night we had dinner together. We talked, danced, and immediately clicked as it happened, we even had a friend in common, Rafael Valls. I told her about my adventures since escaping from Foix but omitted any references to MI6. One could never be too careful. It was love at first sight. We enjoyed each other's company immensely and often went down at weekends to the "Old Bell" at Hurley, where Raf Valls and his girlfriend, Joanna Kinlock-Jones, often joined us. I knew that Raf was with MI6, and he obviously knew that I was, too, but in all our years of friendship, we never once discussed it. Joanna was soon to leave Raf and become romantically involved with her boss. She was the personal assistant to "M", who was also my boss, and who would be immortalized in the James Bond books and films.

In London, we went regularly to The Milroy, which was frequented by Bing Crosby and Frank Sinatra when they were in town. Though we still lived in separate apartments, I felt my relationship with Phryne was healthy, calm, and steady, and so did she.

My cover was that I was working at the Ministry of Aircraft Production and with the job came the privilege of a car, something very rare in those days.

To my surprise, "M" asked me one day to bring Phryne along to meet him. At the time, she was working at the Yugoslavian Embassy. We met at the Savoy for tea. "M" was in his mid-fifties, a tall attractive man with keen eyes and a face like a hawk. To my utter astonishment, he told Phryne all about my work and then said he was certain she could be trusted and could be very helpful to me. He told her never to acknowledge him in public, which of course she never did.

In those days, I had many reports to write and usually prepared them very late at night, thereby indulging in the pleasure of getting up at noon. I went to many cocktail parties and dinners where I mingled with all sorts of people. As in Madrid, I quickly became very popular on the London party scene. I had just turned twenty and was now adept at flirting and charming people into talking. I could be a communist, a fascist or a fag if the situation demanded it. I had become a master of disguise and deception, and I enjoyed myself immensely. However, I gathered so much valuable information that my reports were becoming longer and longer, with the result that I was sleeping less and less.

The news from Cairo was upsetting. The Embassy and the Military headquarters were forced to burn all their papers when an attack by Rommel had seemed inevitable thus that July 1st was known as Ash Wednesday because the air was thick with smoke and ashes as our forces prepared to evacuate the city.

The shopkeepers and hoteliers had prepared red, white, and black streamers and bunting. The pictures of Churchill disappeared, while those of Rommel and their Mohamed Haider popped up everywhere. Mobs took to the streets, chanting "Rommel! Rommel! Rommel!" I felt sorry for the Jewish population in Cairo, and Alexandria was left stranded there by the British to face their fate. I also wondered what fate awaited Irene and Helen, who had done so much for us. All of this disgusted me, as they had all been loyal allies. Fortunately for the Egyptians and the free world, Rommel never made it into Cairo. Had the Germans entered, King Farouk, who was only twenty-two, would undoubtedly have been deposed and the pro-Nazi Prince Abbas Haim, placed on the throne.

On July 26th, 1943, Italy was overjoyed with the news that their king had finally dismissed the Duce and ordered his arrest. The dismissal of Mussolini was excellent news for the Allies, as it meant that Italy would most probably seek immediate peace, but it was too late for poor King Victor Emmanuele to save his crown.

Phryne and I invited Fred Kempler for a drink. He was working for General de Gaulle's Free France government based in London. We went to a well-known club off Park Lane that was run by a hilarious black man who, showing a mass of gold teeth, laughed in six languages while he spent the night playing darts as he drank and laughed. Another evening we went to the Vanity Fair Club in Mayfair, as Phryne was a member. It was the most exclusive club in the city. I met Prince Phillip there and told him that our fathers had been very close friends.

Nightclubbing was an essential part of my job because, after a few drinks, I always managed to elicit some critical information. We regularly went to the Milroy, the Four Hundred, and the Sweevy, which was at the Berkeley Hotel. This club was a rather dangerous place, and it was finally closed as it was considered a security risk.

I finally moved into Phryne's mews flat, where we were

pleased despite my heavy workload. I was thrilled when, just before the Christmas holidays, I received the best present I could have wished for. Finally, my mother, Uncle Jack, and Princess Jane were going to be released from a camp in Albi where they had spent the last two years. A few days later, I received her first letter in almost three years. It was a very emotional moment. She asked me to rent a furnished flat for the three of them, as they would be arriving in London soon. I found one not far from Sloane Avenue.

The day of their arrival finally came, and Phryne and I went to Victoria Station to pick them up. We embraced for a long time. Mama looked wonderful, bubbling over with conversation. Her overwhelming personality had obviously been what had kept their spirits up during all these trying years. Uncle Jack looked even more like Maurice Chevalier than before while Princess Jane looked beautiful with her perfectly set blonde hair and her lively blue eyes. I realized how much I had missed her husky blasé English voice. I was overjoyed at being reunited with my family.

We all wanted to know everything that had happened since we had last seen each other, so we spent all night celebrating our reunion and recounting our trials and tribulations. I told them my story since my escape from Foix, and mother seemed very impressed with my adventures.

"You're a man now, Rodney," she said proudly as she toasted to my health.

✳

Over the next few months, I was extremely busy, as a

Lilian Craig and H.R.H Prince Bertil of Sweden who became very close friends of Rodney Mundy. They were finally allowed to marry on the 7 December 1976, and she became H.R.H Princess Lilian, Duchess of Halland lot was happening on the front. Phryne and I met Lillian Craig at the cinema where she worked and immediately become good friends. She was a petite woman with great charm and personality, who we later introduced to Prince Bertil of Sweden. Theirs was to be one of those love stories that made headlines. It was only many years later, when the prince's nephew, King Charles Gustav, married and had children that they were finally allowed to marry. As Princess Lillian of Sweden, she has gained the love and respect of the Swedes.

I had, however, little time to spend with Phryne or my mother, but I was lucky they were very understanding and supportive. On June 6th, 1944, British and Allied forces landed on the coast of Normandy in an unprecedented offensive against the Germans and their allies. On July 20th, Hitler survived an assassination attempt, led by a group of German conservatives who wanted to overthrow the Nazi regime.

Time flew, and soon it was Christmas. The Germans were desperately trying to stop the Allied advance, and the Battle of the Bulge was their last major attempt to do so. After that, victory would be a matter of a few months. Events were happening at such speed that we all felt victory was not far off.

Late that summer, the British and American forces with the aid of Free French troops finally liberated Paris. How much would I have loved to be in my adored Paris for the celebrations!

M was always full of surprises. He would summon me through coded messages to meet him in the oddest places, being the zoo one of his favourites. One cold December morning in 1944, I found myself feeding the monkeys with him while he explained my next mission.

"Rodney, I need to talk to you about looted art."

"I know nothing about it."

"We've been aware of the scale of looting that has gone on since the very beginning of the war, and last year the War Office set up a specialist department which is responsible to the Director of Civil Affairs. We have created an Archaeological Advisor's Branch with orders to draw up an inventory of all national art treasures and Jewish
private collections in German-occupied countries. A formidable task, I might add,"

"And how can I be of any use?" I asked.

"Does Klaus von Jettenbach ring a bell?"

"I met him some years back."

"That is precisely why you are the man for this job. This charming character has amassed a significant art collection that he has looted from the Jews. As you probably know, and if you do not, you can read this file, numerous artworks were looted from France, Belgium, and the Netherlands. Before the war, Hitler dreamt of installing the best art collection in the world in a museum in his hometown, and Jettenbach and Göring have been working hard on this project, using every conceivable method to acquire the works of their choice."

I listened with interest.

"What sort of paintings does that monster like?" I asked out of curiosity.

"Old masters! We know he loathes late nineteenth century and twentieth-century French paintings. He considers Impressionism degenerate, and consequently, he has forbidden importing such paintings into Germany. Nevertheless, we know the Germans have looted many paintings from this period and then used them as payment for other works of art more to their taste."

I had not been aware of any of this.

"Until quite recently the Baron has been Göring's art advisor, a position he has used to acquire, behind his back, a vast private collection for himself, mainly from Poland, Hungary and Czechoslovakia. The Reichsmarschall also has a large number of agents in the occupied territories who keep him supplied with information about Jewish art collections. As the second most influential man in the Third Reich, he has used his position of power to his own advantage breaking, whenever it suited him, most German laws, those of the neutral countries, and those of Germany's allies. He is a cruel bully who has no qualm about using the Gestapo for his own benefit."

"Does Hitler know about this?"

"Probably not. Göring keeps him happy by giving him, every now and then, some of his paintings as presents."

"Is Jettenbach with him most of the time?" I asked.

"Well, they do spend a fair amount of time together. He

travels with him when Göring is in an acquisitive mood, which, I might add, is most of the time. Jettenbach carries out all the negotiations and makes all the final decisions on acquisitions. Well, that was until recently. Over the past few years, he has been very busy satisfying Göring's vast appetite for art, and in the process has kept for him some magnificent pieces that he has not shown his boss."

"How did he manage that?" I asked unable to believe what I was being told.

"Most of his collection was obtained before the war even started. In those days Jettenbach had many wealthy Jewish friends in Germany, Poland, and Hungary, and knowing what Hitler had in mind, he went to see them one by one and persuaded many of them to hand over to him their unique collections for safekeeping. He can be a very charming man when he wants to! After agreeing to do so, the Jews were then taken away by the Gestapo and have all disappeared.

I remembered then the conversation I had had that first night I went to the Herentals home in Madrid with dear Laszlo. It all made sense now.

"What do you mean by until recently?" I was slightly confused.

"Well, according to our informants, a few weeks ago, Göring found out what the Baron had been up to, and he was livid. The thought that Jettenbach might have a collection better than his own makes the fat pig sick to the stomach. The Baron probably fearing for his life has now vanished, and so, we imagine, has his collection."

"Sounds like a jolly nice chap! I never did feel very comfortable in his presence, and he was certainly anything but charming. What sort of agreement did the two of them have?"

"Göring had promised to appoint him director of his collection at Karinhall, and until now he was acting as his buyer while remaining an independent dealer. He had the right to any work of art that the *Reichmarschall* did not wish to acquire. Being under the wing of the second most powerful man in the Third Reich, he has been free to travel and has given him access to all the art collections in the occupied territories. He has also had access to as much foreign currency as he has needed."

"The war is in its final stages, and it is clear now that we will win. We would like you to find out, and I know it won't be very easy, where the Baron is and where the paintings are. It would be best if you left for Paris tomorrow."

"Ok, M., I shall". I was delighted at the prospect of returning to Paris.

"Here," he said, with a straight face, "have some more peanuts." And we both laughed.

XII

A SHORT VISIT TO PARIS & THE END OF WWII

Paris! It felt marvellous to be back! I stayed at the Powers Hotel on Rue François I, my home in the city of lights even in my old age.

The first thing I did was to call Claude at the *Tour D'Argent* and make an appointment for dinner. I found him in great shape and the Parisians in a festive mood after liberation. Over a glass of champagne, he explained how he had hidden most of his wine behind a brick wall, out of the sight of the heavily German clientele. The city had not suffered too much during the war, but being so proud, most Parisians had had great difficulty in accepting the Germans as their masters.

That evening we went to all the nightclubs, and I drank more than I should have, but I was delighted at seeing my friends again.

The following morning, I went with a slight hangover to the British Embassy. I was introduced to a group of highly qualified art historians who were also seasoned interrogators and wise to the intricacies of the art market. James Plaut oversaw the newly set up Art Looting Unit of the office of Strategic Services. Another member, Theodore Rousseau,

Reichsmarschall Hermann Göring inspecting a looted artwork

Reichsmarschall Hermann Göring, painting in his left-hand sits gazing at two paintings by Henri Matisse being supported by Bruno Lohse. Standing to Göring's left is his art advisor, Walter Andreas Hofer. Both paintings were My had worked at the National Gallery, and Laine Faisan was a professor of art history at Williams College. Their combined knowledge overwhelmed me.

They explained that they had only just started their investigation but had already ascertained that the former German Ambassador to France, Otto Abetz, had been one of the principal architects of the looting programme and had reserved works by Monet, Degas, Bonnard, and Braque to grace his own home and offices. When he had fled Paris, he gave orders to ship these paintings to Germany. The group also had information that Joachim von Ribbentrop, the German Foreign Minister, had hung his Berlin offices with paintings by Monet, Bonnard, and Degas looted from Jewish collections in France.

Göring had organized the *Einsatzstab Reichsleiter Rosenberg*, which he had entrusted to Alfred Rosenberg, the chief party ideologue. From his Paris office, Rosenberg was to take charge of the confiscation of Jewish collections, which ended up in Göring´s private collection.

I wonder why it is that, throughout human history, people on the winning side, in any conflict, have always considered themselves entitled to any spoils of war. This is a very primitive and basic instinct.

The dedicated members of the Art Looting Unit informed me that von Jettenbach had not been seen in Paris since Rosenberg had taken on the Reichsmarschall's affairs in France. So probably only a fraction of his collection came from looted French art unless he had acquired some pieces in Germany, but Plaut thought this was highly unlikely. My investigation would be more complicated than I had foreseen because Central Europe remained occupied. These countries would eventually be 'liberated' by the Russians, who would in turn plunder whatever was left. Thus, I never had the opportunity of travelling to Budapest or Warsaw to continue with my investigation.

It was no secret that many of the prominent Jews from Germany, Hungary, Austria, and Poland had owned excellent collections and that stolen from the PaulRosenberg collection (*Archives des Musées Nationaux*). Jewish Hungarians were particularly passionate about art. The Baron had been to Hungary before the German invasion in March 1944. We had information that he had been able to convince some of his friends to hand over their collections to him. Baron Ferenc Hatvany, for example, had turned over some of his French Impressionist paintings. An art professor, who saw the entire collection before von Jettenbach arrived on the scene, wrote: "There were ten Manets, eight Courbets, twenty Corots and six Ingres, in addition to twenty-five portfolios, each with twenty-five French masters."

I found out much later on that von Jettenbach had at least had the decency to help the baron escape alive. I presumed that he had merely been protecting another aristocrat from certain death, though it was clear that he must have been delighted with the paintings he had stolen from him. After the war, Baron Hatvany had placed sixty of his most valuable paintings in a bank vault, under the non-Jewish name of his secretary, to keep them safe from the Germans. However, in January and February 1945 when the Red Army arrived in Budapest, they had opened all the bank vaults and sent the paintings and everything else they had found to Moscow.

Another renowned pre-war collection was that of Simon Stern, whose father had established a large commercial bank at the turn of the century. He not only had a magnificent collection of old masters, which included five Grecos and three Tintorettos, but also had paintings by Degas, Monet, and Renoir. All Plaut could tell me about this collection was that some of the paintings had been confiscated by the pro-Nazi Hungarian government and were exhibited at the Museum of Fine Arts in Budapest.

What a tragedy for all these magnificent Central European countries to be liberated, only to be placed under the Russian boot for decades. I always thought it was most unfair, and I believe Churchill made a terrible mistake not invading Russia after the fall of Germany. Russia was so devastated by the war and her government was so weak that it would have been an easy matter to install a democratic monarchy that could have saved us all from the Cold War years that were to follow.

I was back in London a couple of days later and decided that I would return to Madrid as soon as the war was over.

XIII

SIMON STERN

Something extraordinary happened just before Christmas when I went on my own for lunch to Bentley's Oyster Bar and there, sitting by himself, was Mr. Scheul, the disgraced Consul. I walked up to his table and smiled.

"Hello, old boy. How are you?" He was rather stunned. Seeing that he did not recognise me, I introduced myself as Meynell Phillips.

"My name is Schubert," he said.

"We met at a few receptions in Barcelona." I said to satisfy his curiosity.

"Do you mind if I join you for lunch?" I asked politely.

We drank some excellent Pouilly and had two dozen oysters each. By the end of the meal, we were best of friends, and I asked him for his address and phone number, which he was happy to give me. I passed the details on to "M" and my dear friend Scheul, was never seen again.

I celebrated Christmas and New Year with my family and Phryne. Everybody felt that the Germans would soon be defeated. The January liberation of the Auschwitz concentration camp by the Russians revealed to the world the full extent of Nazi cruelty and the unbelievable horrors they had perpetrated.

Hundreds of thousands of Jews had been used as guinea pigs in the most appalling pseudo-scientific experiments and many more had perished in the gas chambers. In the camp lay piles of dead bodies waiting to be cremated. The survivors were in a pathetic state: walking corpses who had somehow survived the very worst of nightmares. Similar scenes happened at the extermination camps of Belsen and Buchenwald.

Phryne and I cried when we first saw those images. How could human beings be so utterly cruel and cause suffering to such a degree? The full details of the Holocaust were gradually revealed to the world as the German troops retreated.

It must have been in early February, around the time of the Yalta Conference, when I had one of my regular meetings with "M". He popped by our mews flat for a cup of tea and was in a particularly cheerful mood.

"Rodney, do you know who Simon Stern is?"

"The name rings a bell. Isn't he that Hungarian art collector?"

"Bingo! He was liberated from Auschwitz, and we will be transferring him to a hospital in London. His health is very poor, and the doctors do not know if he will survive. The moment he arrives, please go and visit him and make gain his confidence. He is traumatized and is not speaking, but I am sure you will be able to change that, my dear chap."

Things were moving fast on the war front. On April 25th,

American Forces met the remains of the Nazi Army at Torgau and managed to cut the Third Reich in half. Five days later, Adolf Hitler, one of the most abominable criminals the world has ever seen, committed suicide in his Berlin bunker. By May 7th, the war was over, and we rejoiced and partied hard. We cried with joy at the end of so much suffering, heartbreak, and pain. It had all been such a nightmare that one could only hope that we had all learnt our lesson and that such a tragedy would never happen again. At a personal level, I was also happy because soon I was going to return to Spain to continue with my investigation.

It was exhilarating to be able to tear down the blackout curtains after more than four years. Our eyes had become so accustomed to complete darkness at night that it was almost painful to see so many lights, and we felt quite dazzled. London's streets looked like Fairyland! Restrictions naturally continued for a few more years until we were all back on our feet again. In fact, after the war, there was nothing. Everything was rationed and scarce. During the war, the government had made the enormous effort to keep the morale high, but when it was over, it seemed they did not care anymore. There were coupons for clothes, for petrol, for everything, so the spivs became even more notorious as the black market flourished everywhere. I still clearly remember the line of spivs selling nylon stockings on Oxford Street!

Soon after, I received a call from Sister Mary who had good news. Simon Stern was finally on the mend and had regained some strength; the doctors believed that reasonably soon the time would be right to make his acquaintance.

∗

I was not surprised to learn from M that many Spaniards, including high-ranking members of the army and Franco's government, had reacted to Hitler's death by going to the German Embassy and signing the condolence book. I felt that Franco's regime would not last long and that the allies would finally restore the monarchy in the figure of Don Juan. Franco had only broken diplomatic relations with the Third Reich on May 8th, in a desperate attempt to save his regime.

"Our sources in Spain," M told me, "Inform us that the *Generalísimo* has given orders to conceal Nazi assets there, placing them under an embargo. Over ten million dollars have been transferred to private individuals, and Falangist volunteers have helped to destroy compromising documents from the German Embassy and Consulates. Over two hundred and fifty million dollars' worth of German business assets have changed hands to stooges, and hundreds of Germans who were working for Hitler in Spain have stayed on, becoming Spanish nationals". I could see that his temperature was rising.

"And now Franco is hailed by the Spanish press for his neutrality during the war! He even dares to state publicly that he never supported the Axis, in an attempt to wash away his

Axis stain!"

"But surely, we will be able to get rid of him and restore the monarchy!" I said, sharing M´s indignation.

"That will depend on the politicians. If it were up to me, I would have him prosecuted and executed. Just imagine! In order not to be accused of having granted asylum to war criminals, he has given them Spanish nationality. We've complained to the Spanish authorities, but our complaints just fall on deaf ears."

"It's a scandal! Is there nothing we can do?" I asked.

"I'm afraid not." After a short pause, he continued, "You should go and see Stern as soon as you can. I will arrange everything. Now then, when do you plan to go to Madrid?" He took a long sip of his tea.

"As soon as I win his confidence".

I went to King Edward VII Hospital for Officers, to visit Simon Stern One of the nursing sisters took me to the ward. I had my first glance at him from behind a screen. He was sleeping, but the expression on his face was that of profound suffering, even as he rested. He looked very old and haggard, yet he was only in his late forties. A white blanket covered his frail body. I felt a wave of compassion for him.

I gave the sister my telephone number and soon began my regular visits to the hospital. I spent every afternoon at his bedside. I realised I would have to be extremely patient if I were to succeed in my mission, but luckily, I had a comfortable chair in which to sit, and while I waited, I dozed intermittently.

"Who are you, and what are you doing here?"

The sound of a man's voice drew me back from that pleasant state into which the mind drifts before falling asleep. For over two weeks, I had been sitting for hours in a comfortable chair beside Simon Stern's bed, who completely ignored me. We had exchanged glances, but neither of us had uttered a word.

Shaking off my drowsiness, I now sat up. "I am a friend, Mr Stern."

"But I don't know you. I've never seen you before," he said wearily.

"The British government has asked me to become your friend in England and to help you recover."

"What is your name?" he asked, in a heavy Hungarian accent.

"Rodney."

"Mine is Simon." I could feel that he wanted to talk, but I was ill-prepared for all I was to hear over the next few hours.

"If you are indeed my friend, I need to ask you a great favour."

"Please do."

"You see, they took me to Auschwitz with my wife and my beautiful daughter Rita. She was the liveliest of little girls. When we got there, we were separated, and I have never heard from them again. I cannot bear to think that they are dead. Maybe you can help me find out what happened to them." He was close to tears, and his voice was feeble.

"I will get to work immediately, and I promise you that we will find out where they are. Mr Stern, would you mind telling me about the events that led up to your confinement in Auschwitz? That will probably help me in my investigation."

"If we are going to be friends, you should call me Simon."

"I shall."

"Very well, then. Make yourself comfortable because it is a long story."

I settled into my chair, and within minutes, he immersed me in a terrible story of suffering and loss.

"It all started or rather ended, depending on how you look at it, with the ill-fated attempt by King Carl to recover his throne from the regent. Unfortunately, the attempt failed, and His Majesty had to flee the country, never to return. Admiral Nicholas von Horthy was then free to rule as he pleased, and he soon put Hungary under the influence of the new National Socialist government in Berlin. Hitler had promised to return territory in Rumania, Bohemia, and Slovakia that had been Hungarian before the First World War. Do you follow me?"

"Yes, of course." He was eager to tell me everything.

"At the end of the 19th century, my father had established a bank, which soon became one of the leading commercial banks in the country. He believed in the monarchy and supported the Crown financially, and for his services, he was ennobled and became Baron. Unfortunately the 1st World War shattered these plans and my father's dream. The King and Queen Zita were very compassionate people and would have been enlightened rulers had the situation been different.

"My father was also an art lover and had started a collection that, together with the purchases I made later, became probably one of the finest in Hungary."

"What happened to that collection?"

"By the late thirties, the government had passed anti-Jewish laws that severely limited our activities. By the early forties, with Hungary now one of the Axis powers, thousands of non-Hungarian Jews were rounded up. The fortunate ones went to exile, but tragically most were murdered. We felt that things would only get worse, and we were not wrong. The time had come to act.

I resigned as president of the bank and let the other board members, mostly Hungarian aristocrats, assume control, as I knew that,

"As soon as he sat down, Klaus told me that he had come to Budapest to warn me about Hitler's plan to invade the country and to advise me to place my most famous art pieces in his custody, as he was the only person who could guarantee their safety. He kept insisting that he was taking a considerable risk in safeguarding my collection but as a friend and art lover, it was a risk he was prepared to take.

I did not have many options; so, two days later, I handed over to him my treasures. He signed a document, which my wife sent to her family in England; so maybe one day……." his voice trailed off.

"He did the same thing with many other of his Jewish friends," I said.

"By early March," Stern resumed his story, "German troops had occupied Budapest, and we were arrested and taken to Auschwitz." His kind expression changed to one of terror by the sole mention of the extermination camps. I felt so sorry for him.

"Would you mind handing me another pillow, please?"

I helped him sit up in bed, and he began to recount his trip to hell.

"Things were going from bad to worse, so I had made plans to leave the country with Sarah and Rita and go to England. Some of my aristocratic friends from the bank were willing to help us, but by then it was too late.

The night before our planned escape, we were woken up with great violence and given five minutes to pack our belongings. I feared the worst but tried to remain calm for the sake of my family. We were put on a lorry with other Jewish families and taken to a train station outside the city."

"You must have been terrified", I said.

"Nobody knew where they were taking us. At the station, we forcibly waited for several hours in sub-zero temperatures.

Finally, they crowded us into wagons like cattle, fifty people to a wagon, without food or water. The train journey was the beginning of a terrible ordeal, only made worst by the hours of darkness and the bitterly cold early spring nights. I lost count of the number of days that we spent like this. By the time we reached our destination, several people in the wagon were dead. I had to carry Rita, who pleaded weakly for water. My little princess was only four years old!" His voice broke down, and he started to cry. I felt great pity for him. It was several minutes before he could resume his story as he was a man with a broken heart.

"They rounded up all the men who were physically fit, and we later discovered that they had chosen us to work for the Third Reich. They took the elderly and the weak to a special section of the camp. We never saw them again."

"And the women and children?" I asked.

"They took them to the women's camp. I was heartbroken when my wife and my daughter were dragged, crying, from my side. I have not seen them since then and do not know if they have survived."

A profound silence took over the room. Simon Stern closed his eyes.

"British Intelligence is now investigating what happened to them. Simon, you have my word that you will be informed as soon as we have something."

"Please, Rodney!" he pleaded.

"Life in the camp was a nightmare from beginning to end. The guards stripped us of all our belongings. Can you imagine being deprived of everyone you love and everything you own? Even your name? Well, that is how our life in the camp began."

"I can't even start to imagine how awful it must have been!" I interrupted.

"No one can. We were branded and given a number; thus, ceasing to have an identity. We were allocated bunks; two men, to a narrow lice-infested cot, and given instructions. Everything was forbidden. Once a day we were given a bowl of a disgusting soup, but never any water so that we were always thirsty. Some of us ate insects to survive. Even that was considered a crime punishable by death. We were nothing but slaves, working very long hours, seven days a week. Those who could not keep up were taken away and replaced by new arrivals. The cold was unbearable, and they forced us often to stand outside, naked, for hours on end. Each block had a block clerk. Though prisoners like us, they were German and common criminals and, for some reason that I will never understand, were even crueller than our jailers were. As camp officials, they did not have to work but merely gave orders, and they could be as ruthless as they pleased. They wielded absolute power over the life and death of their fellow prisoners.

One day, our block clerk handpicked my bunk companion and I and took us to a large room in the crematorium, were there were huge piles of corpses. Three prisoners were carefully undressing them while a fourth was removing any gold teeth with a pair of pliers and placing them in a tin. I felt sick, having never touched a dead body before, but if you wanted to survive in Auschwitz, you did as told, however awful that might be.

"For days we worked stripping bodies, before dragging them into the ovens to be cremated. Finally, two of the prisoners could not take it any longer and refused to continue. They got down on their knees and pleaded, but the block clerk beat them savagely with his truncheon, screaming, -You lazy bastards! I'll show you what happens to scum like you! - but they refused to move. I will never forget that scene until the end of my days."

I could see how hard it was for Simon to speak about what he had witnessed.

"The two men knelt motionless, still sobbing. The guards then pulled them roughly to their feet, swung open the oven doors and pushed them inside. They ordered us to continue filling the oven with corpses, and then the clerk, switched the oven. I shall never forget the screams of the two men, as they burnt alive; it will haunt me forever. You have no idea".

After a short pause, Stern went on. "At one point they decided that there were too many prisoners, so the new arrivals were forced to undress before being taken straight to the gas chambers. The SS officers had discovered it was easier than stripping the corpses afterwards. Next, they decided that it was simpler to send prisoners directly to the ovens, without gassing them first. The screams, the moans, the desperate banging on the oven doors were heartbreaking and terrifying. I felt overwhelming horror. Were there no limits to their cruelty?

However, this was not the only way in which they got rid of new arrivals. When groups of less than two hundred prisoners arrived, they forced them to undress, and then shot them in the back of the head in front of the others. Considering other things that I witnessed, this was a far less painful way to go."

"You should write a book," I suggested, "and tell the world in your own words what some human beings can do to others. The world must know, and hopefully, something so utterly horrendous will never happen again."

"Maybe I shall, one day. Because of starvation, my health has grievously suffered, and in the camp, I became thinner and thinner. Then, I had a stroke of luck. Even in the most awful of situations, one's fate can change for the better.

"The Kapo asked around for someone good at accounts. The selected a few of us, we took a test, and they picked me for the job. Working in the camp offices meant less strenuous work and slightly better food.

Nevertheless, shortly after starting my job in the office, I became very ill with a severe stomach infection and was sent to Ka-Be, the camp clinic. The Kapo found my accounting skills very useful. Otherwise, they would have shot me on the spot, as there was no place for weakness or failure in that hell. Turned into non-men, who marched and laboured in silence, they emptied us even of the capacity to feel or to suffer.

Now and then, they gave us delousing orders, which were a cruel joke. For example, they expected us to show the SS officers a shirt that was free of lice or risk death. However, as our bunks, shirts, and bodies were infested with the creatures, it was virtually impossible to be lice-free, and many prisoners ended up with a shot to their heads.

By late spring, Hungarian had become the second language in the camp after Yiddish, as the Nazis were sending all the Hungarian Jews there. By August, after less than five months, those who had arrived with me and I were considered 'the old ones'. The thought of the impending winter made us all shudder. We knew what winter meant. A large percentage of the prisoners would not survive the extreme cold.

The camp was severely overcrowded, and to return to manageable numbers they sent hundreds of inmates to the gas chambers. The crematorium chimney never stopped smoking. When they finally released me from the clinic, another inmate had my accounting job in the office, so I had to return to the impossibly hard manual labour.

"Christmas came and went. The New Year bought rumours that the Russian troops were advancing fast and that the Germans would soon be abandoning the camp. They eventually did, and I was confused as to what to do. Most of the healthy prisoners, about twenty thousand in total, vanished during the evacuation march, but I was too weak; so I decided to take advantage of the chaos and hide in the clinic. We did not know what would happen to us because some SS officers had remained behind. That night the camp was hit by Russian bombs. With the buildings on fire, the remaining prisoners ran outside into the freezing night. Most of us had barely any clothes and some had no shoes, and deep snow lay on the ground. The Germans had vanished. No one appeared for eight days, and we were free to roam around and search for food and wood to burn. I felt very ill, not knowing that I was suffering from typhoid fever. Some days later, armed SS officers suddenly reappeared in the abandoned camp and promptly shot all those who had moved into what had previously been their dining room. Many men were dying of dysentery and the camp littered with frozen corpses. Finally, the Russians arrived, and they moved the survivors to a provisional hospital that they hastily erected outside the camp. I was one of the lucky ones, as most of the inmates perished."

Simon Stern fell silent, exhausted at having had to relive such suffering. A deep sense of grief and sadness overtook me.

"I only saw him once... but I shall never forget that face", he said suddenly, lost in thought.

"Whose face?" I asked.

"The camp Commandant. He was responsible for all those deaths, and his face was the picture of pure evil."

After a dramatic pause, he continued. "Rodney. Please find my wife and daughter! Please!" He leaned forward in the bed and held out his hand. I clasped it in mine for a few minutes while tears coursed freely down his cheeks.

"You have my word, Simon."

"How could anybody give the orders for such a diabolical plan?" He asked, not expecting a reply.

XIV

THE TWILIGHT OF A NIGHTMARE

Phryne and I got our visas for France and Spain. It was June 1946, and we packed our Speed 6 Bentley and drove straight to Paris, where we stayed for a couple of nights. We then headed for Switzerland to change our money as we doubled it by transacting into Swiss Francs and then returning to France and changing the Swiss Francs back into French ones.

As we drove south, I felt how wonderful it was to be back in France with the woman I loved and to whom I then felt so close. We enjoyed every moment of our trip, stopping for a refreshing pastis in the beautiful old village of Cagne, perched up in the mountains between Nice and Cannes.

On our arrival in Cannes, we saw some buildings in ruins, but nothing compared to London. Everybody still remembered me and welcomed us with great affection. Freddy Mcavoy had come back, and we frequently sailed on his superb Black Swan with Porfirio Rubirosa and his famous wife Danielle Darrieux.

For some incomprehensible reason, mother had sold our house, so we stayed at the Martinez Hotel while we looked for a house to rent.

We found Villa Paul on Avenue Benefiat, high up in the town, behind The Martinez. It had five double rooms and three bathrooms, plus an enormous living room, a dining room and, of course, servants' quarters. There was a lovely garden with a swimming pool, and the house came complete with an Italian cook, a butler, and a gardener.

I needed to spend some time with Phryne away from M and London and to disengage myself from the war's shadow whose tentacles were suddenly suffocating me. I wanted to go back to July 1937 and recover that part of myself that died in the war.

I decided that we would use Villa Paul as our home and that I would only return to London when necessary. Spain was close enough, and I planned to go there at the beginning of September. In the meantime, I was determined to lead a carefree life and enjoy it to the fullest; after all, one never knew when death would be calling at one's door.

Most evenings we had drinks on board Stewart Granger and Michael Wilding's boat. I remember meeting Vivian Leigh and Elizabeth Taylor both in their late teens. Vivian was a vivacious young woman, and Liz had a remarkable sense of humour. Her violet eyes were mesmerizing. We all got on splendidly well, and they came to luncheon and dinners at Villa Paul on several occasions.

Raf Valls and Diana, his new girlfriend, came to stay with us. We often took them to Eden Rock, a luxury club perched on the hillside near Cap d'Antibes and the in place to go. Aristotle Onassis could be seen there almost every day, and

The beautiful Elizabeth Taylor

fantastic yachts, two and three-masted schooners, and even large steam yachts, were often anchored nearby, next to the odd seaplane.

To see the sun again and the bright blue sky was very energizing. The emerald and sapphire colour of the sea reflected on the rocks, and the umbrella pines buzzed with chattering tree frogs. Life was merely beautiful again.

When we were not sailing, we used to go to Tahiti Beach, just past St. Tropez. The three kilometres sandy beach was almost deserted. Few people in the nude scattered about in small groups with large spaces in between. We went with friends to enjoy delicious picnics, chilled wine, and refreshing dips in the ocean while the gendarmes, sitting on the dunes behind the beach, watched us through their binoculars. Occasionally they would swoop down and ask us to cover ourselves up, but they enjoyed watching all the pretty girls, and thus they did not sound compelling. The whole thing was somewhat civilized.

We laughed all summer every time Diana and Phryne recounted when walking along the beach, both looking stunning in nothing but a G string, Diana asked a naked young man, who walked past them, for the time. Upon thanking him for the information, the man replied -"The pleasure is mine, madam. I'm so pleased to meet you." She laughed as she looked at his private parts and said, "I can see you are!"

The summer was coming to an end when my mother, Uncle Jack, and Princess Jane suddenly announced their imminent arrival and asked us to postpone our trip to Madrid and spend a couple of nights with them at the Palace Hotel in Monte Carlo. An old friend introduced my mother to Barbara Hutton, who was lavishly entertaining a group of about twenty friends. She was wearing a stunning emerald necklace that I immediately recognised as the one I had sold for Princess Niloufer Mourad at Van Cleefs. What an amazing twist of fate!

The train journey to Madrid was a nightmare. Not only was it hot as hell, but the wagon was packed, and we had to stand for fourteen hours. At one point, a priest gave Phryne his case for her to sit on for a while.

We arrived in Madrid filthy and exhausted, and went straight to the Palace Hotel, where they received us warmly. Although they knew me well, for the sake of appearances we had to take two separate rooms, as in ultra-conservative Spain, it was unlawful for unmarried couples to share a bedroom.

I had come to Madrid on a mission, that of discovering the whereabouts of Klaus von Jettenbach and the art collection he had looted.

Once Spain's neutrality had been guaranteed, Captain Hillgarth had been sent to command naval intelligence in Eastern Europe, where he worked with top-level interceptors. When the war ended, he left the navy and moved to Tangiers to publish an English language newspaper with his friend, Ian Fleming, who later was famous for his James Bond novels. In fact, through him, M became a fiction character.

Samuel Hoare returned to England soon after I had left Madrid, and King George VI knighted him becoming Viscount Templewood. Thus, when I paid a courtesy visit to the embassy, I found I only knew a few of the secretaries. On our first night in Madrid, I called Pepe Ruiz Gimenez, who invited us to dine at Jockey, one of the best restaurants in town. We gossiped about the Spanish friends we had in common, and he told me how the Count of Herentals, devastated by the Nazis' defeat, had followed Hitler's example and committed suicide. I was astounded, and the next morning I called the Count's sons, Pelayo and Gonzaga, who were eager to meet us for lunch.

The brothers immediately fell for Phryne and talked to her about all sorts of things in their perfect English. They both looked well if more mature and were in a very talkative mood, even shy Pelayo.

After ordering some drinks and our food, I asked them how their family was.

"Mother is now a merry widow because our father shot himself last year. He just couldn't cope with an allied victory!"

"I know. Pepe told me. I'm terribly sorry." I said, feeling sorry for their loss.

"We're much better off without him. He made our lives

a misery. Now Gonzaga is the new Count, and I am free to paint and study at the *Academia de Bellas Artes*".

"So, it was you who painted those two lovely oil paintings that Rodney bought from Spain? They are hanging in our living room in London," Phryne exclaimed admiringly.

Pelayo grinned with pleasure at the compliment. And Gonzaga raised his glass in a toast, "To friendship!"

"Gonzaga, now that the war is over, what do you know about your father's dealings with the Germans?" "Father admired the Third Reich and what the Führer wanted to achieve. Even Franco did," he added as a matter of justification, "which is why he offered his services to the German Embassy.

"And what exactly did he do for them?"

"He organised parties in their honour and passed them information about his pro-Ally friends. He helped them in whatever capacity he could, as he was devoted to their cause. For example, when Göring wanted to sell about sixty paintings to the Prado Museum, my father arranged a secret meeting between two of his friends, José Uyarte, Director of the Museum, and a friend of Dad's called Klaus von Jettenbach."

It was a sheer stroke of naked luck. I was right on track.

"And did the deal go through?" I asked.

"No. Despite my father's assurances as to the legitimacy of ownership, Uyarte was not convinced and refused to continue with the negotiations."

"I met the Baron the very first time I went to your house.

Whatever happened to him?"

"Oh, he came back to Madrid just before the end of the war.

He managed to smuggle with him many crates containing his entire collection, which we kept in our cellar until he disappeared."

"What do you mean?"

"I heard my father tell mother that the Baron had fallen from grace with Göring and could not return to Germany as it would have been unsafe for him. He stayed with us for several months, and it was my father who asked Franco to grant him a Spanish passport, which he did."

"Why would Franco do something like that when by that time he must have known that we would win the war?"

"Well, he received a magnificent Rubens as a gift."

"How did the Baron disappear? It must have been difficult without the Gestapo's aid?"

"Don't forget that by then he was Spanish and very wealthy. We think he left for South America as soon as the war was over, taking advantage of his Spanish nationality. Father was furious at his leaving without even bothering to say goodbye or thank him for his hospitality. He left like a thief, taking everything with him when father and mother were in the countryside."

Phryne and Pelayo were silent, listening with interest to our conversation.

"Do you know if he changed his name in his new passport?"

"Yes, of course, he did. He changed his name to Claudio Jiménez de Bach. Our father made us call him 'Uncle Claudio'."

I planned to stay in Madrid for a couple of weeks before flying back to London, and I intended, in those two weeks, to make Phryne love Spain as much as I did.

I took Phryne to visit the Monastery of the Escorial and the Roman Aqueduct in Segovia. I also took her to her first bullfight, at which the hitherto *novillero*[31], Luis Miguel Dominguín, took his *alternativa*[32] at the hands of Aruza and became a fully-fledged *matador*[33]. He and I were to become friends, and I was later to meet him on many occasions in London in the company of Ava Gardner. To my relief, Phryne was enjoying Spain and its people. She loved her stay at the Ruiz Gimenez country estate, outside Madrid, where we went boar hunting. Pepe was a charming man and an excellent host.

As soon as I had an opportunity, I called Felisín. I had never mentioned her to Phryne, and I was not about to do so at this stage. I had asked the Herentals brothers, but they did not seem to know. I could not get through to her, so I walked from the Palace Hotel to her apartment, which was nearby while Phryne went shopping. The doorman recognised me immediately, as I had been generous with

---

[31] Novice Bull Fighter

[32] Presentation of novice bullfighters

[33] Fully fledged bullfighter

tipping in the past.

"Señor Mundy. It has been a long time. Where have you been?"

"In London, Antonio. How is Señora Felisin?"

"Oh, Señor Mundy. You did not hear about the tragedy?"

My heart skipped a beat.

"What tragedy?"

Antonio passed his arm around my shoulders and whispered, "Señora Felisín was murdered about two years ago. Her killer shot her in the back of the head."

I was speechless and felt utterly devastated. My tears began to flow as I remembered all the good times we had spent together. I recalled her sweet laughter and sense of humour. She was such an extraordinary woman, beautiful and full of the most exceptional human values, and I had failed her.

After a few minutes, Antonio brought me a glass of water and patted me on the back.

"I know how fond of you she was," he said.

"Was anybody prosecuted?" I asked.

"No, Señor Mundy. The police closed the investigation after a few days."

I knew it must have been Vogel. If only she had listened to me, she would be alive now, but the temptation of a bloody hundred thousand wretched pesetas had been too great to resist. The next few hours I spent alone walking in the Retiro Park. Alone with my thoughts reflecting on what my life had been until now. I realized that I had really loved her, and I cried in silence again at the loss.

XV

A MARRIED MAN

Phryne had not felt too well during our stay in Madrid, so as soon as we got back to London, I took her to the doctor who told us she was pregnant with a dead baby. This was devastating for her, especially as I was not sympathetic enough, for I had never really thought of becoming a father, and I felt overwhelmed by the whole situation. I guess, at the time, those were too big shoes for me to wear.

My mother, Uncle Jack, and Princess Jane had returned to London in time for my birthday on the 27th. It took her only a few days to sell our magnificent estate in Farnham and buy a beautiful large house in London, at 76 Cadogan Place on Lord Cadogan's estate. She moved in with all our furniture from both Farnham and the South of France.

M was delighted with my information on the whereabouts of Klaus von Jettenbach, now going by the name of Claudio Jiménez de Bach. He believed that eventually, our secret services would track him down wherever he was in South America.

The Nuremberg hearings were going on since November 1945 but, unfortunately, many prominent Nazi figures were being tried *in absentia* as they had mostly disappeared to South America where the local dictators received them with open arms. Those brought to trial had been chosen largely to ensure representation of all major administrative groupings of the Reich. However, the lawyers, the press and the public came to focus mainly on the human dimension of Nuremberg considering it a trial of humiliated Nazi bosses and a record of their victims' sufferings.

I went to see Simon Stern, who, though still in the hospital, was to be soon discharged as he had made a remarkable recovery. I regaled him with stories about the South of France, and for the first time since his death, I spoke to someone about my father.

"Do you know Simon, I remember when I was home on holiday, and my Papa told me fascinating stories about when he was young. He had been a very close friend of Prince Andrew of Greece[34]. They both were wild in their early manhood and had spent a lot of time together in Paris, mostly broke. They were known as the *"Papillon Gris"* because of their grey hair at such an early age, and they modelled for a well-known artist to make ends meet. The result was a famous bronze statue of two polo riders!

"Your father comes alive every time you think of him as do my adored wife and my little Rita." Simon said sadly.
I liked Simon. He had a good sense of humour despite his underlying sadness, and he, like my father, was a true gentleman. I yearned to give him news about his family. He had such a generous spirit that he never again mentioned

---

[34] Was married to Princess Alice of Battenberg and was the father of H.R.H The Duke of Edinburgh

H.R.H Prince Andrew of Greece, father of HRH The Duke of Edinburgh them, but his silence was more eloquent than words. Then one day, just before Christmas and to my relief, I was finally able to give some news, albeit sour-sweet ones. M called to tell me Rita was alive and living in an orphanage outside Budapest. Our government was flying her to England as her mother had been British, the girl now nearly seven, was one of us. God alone knew what ordeals she had endured. She had only survived the camp because a childless wife of a German captain had found her very pretty and had arranged for her 'adoption'. Fortunately, for Rita, her devoted new parents had abandoned her when they hurriedly vacated the camp. Her mother, unfortunately, had ended her days in the gas chamber.

Upon his release from the hospital, Simon Stern rented a room in the home of a Polish refugee couple now living in London. Tadeusz and Malgorzata Zawidski had a small boarding house at 86 Onslow Gardens. I was to become very close to them; they were the loveliest of people. The Zawidskis had been members of the Polish underground of whom over 200,000 had died in their desperate fight against the Germans. Unknown to them at the time, also against their allies, the Russians. They had managed to reach safety by walking through the city sewers, full of human waste that sometimes reached up to their necks. They walked for over a day, and they lost their sight for several days due to the fumes given off by the sewage.

I visited Simon at their flat, which was beautifully

decorated for Christmas. The moment I walked in Tadeusz offered me a glass of Polish vodka while Mrs Zawidski went to tell Simon Stern, he had a visitor. No words were necessary between us. As he entered the living room and saw my smile, he asked in disbelief, "Have they found her?"

"Yes, Simon. She will be in London for Christmas."

"What about my wife?

I'm afraid we have no information about her. We must assume she has not survived."

∗

I believed the time had come to leave MI6. I had concluded my mission and was planning to marry Phryne. I felt I wanted to start my own business and make real money, so I went to see "M" at his office and handed in my resignation.

"Once you are MI6, you will always be MI6," he said, making it sound like a courteous expression of formality as if we belonged to a prestigious fraternity. At the time, I could not grasp the full meaning of his words.

We set our wedding for April 28th, my mother's birthday. It was a quiet affair at the Kensington Register Office, and it was only then that I discovered Phryne was four years older than I was. We had a family lunch at the superb Belfrey Club, and in the evening, we gave at Raf and Diana's flat, a large party for about forty-five friends including M.

Having no job, I soon ran out of money, so we went to

live with my mother at Cadogan Place while we planned a tourism venture in Santa Margherita in Italy.

It soon became clear that the United States did not intend to permit the spread of communism, once more, throughout Spain. President Truman had concluded that, despite Franco's continuous human rights abuses, he was a lesser evil as he was, at least, ferociously anti-communist. One of the paradoxes of history is that Stalin´s policies were to keep the Spanish dictator in power until he died of old age in 1975. Within a few months, Spain, to the great relief of the Caudillo, was included in the reconstruction project known as the Marshall Plan. I felt sorry for the Spanish democrats and for Don Juan, whose chances of recovering the throne were now shattered.

In 1947 Phryne moved to Italy to get everything organized, and I followed in late July. Things began going well for us until the British Government suddenly passed a law that cut the travel allowance right down to £25 per head, which was virtually nothing. Nobody could go abroad on such a pittance so we had to sacrifice our new business venture at infancy.

Without a business, soon we were broke, and I had to leave Phryne at the hotel and go to Milan to get some money pay our hotel's bill, as it was promptly closing for the winter. With some money still left in our pockets, Phryne and I went to Cervina, a mountain resort on the Italian side of the Matterhorn. I immensely enjoyed skiing and teaching Phryne how to do so. By the end of our alpine holiday, we were again practically penniless, so Phryne, to pay for two first class tickets on the Orient Express to Paris, sold her gold watch and some ruby earrings. One precarious and exciting adventure was over, but another was just about to start.

To celebrate my twenty-fifth birthday, I took Phryne to the Scala in Milan to hear De Steffino make his debut in Puccini's "Manon". It was a memorable evening. My mother inculcated me with the love of opera since a very tender age, and I spent many evenings with my father sitting by her piano. At the same time, she played and sang her favourite arias.

Our first-class couchette on board the Orient Express adjoined that of Jacques Fath, the well-known gay couturier from Paris, who spent the whole night trying to seduce the guard on the Wagon Lits. It was very entertaining listening to their conversation while we dined, and I feel sure he succeeded in the end. As we could not afford to go to the restaurant car, we had bought a bottle of Chianti, a loaf of bread, some salami, and a dozen oysters plus a lemon to eat in our compartment. It was a perfect arrangement, as far as we were concerned, for it provided a romantic night with jolting love sessions on board a train quite unlike any other in the world. We arrived in Paris in November 1947 with precisely 50 Lire and 2,000 Francs and went straight to the Powers Hotel where we were welcomed with open arms. We took a beautiful light and airy room in the attic with a slanting roof, chintz curtains and a large bathroom. Whenever we ran out of money, which was very often, we would order a bottle of champagne to see if our luck changed. We would drink it in our room, laughing and chatting over our latest adventure.

However, our luck was not quick to change, and we were stuck in the charming hotel for over three weeks. I loved France and was determined not to return to England. I was not missing my work at MI6, and despite our precarious financial situation, we enjoyed every moment.

Finally, my lucky break came when one day, of all people, I ran into Fred Kempler. It was marvellous to see him again. He was now living in Paris and made a living by wheeling and dealing. He immediately lent me some money, and we ventured into the cloth business together.

In France things like material, except those destined for export, were still rationed. So at least on paper, I became an English agent. Fred would buy the cloth for manufacture and then he would export it to England through me. However, what happened was that Fred bought the material very cheaply and then promptly flogged it by the baleful on the black market for a small fortune. The article never saw a manufacturer and never left France while Fred and I split the profits of our highly lucrative business. I knew he was doing on the side all sorts of dodgy deals but preferred not to know too much about them. After a month in the cloth business, Phryne and I moved into a divine little house with a garage and a garden at N° 10, Rue Donne, very near the *Bois du Boulogne.* Beautifully decorated it even had three Renoirs on the walls. We rented the house for an entire year, as the owners had gone to the United States to sell a theatre curtain painted by Picasso, which they had managed to smuggle out with them!

The business was booming, and we gave many parties. Edith Piaf and Yves Montand were regulars. She was an amazingly scruffy little person, always dressed in black, but what a lovely voice and personality she had!

One day Fred came roaring into the house, saying that the authorities had caught a partner of his in some other business for some tax fiddle. He suggested that I return to England for a while until things cooled down in case, they came asking awkward questions. Thinking this a sensible idea, I returned to England, leaving Phryne with quite a bit of money but with a garage full of material. Fortunately, nothing happened. After I had only been in London for a few days, Phryne phoned me, sounding desperate. The French government had suddenly called in all 5,000 Franc notes. I rang Fred and arranged for him to go to the house and collect all the banknotes in that denomination. As I had hidden the money between the pages of over a hundred books on the bookshelves in the drawing room, I sympathised with poor Phryne who had a hard job ahead of her.

I was very relieved when the next day Fred told me that he had successfully changed the money through a South American Embassy. I guess Porfirio Rubirossa helped him.

*

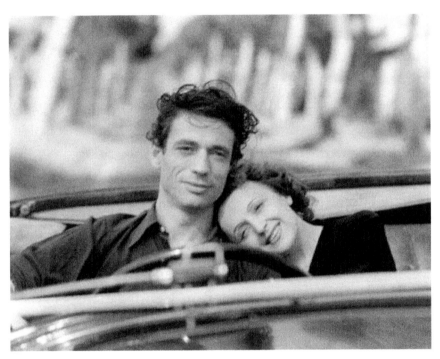

Yves Montand and Edith Piaf

Phryne Mundy nee Alabaster, Countess of Mondaye and her son, Simon
Godfrey Mundy

Time flew and soon an entire year had passed since we moved into 10 Rue Donne. We were now moving out. Phryne was pregnant and we decided to spend the summer at Villa Paul, but at the end of September we returned to England, as I wanted the baby to be born there. I reasoned that if the baby was a son and born in France, he would be My son was born on my birthday, which was the very best gift I By February, I needed a holiday and was ready to go skiing, so I convinced Phryne to leave Simon with her sister, and off we went to Alp d'Huez, about fifty kilometres from Grenoble.

On our way back to England, we stopped in Paris where we met Prince Mahabir of Nepal. He was a charming little man with whom we spent a couple of days enjoying the Paris circuit. On our last evening, having a drink together at the Ritz, he suggested that we take his private plane to Kathmandu and stay at his palace for as long as we wished. Unfortunately, we could not accept his kind invitation for both Phryne and I were missing Simon, but I have often wondered what it would have been like. However, we became good friends and whenever the prince came to London, which was often, he called on us.

Within a year, I was flat broke again. My mother and Uncle Jack had been living well beyond their means for some time, so she decided to sell her lovely house, and we all moved into a flat in Sloane Square. She had to sell most of the furniture as there was little room, but this did not include the Bluthner piano, and we still enjoyed many a musical evening.

My relationship with Phryne was becoming rather tense. What made matters worse was that we could not take any holidays because we had no money. To escape from the very unpleasant situation at home, I began playing golf at the weekends. My mother, as usual, gave me enough money to make ends meet until she decided to return to the south of France.

By now, I owed £600 in debts, and there seemed no alternative but to get myself a proper job, especially as I now had family responsibilities, so I entered the motorcar business. My friend, Ian Metcalfe, and I became sole distributors in the United Kingdom for the Borqward, a German car.

Things soon changed for the better. I paid off my debts, and we were able to live quite well despite many things such as material, clothes, and petrol still being rationed. Life with Phryne improved considerably, and in the summer of 1951, we returned to the south of France for an extended family holiday, this time in St. Maxime, in the Villa *Le Mas de Saccade*, right up in the hills.

We sailed daily on the Black Swan, until one day Fred announced that he would be sailing back to Australia with his beautiful and wealthy girlfriend. He went down to Marseille and having difficulties finding personnel for such a long trip, he got himself a rather dubious crew. He then filled the vessel with all the jewellery and furniture he possibly could and set a date for their departure. When the day came, it was very stormy, and he was advised to delay the trip a few days but being a seasoned sailor, he insisted on leaving. We were shocked to read in the newspapers the following day that the Black Swan had sunk, and Fred and Marianne had drowned. How could that have happened when both were excellent swimmers and, strangely enough, all the crew had managed to swim ashore?

The police, once they found their bodies tied to the mast, finally concluded the crew had murdered them, but it was too late, as by then they had disappeared taking with them all the jewellery. It was a tragic ending for a wonderful friend.

After the summer, I had an argument with Phryne because we had not been making love regularly. She blamed it on the fact that she was now a mother but insisted that she still loved me. As proof of her love, he gave me the green light to see other women, with the sole condition that I not fall in love.

We used to go to many parties at Raf and Diana's. One evening, Ava Gardner and Luis Miguel Dominguín were there, as well as the Spanish Ambassador. Ava walked straight up to the ambassador, kissed him on the lips and then sat on his lap! That night I was introduced to a beautiful young Spanish student who was staying at Raf and Diana's. She was called Pepita and was stunning, with a bubbly personality. She reminded me of Liz Taylor, as they had the same colouring of the eyes. Pepita was a friend of Jorge Juan, a young Spanish lawyer who was doing his articles in

Luis Miguel Dominguin and Ava Gardner

Villa Le Mas de Saccade in St.Maxime

international law at Raf's office, and the two of them soon joined Phryne and I, regularly for cocktails and picnics.

One night, after spending a blissful evening at Pepita's new apartment, I drove around the corner only to see Phryne standing there. I drove a short way past, then pulled up and waited for her to come alongside. Opening the door, I told her to get in.

"I want to walk home. Don't you remember we have a son?" she said on the verge of tears.

Back home, we had a terrible scene. In her rage, Phryne threatened to shoot Pepita, but soon she calmed down, and we agreed to continue living together for at least another year, for Simon's sake.

I tried everything to get Pepita out of my system but failed miserably. She was the woman I loved. The love of my life!

It was soon May 1952. I sent Phryne and Simon to St. Maxime to stay with my mother and Uncle Jack and joined them a few weeks later in a last attempt to salvage my marriage. We spent most of the days with Gregory Peck who had rented the villa next to ours. By then, I really could not face being alone with Phryne, and always tried to surround myself with friends.

While all this was happening King Farouk lost his throne. I felt really saddened by the news as he had been a good king in many ways. With the creation of the Arab League in Cairo in 1945, he had become the de facto leader of the Arab world and was at the pinnacle of his popularity. He had been very active in inter Arab politics, had increased the Arab orientation of Egypt and had taken a keen interest in the aspirations of the Palestinian people. Egypt had developed economically during his reign, and he had founded many institutes of higher learning. In 1950, young Queen Narriman gave birth to the most desired heir, Prince Ahmed Fuad but by then the elements in the army had been working against their king. Farouk instead of confronting them ran off to Alexandria with his young family to escape the heat. On July 29, the king was forced to abdicate, and his baby son proclaimed King Fuad II. The royal family left the country that same day and the army eventually abolished the monarchy on the 18th of June, the following year. I never met Farouk again.

A few months after this holiday, we got divorced. Our break-up was tough for her, but we have managed to stay friends all through the years. Soon afterwards, she moved to the Costa Brava and ended up having an affair with Jorge Juan, Pepita's friend. She has lived there ever since.

Pepita took a room at the Zawidski´s boarding house, and we saw each other every day. By then Simon Stern had left the country. The Zawidski's were very fond of her, and we used to sit with them over a glass of their excellent Polish vodka and listen to what they had to say about Poland's past and present hardships. They were very embittered about Churchill having sold Poland's freedom to Stalin. Their country had fought the German war machine for sixty-three days with no outside help until the Germans crushed the resistance and Warsaw was completely destroyed as a lesson to the rest of Europe. We felt extremely sorry for them because they had both suffered enormously, and their deep-set nostalgia for their country would never leave them.

Pepita and I were very much in love, but she always felt guilty and blamed herself for the break-up of my marriage to Phryne. She came from a conservative Catholic Basque family and was very religious. I was glad that she got on well with my mother and Uncle Jack, as that made things easier for everybody.

I finally proposed to her, and she accepted. However, there were quite a few problems to solve before we could get married. I belonged to the Church of England, and the Catholic Church was against marriages between different faiths. To make matters worse, I was divorced, which was equally unacceptable. As far as Pepita´s family was concerned, I was entirely unsuitable as a husband for all the above reasons and because I had a son it was even worst in their eyes.

After much consultation, a lawyer specializing in Vatican Law gave us the good news: as far as the Catholic Church was concerned, I had never been married to Phryne at all, because she had been a divorcee at the time. Therefore, the Church considered her still married to her previous husband; in the Church's eyes, our marriage had never existed. This was a surprising way of erasing ten years of our lives, but it suited us just fine.

In the summer of 1954, I invited Pepita's mother and her sister to the South of France to spend with us a few weeks

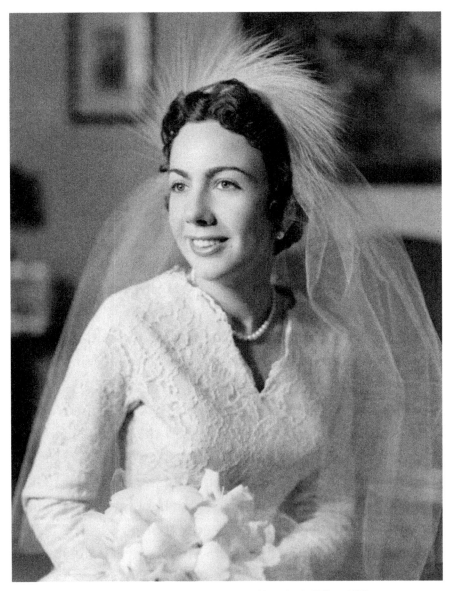

Pepita de Orueta y de Arrese on her wedding day in Bilbao 1955

Pepita Mundy and her new born son, Carlos

in the delightful atmosphere of the Mediterranean. Everything went very smoothly as our respective mothers sat down to arrange the details of our wedding, which were to be celebrated in the Church of *Nuestra Señora de Begoña* in Bilbao in the spring. I was very excited and much in love.

The wedding was an incredibly lavish affair with over five hundred guests. As I stood waiting for over half an hour at the altar of the Basilica, which Pepita´s mother had decorated with hundreds of white flowers, I felt rather uneasy. Had Pepita changed her mind?

Luckily, she had not. She arrived at the church holding Uncle Jack´s arm and looking ravishing in her stunning light mauve long-tailed wedding dress. The Duke of Primo de Rivera, Spanish Ambassador to Britain, Ian Metcalfe and Jose Luis de Arrese, Pepita's uncle, all signed as witnesses, together with other friends.

That night after the banquet, we drove to San Sebastian where we stayed at the *Hotel de Londres* and then travelled through France.

*

Back in London, we stayed for a few weeks at the Zawidski's, who by now had become very close friends. Every Christmas we went with our children to see them and we all enjoyed listening to old Polish tales.

As the motorcar business was thriving, we decided to buy a beautiful house in Putney. 9 Westleigh Avenue was to be our home until we left England. Pepita hired Spanish staff, and we entertained constantly.

My son Carlos was born in May 1956. Pepita went to Bilbao to give birth to be close to her mother. I had not been too keen on the idea, myself, but she was a stubborn woman and insisted on giving birth to all four of our children in her hometown.

I received a heavy blow just before my second son was born. My mother died from a stroke while taking a nap. I would miss her very much, as she had been an important person in my life. Not only had she been an excellent mother, but also one of my closest friends.

For the next few years, I led a life of domestic bliss, until one day the harmony was shattered, and the past returned to haunt me.

XVI

THE SWINGING SIXTIES

Life in London in the Sixties was great fun because if the Sixties were a social revolution, London was its centre. Yuri Gagarin's becoming the first man in space in 1961 had led to a new way of thinking.

People somehow felt they were no longer limited exclusively to this planet, and this idea of grander space and freedom reflected in everything else.

We entered the decade in black and white, and we came out in colour. Mary Quant had invented the mini skirt, and the Beatles and the Rolling Stones had taken the music world by storm. The British Establishment was reeling with shock, having been wholly unprepared for such a radical change, a change that was visible everywhere. Everything now geared to the taste of the younger generation.

With the Bay of Pigs incident, the world had been poised on the brink of a major conflict, and President Kennedy's assassination a year later in 1963 came as a dreadful shock.

I feared MI6 would come knocking on my door, but luckily, they failed to materialise and allowed me to continue living my life in peace. I heard through Raf Valls that M had finally retired, as by then my contact with the Firm was non-existent.

I was enjoying life in the company of my beautiful wife

and children. Simon was attending Kings College in Canterbury, and I saw him on occasional weekends and holidays.

Time flew, and in 1965 Winston Churchill, the most exceptional political leader of the 20th Century died. The entire nation went into mourning. I admired him enormously, considering him a keystone to the Allied victory in the War. But I am sure history will also judge him for his mistakes, especially that of handing half of Europe over to Stalin.

Back in 1947 Simon Wiesenthal, a Jewish Holocaust survivor, and thirty others had formed the Jewish Historical Documentation Centre, based in the town of Linz in Austria. The Centre aimed to compile evidence in the hope of bringing Nazi war criminals to trial.

"M" had passed Klaus von Jettenbach´s file on to the Centre years ago, and for a while, I waited for his detention, but by now I thought the case had been forgotten. Although the original office had closed in 1959, Wiesenthal had carried on with his investigative work and had opened the Jewish Documentation Centre in Vienna, concentrating his efforts exclusively on hunting down Nazi war criminals. His painstaking efforts and investigations were soon to prove very fruitful. Not only was Wiesenthal responsible for the capture of Adolf Eichmann, the man who had supervised the implementation of the Final Solution and who had been living happily in Buenos Aires as Ricardo Klement, but in

October 1966, he had nine SS officers arrested and tried in Stuttgart for their part in the extermination of Jews in Lvov. A year later, after three years' patient undercover work in Brazil, Wiesenthal had Franz Stangl arrested and sentenced to life imprisonment. Stangle had been the commandant of Treblinka and Sobibor concentration camps.

After Stangl's arrest, the international press ran articles about him and the luxury in which he had been living. In one of the photographs taken in his home, I recognised a painting that had been part of Simon Stern's collection and included in the list of works he had given the baron for safekeeping.

The discovery exhilarated me. I contacted the Jewish Documentation Centre in Vienna and gave them the information that was to lead to the baron's arrest.

Fleeing from Spain as Claudio Jiménez de Bach, the baron had settled in Asunción, Paraguay, where many high-ranking Nazis joined him, seeking the protection of President Stroessner, who had turned his country into a home for ageing Nazis. The baron soon became a Paraguayan citizen and changed his name once again, as the name given to him by Franco made him very easy to trace. He also underwent plastic surgery to erase any features that might remind anyone of Klaus von Jettenbach.

As Gerardo Echevarría, he lived in style in Asunción and was a prominent member of Paraguayan society. He had become a patron of the arts. His donation of some of the minor works in his collection to the city's Art Museum had won him the favour of the dictator and to add lustre to his altruism, he sponsored young Paraguayan artists. It was thanks to Stangl's testimony that the Jewish Documentation Centre was able to trace the Baron but bringing him to trial in Israel was not so easy. The Paraguayan authorities, as was to be expected, refused to either arrest him or grant his extradition. To them, officially, Gerardo Echevarría had been born in Asunción and could not possibly be a war criminal. However, irrefutable the proof presented by Israel, it was all to no avail.

The Israeli government finally lost its patience and decided to act. Israeli agents promptly abducted the baron on his return from spending a weekend with his wife and son at his country estate in the north. It was there that he kept his magnificent art collection for the enjoyment of his family and closest friends.

I knew the capture of Klaus von Jettenbach would land me once again with MI6, although I hoped they had forgotten me. A few days later, however, someone from the firm came to see me at my office. A man called Miles.

"Mr Mundy, the Israeli government has requested that you go to Jerusalem to attend Mr. von Jettenbach's trial once they set a date. And as a former member of this organisation, we also request that, when the time comes, you attend the trial."

"But these events took place over twenty years ago!" I protested, "I only met Jettenbach a few times, and I don't even recognise him now in the photographs."

"You were involved in the investigation that took place at the time, and you became a good friend of Simon Stern, so I think you owe it to him, at least. Your testimony will undoubtedly help to get that bastard convicted!" Miles added, convincingly.

"All right then. I'll do it," I conceded. "Tell me, whatever happened to Stern?"

"He finally moved to Costa Rica with his daughter. He died a few years ago. The suffering he endured in those camps must have finally taken its toll."

"What will happen to the Baron's art collection?" I asked.

"Stroessner is so angry at what has happened that he refuses to admit that his buddy was a former Nazi. The official position is that the collection belongs to Paraguay. We will do everything legally possible to have the paintings returned to the families of their former owners, although it is going to be difficult and costly.".

"Very well, then. I shall have to speak to my wife, of course, whom no doubt won't be happy that I have never mentioned any of this to her."

"Rodney, one more thing... we would like you to go and live in Spain. Franco cannot live forever, and we need you there."

I could not believe it! I was back in MI6 again! To my surprise, Pepita was most understanding. She loathed the Nazis with a passion, influenced no doubt by the Zawidskis horrific stories about what went on in Poland. I, myself, believe that sometimes one must let go of hate for the wounds to heal, but, of course, every human being is a world unto himself. Pepita decided she would accompany me to Jerusalem whenever the trial would take place; moreover, she was willing to go and live in Madrid and be closer to her family.

We stored our furniture in a warehouse, put Westlcigh Avenue up for sale, and made our travel arrangements back to Spain, to Berria Beach, not far away from Santander, where every summer we spent the holidays with Pepita's mother and her sister's family.

When the summer was over, we settled into our new home at *Calle de Cinca 16*, in the residential district of *El Viso*. Pepita had chosen a lovely big house with a garden so that our children would not feel too unsettled by the move.
Madrid had changed enormously since my last visit, and a new air of freedom could be sensed everywhere. Franco was getting old, and in time, there would be a change of regime. As soon as I arrived, I called Joaquín and Pepe who were now prominent members of society. They loved Pepita.

As a cover, MI6 had arranged for me to work for a company called *Hierros y Aceros Europeos*, which was a subsidiary of Harlow & Jones. Our job was to advise the Spanish steelworks on the purchase of scrap metal from the US, the UK and other European countries, chiefly Belgium and the Netherlands. Initially, I knew absolutely nothing about scrap metal, nor did I ever have the slightest interest, but I soon learnt to enjoy it and eventually became very good at it. To cap it all, I got a generous salary, and I had a charming assistant, Count Peter Potocki, whose family had given Poland several kings and who was now living in exile in Madrid.

My work for MI6 was once again to infiltrate Spanish society and find out who would support the restoration of the monarchy because a lot of support would be necessary if the institution were to survive. We eared the extremists would react against it. Neither Santiago Carrillo's outlawed Communist Party nor the Socialists wanted a monarchy, and they both mocked the future king from their headquarters in exile. They referred to him as Juan Carlos 'the brief'! On the other hand, Franco's acolytes were not very keen on the idea of the monarchy either, although they said nothing in public. MI6 had briefed me that they feared that after Franco's death, there was a real danger of another civil war breaking out.

Pepita was a great asset in my work because after only a month in Madrid she started giving her extravagant and amusing dinner parties, which became the talk of the town, and which our *madrileño* friends found very entertaining.

I was in contact with Miles through my office, and I told him everything I learnt, which, in truth, was not very much, because nobody wanted to discuss the future. After so many years of Franco, who did achieve a reasonable level of prosperity for the country, the population was apprehensive of any change, and they all agreed that the king's task would be anything but easy.

No date had yet been set for the trial in Jerusalem, so at

Easter, we decided to rent a house in a sleepy fishing village on the Costa del Sol, called Torremolinos. We took the children and their Spanish Governess, Beatriz, with us. Pepita and I were planning to go afterwards to Seville for the April Feria, having been invited by Pablo Atienza, she took most of her precious jewellery with her.

One afternoon we drove with the children and the governess to the nearby village of Marbella to visit some friends. On our return, we discovered the apartment had been visited by burglars. We were upset by the loss, as many of the jewels stolen had been gifts from her mother, others were Mundy heirlooms, and the rest were expensive gifts from a devoted husband. The police concluded that the thieves were just common criminals who had had a stroke of luck, but I knew better. From how they had searched the apartment, I knew the burglars were highly trained. I said nothing about my fears to my wife. Instead, I contacted Miles, who told me that the Israelis had set a date for the trial in October of the found that burglars had entered the house. The place had been ransacked and, naturally, Pepita's jewellery was missing. She was very distressed. Now I understood!

In the spring of 1968, France was in turmoil. The students had taken to the streets of Paris *en masse* and were bringing about a veritable revolution. Naturally, the Spanish press censored all news from Paris, while giving ample coverage

Their Royal Highnesses Prince Juan Carlos and Princess Sophia, Prince and Princess of Asturias in the late 60's. General Franco made them use the title of Prince and Princess of Spain which was non-existent title. He loathed Prince Don Juan who was considered King Juan III by the Royalists and thus did not want his son to use the traditional title of the heirs to the Spanish throne of Prince of Asturias.

to the communist regime's brutal repression of the pro-democracy movement in Prague.

Spanish summers were three months long; so we prepared to shut up the house in *Calle de Cinca* for the holidays. It was a lot of hard work; all the furniture and paintings had to be covered with sheets to protect them from dust, and the smaller objects wrapped in newspaper, but under Pepita's guidance, the servants managed to get everything done.

As every summer, we went to Santander, driving up in two cars. In mid-August, feeling like a change of scenery, Pepita and I accepted an invitation to spend a few days in *La Manga del Mar Menor* in Murcia. We took Carlos with us and drove down, stopping in Madrid for an overnight stay at home. Madrid was unbearable hot, and the house felt ghostly. We enjoyed our week in La Manga, which had only recently begun to be developed. Our host, Jaime Royo-Villanova who would eventually marry Pepita's niece, took good care of us.

For our return journey, we planned the same route, once again with a stopover in Madrid. However, the minute we arrived home, I knew there was something terribly wrong. The front door had been forced open, but my worst fears were nothing compared to the nightmarish sight we found inside. Whoever had broken in had turned the house upside down with premeditated violence, they had slashed all the valuable paintings, destroyed and thrown about many of the children's toys. The mess left behind was unbelievable. Pepita broke down in tears. We called the police and booked into a hotel. The police thought it most likely that a group of gipsies had broken in and stayed for a few days, as there were signs that lead them to believe they had cooked themselves meals and slept in the house. As one would have thought in a burglary many priceless objects, including the rest of Pepita's jewellery, were missing but what was not in character was the evident hate factor. Why had they destroyed the paintings rather than stolen them?   Littered around the house were packets that looked like gifts, but when the police opened them, they turned out to be full of human excrement. I realised that whomever these people were, they were delivering a message on behalf of others who passionately hated me and wished to intimidate me. Once again, I kept my thoughts to myself, as Pepita was worried enough as it was.

We decided for safety sake to move to a rented, vast, flat on *Raimundo Fernández Villaverde*, 61, and had the rest of our furniture sent out from London.   It was already late September, and shortly we would have to fly to Jerusalem for the trial.

It was then that I started receiving hate letters and threatening phone calls at the office, and I became seriously worried. I naturally had to speak to Pepita, who pleaded with me to forget the whole affair and not go to Israel. I was obliged to explain that I was active with MI6 again, at which she became distraught and sincerely concerned about the children's safety.

"You had no right to hide that from me. We are a team,"

she said: "These Nazis won't stop at anything to achieve their goals. And their goal is that you stay here."

"I know that my love, but I have to go."

"Fine! In that case, you can go alone. I do not want to have anything to do with it. I shall take the children to Bilbao, to my mother's, until it is all over. I hope you never live to regret this decision." She stormed out, slamming the door behind her. It was our first significant row since our marriage.

In a few days hence, I would be on my way to Jerusalem. In the meantime, the British Embassy provided some guards to protect my family.

*

The day before my departure, I invited Pepita to lunch at Horcher, the celebrated German restaurant that Otto Horcher opened in Madrid in 1943. She was barely speaking to me, but I needed her blessing before I left, as I knew that my stay in Jerusalem would not be relaxed. She accepted, and we walked into Horcher at precisely 2.30 pm.

We sat at an excellent table, and the *maitre* placed a cushion under Pepita's feet. I ordered a bottle of vintage Krugg champagne, and we drank a toast. We were chatting away happily when I noticed an older man sitting by himself. He was fairly close to us. The face was very familiar, and after observing him, I realized that he was Vogel. He had to be following me, and I was sure he was responsible for everything that happened to us. Instinctively, I got up and walked over to his table. Though he, of course, knew very well who I was, he pretended otherwise, feigning surprise.

"Hello, Hans. It's been a long time." He played his role with excellence and continued to act as if he did not know me.

"Inform whoever is in charge to get off my back! "I said firmly, but in a whisper. "If you hurt my family, I'll destroy you."

He started rambling in French, "But *monsieur*, you are crazy, I am a French tourist, my name is not Hans, and I have never met you. My name is Pierre Dupont. You must be mistaken."

Vogel started calling the *maitre* and complained about my harassment in fluent French and without a trace of his former heavy German accent. I turned and, without another word, walked back to my table. The sight of him had much disturbed me. I remembered Laszlo's murder.

"What was all that about?" asked my wife. "Everybody is looking at us!"

I recounted the whole story. "I told you before, Rodney, these people are perilous and will stop at nothing to save the Baron. What do you intend to do? You cannot possibly go to Israel. You must think about your family."

"My love, I must do my duty. I shall inform my boss in London, and the Simon Wiesenthal centre."

"What about your duty to your family?" Tears rolled down her beautiful cheeks. I could not bear witnessing her pain. However, I had no choice.

XVII

THE BARON'S TRIAL

In mid-October, Pepita took a night train to Bilbao with the children and Bea as planned. She had made me promise that I would be back for my birthday, although I was not at all confident that the trial would be over by then.

The flight to Lod airport was uneventful. The Israeli Government had bought me a first-class ticket on El Al, the national carrier, and on arrival, the British Consul and several members of the Mossad collected me.

The weather was delightful. It was sunny and warm, as only Mediterranean capitals can be in autumn. We drove to Jerusalem, the city of peace and they took me straight to the King David Hotel, where a comfortable suite was waiting for me. I called Pepita, who had arrived safely in Bilbao. I felt a faint sensation of uneasiness and promised myself that this would be the last mission of this type. My work in Madrid was not dangerous, so in future, I would stick to that.

Isaac, a member of the Mossad, had been assigned to me during my stay, and when I had unpacked, he escorted me to the Consulate, where members of the Israeli secret service would brief me on the details of the trial.

The residence of the British Consul was situated in one

of the best areas of the city. As we drove there, I marvelled at Jerusalem, a city that was three thousand years old and sacred to the world's three most important religions.

I hoped I would have time to do some sightseeing during my stay. Talbot Mundy, the great author, that as a sign of friendship to my father, had taken our family name as his *nom de plume* wrote in the twenties that Jerusalem was a ludicrous, uproarious, dignified, pious, sinful, naively confidential, secretive, altruistic and realistic city. A city proud of its name and its unique history.

The gates of the residence opened as the car approached. After we passed security, I was escorted to the Consul's study. He rose from his chair as we entered, looking distinctly worried.

"Welcome to Jerusalem, Mr Mundy," he said somewhat gravely, and I realised all was not well.

"Please call me Rodney,"

Isaac and two other members of the Israeli Secret Service sat down, and the Consul introduced me to the Ambassador.

"Rodney, I am afraid I have news from Spain that you are not going to like."

My heart sank, and my distress was visible to everybody in the room.

"Your family is fine," he quickly reassured me, "however, your ex-wife has contacted the embassy in Madrid to inform them that Simon, who was spending the weekend with her, met a middle-aged man fluent in German who threatened him.

"What did he want? Is my son all right? I was beyond myself with worry. I could not believe that I had put duty before my family.

The consul rose from his chair and approached me.

"Whoever it was, wants you to return to Spain and that you don't testify."

"I can't go ahead with this."

"You have a duty to perform, Rodney. You must stay. Both, your family in Bilbao and your ex-wife and elder son now have extra protection. They are safe."

"That's not much of a relief! I would never be able to forgive myself if anything happened to them."

"The man told your son that he was an old friend of yours. Do you have a clue as to who he could be?" the Consul said.

"Yes. He was probably Vogel. He was a member of the Gestapo. He is a cold-blooded murderer. How is it possible that these Nazis move around with such impunity? It's been over twenty years since the Reich collapsed!" I cried out in bewilderment.

"Though very discrete, the Nazis are still very active. We know they have a clandestine organization that operates worldwide, but it is so impenetrable that we have been unable to infiltrate it. We do not even know where it is based. Former members of the Gestapo, the SS, and Nazi sympathisers belong to it. They have vast amounts of money, which they managed to get out of Germany mainly through Spain, and they use it to help those in need to protect their identities and they finance neo-Nazi groups. Their main goal, of course, is to establish the Fourth Reich. So, you see, Rodney, the Nazis are formidable enemy, which is why you must stay for the trial."

"Why are they so concerned about the Baron? After all he is a disgraced Nazi!"

"Well, after the fall of the Reich, he used his money and influences to regain the organisation's respect."

"Ambassador, Captain Vogel murdered two good friends of mine. I would like us to do whatever it takes to have him arrested and prosecuted for his crimes."

"I will speak to the Israel Government and our Secret Services, and hopefully we will find him."

"I saw him in a Madrid restaurant only two days ago. He is pretending to be French, and if he was with my son he is probably still in Barcelona."

✳

The trial was set to begin on the morning of the 17th. Jerusalem was abuzz with expectation, and stringent security measures were in place everywhere. Close to a hundred journalists had come to cover what was dubbed, "The Trial of the Decade". To add to the excitement, it was going to be televised, as the Israeli Prime Minister, Levi Eshkol, wanted to ensure that the world did not forget the atrocities committed by the Nazis.

This would be the second Nazi trial to be televised, the first having been that of Adolf Eichmann. There were similarities between the two cases. The Jewish state had kidnapped both men in South America, rather than being arrested and both put on trial by a Jewish court in Israel. The difference was in the scale of their crimes. Eichmann had been responsible for the deaths of millions of Jews and had been the mastermind behind the Final Solution, whereas the Baron had arranged the disposal of some of his wealthy Jewish friends out of pure greed. I walked into the courtroom and sat at the designated place. I looked around to see if I knew anybody. Over in a corner, I spotted a beautiful blonde woman in her thirties, accompanied by a boy of about twelve, who with his blonde hair and bright blue eyes was the epitome of the ideal Aryan. He looked very much alike to the Baron when we had first met in the south of France. It had to be his son, and it only confirmed that this man, about to be tried for crimes against the Jewish people, was, in fact, none other than Klaus von Jettenbach, whatever the Paraguayan Government said.

The accused entered the courtroom and took his place inside a glass booth to protect him. I had to admit that he had changed beyond recognition, his piercing blue eyes being the only vestige of his former self.

The chief judge entered the courtroom, and the proceedings began. He read out the accusations and asked the accused if he declared himself guilty or innocent.

He stood up, defiantly, and said, "you have made a mistake! I am not the man you say I am! My name is Gerardo Echevarria, and I am a citizen of Paraguay."

His German defence lawyer, who had defended many former Nazis, asked to speak to the judge. After a few minutes, the judge spoke again.

"As the identity of the accused is in doubt and the representatives of the Government of Paraguay insist that the accused is, in fact, Mr Gerardo Echevarria, the court will subject him to some tests to establish his identity and will study the documents submitted by the Paraguayan authorities. The trial is thereby adjourned for five days while the experts reach a conclusion."

I was rather put out by this decision, as a delay meant that I would probably be unable to keep my promise to my wife, but Isaac reassured me, saying it would only take a few days for the baron's identity to be proved beyond doubt.

"Although he has had much plastic surgery performed on his face, in addition to dental work, we are submitting photographs of the baron as a young man and pictures of him today, to an eminent German forensic expert who has developed the PIK ear identification. The baron can't have changed his ears!" he said laughing.

"What other tests will they do?"

"He has no fingerprints, as he has had them erased, so we have requested a graphological report. We are not worried, as we have no doubts. If it shows positive, the PIK test is irrefutable."

I spent the next few days sightseeing with Isaac, eating kosher food, and enjoying one of the most fascinating cities in the world. The dinner with the Consul was very pleasant.

Every day I spoke to Pepita, who was fine, and I heard through the Embassy that Phryne and Simon were also well. I had given him instructions not to return to university until after the trial.

Five days later, we were back in the courtroom. The silence was absolute. The judge entered, at last, with a broad smile on his face.

"The identity of the accused has been established beyond doubt." He paused for greater dramatic effect, and I could see he was quite a character. Handsome and in his early fifties, he had a boyish look that was enhanced by his straight blonde hair, but I felt sure that behind his amiable and mild-mannered expression lay a sharp mind.

"Since there are no fingerprints or dental records, we have had to hire the services of Dr Moritz Furtmayer, who has developed the PIK test, which compares the anatomical points of the ear. For a person's identity to be confirmed, a minimum of twelve points must be identical. The professor has compared photographs of the right ear of the young Baron with pictures of the right ear of Gerardo Echevarria, and he has found fifteen identical anatomical points. Therefore, the trial will now proceed."

There was an uproar of approval in the courtroom. Only Mrs Echevarria and her son looked miserable. She was devastated. After all, she had not known to whom she had been married all these years. I felt sorry for her as she too had been a victim of deception.

"Do you have anything to add?" the judge asked the

accused. The Baron remained silent.

The prosecution called on several witnesses who recounted everything they knew about the baron's activities, and whose testimonies the defence lawyer weakly refuted. Many of them were descendants of the baron's victims and, deprived of their inheritance, lived in semi poverty while trying unsuccessfully to obtain compensation from the German Republic. The outcome of this trial could change their lives, as it would enable them to recover eventually some of their works of art. Then Gonzaga Pérez de Sanchís was called to the witness stand. To my surprise, it was Gonzaga Herentals but addressed by his family name. I had not seen him in years, as both brothers left Madrid and went to live in New York. He looked well and was still very handsome. I hoped I would have the chance to talk to him, but as witnesses, we were kept somewhat isolated, and we could not mingle with each other.

Gonzaga told the court about his father's relationship with the baron, and how he had secured a Spanish passport for him just before the end of the war. He recounted everything he knew, including detailed information on the crates of paintings that had at one time been stored at the Herental's palace.

They adjourned the trial until the following day. Things seemed to be going smoothly, and the defence lawyer's attempts to discredit the witnesses presented by the prosecution were all proving unsuccessful.

The next morning, I was called to the stand. I confirmed

Gonzaga's testimony and recounted how I had first met von Jettenbach and became aware of his activities. I also told the court what Simon Stern had said to me about the baron's acquiring part of his collection, which was now in Paraguay, an indisputable proof of his guilt. There was no doubt to anyone present that the accused was guilty, and it looked as if the trial would be a brief one.

On the third day, after listening to over fifty witnesses, the judge asked the accused to make a deposition. The baron stood up in his glass booth and in a dignified manner proceeded to defend himself. After a sip of water, he cleared his throat.

"My detention is illegal. It was an act of terrorism. I am the victim of an error of judgement. The Mossad has kidnapped me and brought me here against my will, which makes this trial illegal. My lawyer has already explained to the court how President Stroessner's government has filed a lawsuit against the Israeli government. I trust the judges will consider these facts.

"In my defence, I can only say that I never persecuted Jews with avidity and passion. The reality is that I never persecuted Jews at all. I, myself, had many Jewish friends, whose names have been mentioned in this court. I tried to save them through my close relationship with *Reichsmarschall* Göring who, like me, was a lover of art. My intentions were honourable. I tried to protect my friends by warning them about what was going to happen and by protecting their collections.

A roar of disapproval greeted his words. He paused and took another sip of water. I could see that he was only too aware of the importance of what he was saying. He knew his life depended on it.

"In those days, I was an art advisor to the *Reichsmarschall*, and I merely obeyed orders. We all did. If I am guilty of anything, I anything I am guilty of obeying orders."

The deposition was somewhat like the one Eichmann had made at his trial a few years earlier, where he had been found guilty of crimes against humanity and had been hanged.

"When I discovered what was happening, I was horrified by the extent of the killing of Jews. I did not hear about the Final Solution until just before the end of the war, and I was so disgusted that I left the Third Reich and moved to South America. The Court has to believe that I had anything to do with those fanatics. I assure you that during my days of service to the Third Reich I never had the power or responsibility to have anyone killed. I have always lived my life according to ethical principles."

A lone laugh was heard somewhere in the courtroom.

Though the baron was giving an excellent performance and he sounded quite convincing, I, of course, knew better.

"I have a son whom I love and a wonderful wife whom I cherish. I am a respected member of society in Paraguay, a patron of the arts. I am no danger to anybody. I beg this Court to consider this. If I am declared innocent, I shall ask the Government of Paraguay to permit the export of those paintings that were given to me by my friends for safekeeping."

An irritated elderly man cried out, "It's a bit late for that!"

The judge demanded silence in the Court and then addressed the accused.

"Baron Klaus von Jettenbach, have you finished?"

"Yes."

"Very well then, the court is adjourned until tomorrow at ten, when we will pass the sentence."

The next day the courtroom was buzzing with excitement.

Although it was clear that the baron had not murdered anybody himself, there was overwhelming evidence of his involvement in the disappearance of some of the most prominent Jewish art collectors in Europe. I very much doubted that the sentence would be a mild one.

We all rose as the three judges entered the room, with the verdict inside an envelope. The excitement was palpable. The chief judge ceremoniously opened the envelope and, with even greater solemnity than on previous days, proceeded to read the verdict.

"When deciding upon the appropriate sentence for the accused, this Court has been more than aware of the enormous burden of responsibility laid upon it. Since the accused has enjoyed over twenty years of impunity under a false identity, the Court has decided to give him the maximum sentence permitted by the laws of the State of Israel. In its judgement, the Court has detailed the crimes in which the accused took part. Although it is a fact that he is not directly responsible for the murder of the Jewish art collectors whom he insists on calling his friend*s*, the accused has been found guilty of stealing their collections before having them sent to extermination camps. As the Court is aware, most of these Jews did not survive their ordeal.

When considering the sentence to be passed, this Court has also, and perhaps most importantly, considered the injuries inflicted on the victims of these crimes as individuals, and the immeasurable anguish which they and their families suffered and still suffer to this very day. Whether the accused was following orders or whether he acted out of irrepressible greed is mostly immaterial. The fact is he acquired one of the best art collections in the world by illegal means. If, as he claims, he did so out of altruism, he should have returned all the paintings after the war. Had that been the case, this Court might conceivably have treated him with greater leniency. Therefore, after due consideration of the testimonies presented, this Court hereby sentences Baron Klaus von Jettenbach to life imprisonment for crimes against the Jewish people, and the theft of art collections owned by Jews. He is also guilty of membership of an organization that is hostile to Jews and to the State of Israel. This is the Court's verdict and sentence. Baron von Jettenbach is entitled to appeal and has ten working days in which to do so. I declare this trial closed."

The crowd burst into applause. The only person sobbing in the courtroom was his deceived wife. She understood she had suddenly become a social pariah. Her son sat beside her expressionless.

The judges left the courtroom, and everybody started talking at once. I was relieved that everything had gone so fast, as it meant that I would be flying back to Madrid the next day, in time to celebrate my birthday with my family. It was all over, at last.

XVIII

AN IRREPARABLE LOSS

My return to Madrid was uneventful. Pepita and the children arrived from the north so that they were home for my arrival. She had arranged a surprise party as only she knew how to do, and to all our friends were invited to celebrate my forty-sixth birthday.

Less than a fortnight later, I was having breakfast when the maid brought me the morning paper, the ABC. On the cover was a photograph of Baron Klaus von Jettenbach. The article said that, after losing his appeal against the sentence, they had found the baron dead in his cell. He had cut his own throat with a boy-scout knife that his son had somehow managed to give him before returning to Asunción.

"What a finale!" I thought. I felt sorry for the baroness or Mrs. Echevarria. Until her husband's abduction, she had not been aware of his identity or his activities.

The next few months went by very quickly. I had to travel extensively for the company, and now and then, I would send a report to Miles.

However, in early June, I once again started receiving threatening letters and phone calls, so I immediately notified London.

The long arm of the hostile organization that I had heard about in Jerusalem seemed to be quite active. In the letters, I was insulted and called a murderer, while the voices on the phone kept repeating that I should always look behind me. It made me so uneasy that I again requested protection for my family and for Simon, who was now studying in Germany.

Pepita was beside herself with worry and told me she could no longer live like this. Neither could I, so I promised her that by the end of the year, I would quit my espionage activities. We decided to spend our summer holidays in the north as usual, but starting in late May, so we set about closing the house. If I had to return to the office during the summer, I would stay at a hotel.

The summer was glorious and the weather excellent, which was not too usual in the north of Spain, where rain and cold temperatures are the norms. We fell into a delightful routine of swimming, fishing, going for long walks, playing golf and dining in excellent rural restaurants. My sons Carlos and Ivan were sent to Broadlands in Hampshire to improve both their English and their riding and would be back by mid-August. The girls remained with us, enjoying the company of their cousins, aunt, and grandmother.

That summer, we witnessed the fantastic the feat of men walking on the moon, and no one can deny that the sixties were significant years for humankind.

In early September, Pepita and I were ready to return to

Madrid to re-open the flat. We took two cars. For the children's sake, we always drove separately as a precaution against both of us being involved in an accident. We did not take Carlos with us despite his insistence, and he was distraught when we drove off without him.

In those days the roads in Spain were very second rate, so we stopped for the night in Burgos. The *Hostal Landa* had a charming atmosphere and offered excellent food, and that night Pepita and I made love with a passion that surprised us both.

We spent two days in Madrid, busily preparing the house for the family's arrival, before driving north again, via Burgos. That night at the Hostal we had a major row, probably the first in our entire marriage. Pepita blamed me for all the stress she was under, due to my activities with MI6, and threatened to leave me if I did not stop the minute we returned to Madrid. I tried to calm her down but was not too successful. In the end, she fell asleep in my arms. I felt terrible at being the cause of all her worry and anguish.

The following morning, we awoke to appalling weather and heavy rain. "Drive carefully," I said, as I kissed her tenderly on the lips. "I love you."

The weather was foul all day, with pouring rain and strong winds, and it took me five hours to reach the north. The children were happy to see me, and I to see them.

"Papa! Papa! Did you bring me a present?" asked my lovely little girls, as their grandmother looked on, smiling indulgently.

"Has Pepita arrived?" I asked.

"No, not yet" my mother-in-law replied.

"Well, she should be here very soon, as we left at the same time. She's probably driving carefully because of the rain." I said.

An hour passed with no sign of Pepita, then another and another. By then, we were seriously worried, and I called the Civil Guard to find out if they had a report of any accidents. They promised to call back if they received any.

Shortly afterwards, the phone rang. "*Señor*, I'm afraid a car with the description you gave me has gone off a cliff in the mountain pass of *Los Tornos*. An ambulance has taken your wife to Bilbao."

"How is she?"

"I am sorry to tell you that she is in a critical condition."

"Pepita! Pepita! No! Please hang on!" I muttered to myself. From the tears running down my cheeks, my mother-in-law and Carmen knew that something was terribly wrong. We hugged and cried until I managed to regain my composure. I called Dr Jose Mari Herrasti, who had been Pepita's gynaecologist and was a close friend of the family and asked him to go to the hospital. I did not want to tell the children anything until we knew more about the situation, so we left them with a neighbour, their cousins and the faithful Beatriz Ruiz.

Before leaving for Bilbao, I went to say goodbye to them.

"What's happened?" Carlos asked. He was already thirteen and very intuitive.

"Everything is fine. Your mother has had an accident, but she will soon be well. Don't worry. Now, make sure you take good care of your brother and sisters."

"OK, Papa." I knew he did not believe me because he started to cry. He was heartbroken.

My sister-in-law drove her mother and me to Bilbao. It was only a distance of sixty-eight kilometres, but it took us nearly two hours because of the rain and the bad state of the roads. Dr Herrasti was waiting for us at the hospital with a gloomy expression on his face.

"I'm afraid it doesn't look good at all," he told us, "Pepita is in a coma, in intensive care. There is only about a ten per cent chance that she will survive."

My mother-in-law, usually a paradigm of strength, half fainted.

"The best thing is for you to go home and fetch the children. And pray."

"May I see her?" I asked.

"I wouldn't recommend it. Please trust me."

As the situation began to sink in, I started asking myself many questions. Why had Pepita taken that particular mountain pass, dangerous even in the best of weather? Did the threatening letters and phone calls have anything to do with the accident? I called London from my mother-in-law's flat and informed my superiors.

"They have murdered her, Miles. I know it. It's the dark hand of Nazism."

"Rodney don't jump to conclusions like that. We will

send a team of experts to work with the Spanish police and the Civil Guard and I will get a report to you as soon as we know anything."

"But, Miles, those letters and the phone calls…. They are making me pay for Jettenbch's death. Fuck Miles, it is your responsibility. This was not supposed to happen. You gave me guarantees!"

"Calm down, Rodney. Let us wait for the results of the investigation before you jump to any conclusion. Just remain calm, and we will contact you soon."

I was broken inside and felt an uncontrollable rage inside me. I promised that if the Nazis were behind this, I would seek them out and destroy them even if it was the last thing I did in my life.

I took refuge in my work for the company, and visited the steelworks, spending very little time at home. The children were in Bilbao, but I hardly saw them. I just could not face them. I ate in restaurants and tried to hide my pain. However, when I came home late at night, my mother-in-law berated me, saying that my behaviour was disgraceful and that my children needed their father. I knew she was right, but my distress was so great that I did not know how to cope with it. The idea of losing Pepita was driving me crazy.

A week after the accident, and without her ever regaining consciousness, Pepita's heart failed her. We were all devastated.

They buried her in her mother's family vault. A few days

later, a Requiem Mass was held at the *Basilica de Nuestra Sra de Begoña* where we had been married. Hundreds of our friends attended. I went through the motions like a zombie, only managing to cope with the ordeal thanks to the tranquilizers given me by Dr Herrasti.

Miles was there and I remember him telling me that all the evidence pointed toward an accident. His experts said that the car had not been tampered with, and the Civil Guard and police agreed. Pepita had simply taken the wrong road and, due to poor visibility, fog, and rain had gone off a cliff. The report was final, and the findings somehow made me feel less miserable.

As soon as all the funeral ceremonies were over, I returned to Madrid with the children. It was already late September, and, for the sake of my family, life had to go on.

After the conclusions of the investigation, I was ill-prepared for the letter that Rafael, the porter, handed me on our arrival in Madrid. Written in capitals, the letter said: "WE TOLD YOU SO............"

I was so confused I did not know what to believe anymore. I called Miles. I was very, very angry and frightened.

"Don't let this bother you. All they are doing is playing mind games. They know you are very vulnerable, and these notes are simply to undermine you. They want you to break down," he said, trying to reassure me.

"But after all these years, how can they still be active?"

"Rodney, you know as well as I do that one of the Nazis'

specialities were psychological torture. They just want to drive you insane. So please try to stay calm. Be reasonable. There is no doubt whatsoever that your wife's death was a most unfortunate and terrible accident.

"That's an easy thing to say from London!"

I was now beginning to get angry, and I was confused. The formula to personal disaster Why hadn't I killed those bastards when I'd had the chance? Vogel, Gisella….. every one of them! However, Miles was right. They were just trying to make me lose it and I was not going to let them. I had to be strong and keep my bearings.

*

Returning to the flat with Pepita gone was not easy. I had four young children to take care of and had no idea how I was going to manage. I took Carlos under my wing, for he was terribly distressed by his mother's death; he was depressed, and for some reason blamed himself.

Nevertheless, time cures all, and after a few months, although I missed Pepita dreadfully, I was back, leading my regular routine. I had loads of work in the office, and I travelled a great deal, having taken an extended leave from MI6.

My in-laws came to visit the children on several occasions. I could feel a certain tension in our relationship, which I could not understand, as I had always enjoyed their company and felt genuine affection for them.

They began to put pressure on me to send the children to

Pepita Mundy, Countess of Mondaye in London 1965

Rodney Mundy and his wife Pepita in Cortina d'Ampezzo (Italy) in 1966

live with them in Bilbao, but I refused. I had already lost my wife and was not prepared to lose my sons and daughters, as well. However, eventually, as a compromise, I agreed to send my two daughters to spend a year with them and see how it went. I would always regret that decision, not because they were not kind to the girls but because I later realised that a father must be with his children, especially at that age.

I bought a 1,000-sq-metre flat on Calle Rafael Calvo, 7, to be our new home, and moved my office there, too. It was a lovely apartment with a large terrace, and I felt we could be happy there.

Simon had now finished his studies, and I asked him to come and work for me in Madrid. The boys were very excited at the idea of their elder brother whom they hardly knew coming to live with us. They all got along splendidly from the start, and he was a great support to them and still is.

Beatriz, the governess, had taken over the household and now managed everything, and I really did not know what I would have done without her.

XIX

MY THIRD MARRIAGE

I am a man who needs a woman by his side in life, and I started dating a delightful widow, but she had four children of her own, and the relationship failed to take off.

However, soon another woman entered my life. Pepita and I had often played golf and dined with her among other friends. We had often played golf and dined with her among other friends. We both shared a love for golf, the opera, and travel, and I found her very appealing. Her name was Rosa Cuito. She was born in Cataluña and was the daughter of a wealthy textile entrepreneur.

My sons got on quite well with her from the beginning, but for some reason, the girls did not warm up to her; so it came as something of a respite for me when my daughters finally went to live in Bilbao, whereupon I fired Beatriz, who promptly joined them.

I travelled to Bilbao every week on business, so I saw my daughters regularly, but I could feel I was gradually losing their love. They were too small to understand my situation, and unfortunately, I was too selfish to understand theirs.

At the beginning of 1972, I asked her to marry me. I did

Rosa Mundy nee Cuito on her wedding day

not dare tell my daughters but through a letter to their aunt, in which I informed her of my marriage and asked her to pass the news to the girls in the most delicate of manners.

My new wife had no siblings, nor had she had any children in her previous marriage. Living in a big household with teenagers became too much of a strain for her, so we built a house in the country, twenty-five kilometres outside the city. I left my three sons in the big flat with a cook and a butler. They were free to do as they pleased and I gave them plenty of money, which was no doubt not the best thing to do.

By now, I felt half-Spanish and really loved my adopted country, so as Franco's health was deteriorating rapidly, I resumed my work for MI6.

The *Generalissimo* had become a pathetic and fragile old man who clung to power despite the changing world around him. This fragility was an ideal breeding ground for all sorts of intrigues, such as the arranged match in March 1971 between his granddaughter Carmen and Alfonso de Borbon-Dampierre, the eldest grandson of King Alfonso XIII. Despite Alfonso's having no rights to the Spanish throne[35], the wedding was organized with all the pomp and ceremony of a royal wedding. Franco persuaded Prince Juan Carlos and Princess Sophia to attend and invited the Queen Geraldine of Albania, King Leka II of Albania, King Simeon II of

---

[35] His father H.R.H Infante D. Jaime abdicated his rights to the throne on the 23rd of June 1939. He was born deaf and later made a morganatic marriage with Emmanuela Dampierre, daughter of the Duke and Duchess of San Lorenzo. They were known as the Duke and Duchess of Segovia. In 1941, after the death of King Alfonso XIII, the French legitimist considered him as Head of the Royal House of France and Duke of Anjou.

An ailing General Franco, his granddaughter Carmen, Prince Alfonso of Borbon-Dampierre and Doña Carmen Polo de Franco, the dictator's wife on the day of the wedding at the Palace of El Pardo on the 8th March 1972. The wedding opened an entirely new world of worrisome possibilities.

Bulgaria and his wife Queen Margarita, Grand Duke and Grand Duchess Wladimir Romanov of Russia, who all lived in exile in Madrid, Prince Rainier and Princess Grace of Monaco and the Begum Yvette of the Ismaelites whom I had met in the South of France with the Aga Khan many moons ago. This marriage opened an entirely new world of worrisome possibilities.

To me, it seemed improbable that Franco would renege on his designation of Prince Juan Carlos, son of Don Juan, as his successor. However, through some friends of mine within the regime, I found out that Franco's inner circle, comprising his wife, Dona Carmen; his son-in-law, the Marquis of Villaverde and the most extremist of the *falangistas* were putting enormous pressure on the ailing dictator to designate Alfonso de Borbon as his successor. I could understand the attraction that such a possibility might have for Franco. The inner circle argued that the future heir of this marriage would be a grandchild to both the dictator and the late King Alfonso. London was anxious, fearing that if this were to happen, it might lead to a revolution shortly after Franco's death or worst, another civil war.

Despite very tight censorship, things in Spain were changing rapidly. This was partly due to the tourist boom, as in summer Spaniards mingled with the increasing number of foreigners who came to the coasts. The Spanish people were waiting patiently, and in silence for the freedom and democracy, they so desired, while the most important of the banned political parties - the socialists and communists –

were likewise buying their time before reappearing on the scene and fighting for their goals.

Prince Juan Carlos had very little support within the regime - only Torcuato Fernandez Miranda, Laureano Lopez Rodó, and a few others – but if became king, he would inherit absolute power, enabling him to go in whatever direction he wished. The only problem was to manage to stay in control long enough to do so. On the other hand, the leaders of the political parties were in contact with his father, Prince Don Juan, the Count of Barcelona, who was still living in exile in Portugal. They believed that his restoration to the throne was the only option that would guarantee a return to democracy in Spain. In those days, the democratic opposition did not believe in Franco's designated successor. The fact is that they did not know him at all.

The royalists, the monarchy's natural supporters, were divided among themselves. The traditionalists would not accept Prince Juan Carlos as King unless Don Juan abdicated, whilst others, whom I called the practical, wanted the restoration of the monarchy at all costs, even if this meant sacrificing Don Juan. The only thing they had in common was their loathing of the Don Alfonso option.

In the summer of 1973, Franco named a prime minister for the first time, Admiral Carrero Blanco who ETA, the terrorist group, assassinated three months later. At least that was the official version then. I had my doubts as the murder of Carrero was incredibly well planned. I doubted that ETA had the means to carry out such an attack on the regime.

Considering that Carrero Blanco, with the Army behind him, would have blocked any democratization of the regime under the young King, it is evident that he was an obstacle for democracy. I asked Miles on several occasions if he really knew who was behind the assassination, and he always shrugged his shoulders and smiled. I was sure then and still am to this day that it was a CIA operation, probably with some help from us.

Influenced by his inner circle of family members, Franco then chose Carlos Arias Navarro as the new prime minister. This was a blow for the monarchists, as it was common knowledge that the hardliner Arias was utterly opposed to the idea of the restoration. The prince now found himself in a difficult situation. Franco was very ill, old, had no will of his own. His inner circle did not look forward to losing their privileges, everyone having ambitions of their own. Alfonso de Borbon, however, instead of remaining loyal to his family and the institution, went along with them and with the hostile prime minister.

By the summer of 1974, Franco was so ill that he named Prince Juan Carlos as acting head of state. In the inner circles of Madrid, we knew that his wife and son in law were furious at this decision. Their weight was felt when only five weeks later; Franco decided he was well enough to resume his responsibilities as head of state. Everyone knew better, and the situation became very tense, with rumours and jokes abounding.

MI6 had informed me that the leaders of the democratic

parties were flocking to Estoril and holding talks with Don Juan to discuss Spain's future, which would ultimately depend on the attitude adopted by the Army. I had been told by Generals Galarza and Cuadra, that with Carrero Blanco gone, the Army would be loyal to Prince Juan Carlos as their chief commanding officer's designated successor. That was great news, and I informed London that the prince stood an excellent chance of remaining king if he democratized the regime shortly after the dictator's death. It was clear that an undemocratic monarchy would have very few chances of surviving and could only hope to do so using force, which would be unacceptable to other European democracies. I was certain that the prince was well-aware of this, as he seemed a brilliant man. I had met him once at a golf tournament, where I had had the chance to chat with him.

The end of nearly forty years of dictatorship was fast approaching. On November 20th, 1975, Francisco Franco Bahamonde, *Caudillo* of Spain and Generalissimo of the Army died after weeks of being kept alive artificially by his family, who still clung to the hope of persuading him to change the succession. Nevertheless, though Franco had many failings, he was not a fool. Quite the contrary!

On November 22nd, Parliament proclaimed Juan Carlos as King of Spain. His father, Don Juan, remained silent in Portugal, waiting to see how events turned out. If this attempt at restoring the monarchy failed, as the legitimate king, the throne, eventually could be restored on him. After a year of brilliant political decisions amid high tension, and thanks to the sagacity of, first, Torcuato Fernandez Miranda and, secondly, Adolfo Suarez, the young king legalised all political parties. He announced that democratic elections would be held in June 1977. By doing so, the monarchy was bringing democracy to Spain in a move that would guarantee its survival.

After seeing his lifelong dream realised, and democracy established in Spain, Prince Don Juan, who was primarily a great patriot, abdicated in favour of his son on the 14th of May 1977, thereby granting him dynastic legitimacy. It was an act of great love and personal sacrifice, and it touched and moved me profoundly. This extraordinary man that had lived most of his life in exile, was insulted and loathed by the regime. I had played golf with him on several occasions, and I admired him greatly for his values and his patriotism. He was also a very charming man with an extremely good sense of humour. A true gentleman as had been his father, King Alfonso XIII, my father's friend. The man who had always put his life at the service of Spain had passed on the flame to his beloved son. A week later, having accomplished my mission, I handed in my resignation.

The following year I had the great honour of being received by His Majesty King Juan Carlos I in the Zarzuela Palace accompanied by my son Carlos. It was a very moving audience, and I told His Majesty how proud I felt by his achievement.

The emotional ceremony of abdication of Don Juan de Borbon in favour of his son on the 14th of May 1977. By doing this act, the staunch royalists transferred their support from whom they considered their King Juan III, to his son and heir King Juan Carlos I.

XX

A PLACID RETIREMENT

By 1954, the year the Marbella Club opened. Two men with an eye for business had bought up most of the property and orange groves between the charming sleepy fishing village of Marbella and the Guadalmina River.

One of them was Prince Alfonso von Hohenlohe, whose father, Prince Max, had tried so eagerly to persuade the British Embassy to sign a peace treaty with Germany during the war. The family discovered Marbella soon after the war, immediately saw its potential and bought a large amount of land. Prince Alfonso's idea was to build a haven by the sea for all his rich and famous friends, which is precisely what the Marbella Club would become.

The other astute businessman was Norberto Goizueta, who bought all the land between the village of San Pedro de Alcántara and Guadalmina, where he developed the Guadalmina Golf and Hotel and sold plots of land to all his wealthy conservative Spanish friends. I bought a lovely flat there, overlooking the sea, where we spend three months every summer.

1970 saw the construction of Puerto Banús, a splendid leisure port against a stunning backdrop, the mountain of La

Concha. The port would soon attract some of the largest yachts in the world.

It was during the seventies and eighties that Marbella enjoyed its heyday. During those happy years, some extraordinary characters appeared on the scene and dominated the nightlife. Pepe Moreno's discotheque catered mainly for the Guadalmina crowd, while Menchu Escobar established her equally famous Menchu's Bar in Puerto Banús. I had met her years before in London when she had struck me as a beautiful redhead with a very outgoing personality. My wife and I used to go to her bar nearly every evening, as the mixture of people from Guadalmina and the Marbella Club made it very entertaining. Everybody went there, and it was a matter of great importance where Menchu sat you.

One evening in the summer of 1980, I went to Menchu's Bar by myself. Even though the place was packed, Menchu gave me our usual table on the terrace. A few minutes later, she returned, accompanied by an extravagantly dressed woman in an enormous straw hat that completely hid her face.

"Let me introduce you to my dear friend from Paris, Mimi St Claire."

The faceless lady extended her hand for me to kiss.

"Are you alone tonight?" Menchu asked, "If you are, I'd like to ask you to invite Mimi to your table."

"Yes, I am. Please, Mimi, take a seat", I said, moving a chair back.

"Champagne is on the house!" said Menchu, pleased with herself.

After Menchu left, the mysterious Mimi made herself comfortable and proceeded to take off her hat. She had not yet said a word when I saw her face and immediately recognized her. She had quite a few wrinkles, though not as many as I would have expected for a woman in her seventies, but those unforgettable sensual green eyes and red hair were still there.

"Gisella!" I cried, quite startled.

"Monsieur!" She paused to whet. "You are mistaken. My name is Mimi," she said in exquisite French with no trace of a German accent.

Surprised, I said, "Cut the crap, Gisella, and let's try to have a drink in a civilized manner. It's been a long time."

A pretty waitress uncorked the champagne and filled our glasses. I knew her well, as her father, Brian Walmsley, was a good friend who had also been in MI6. Her name was Tessa, and I introduced her to Mimi. She now runs a fashionable restaurant in Madrid called La Parra in Calle Montesquinza 34.

"Her father was MI6," I said after Tessa left.

"And so were you," she added softly and then sighed.

"So, you knew!"

"We knew everything, my dear. As I suppose you did, too; anyway, in those days you either fought or spied, so it was rather obvious. It was all a big game."

"A terrible game! So many lives were lost. Over fifty

million people! I've often wondered how you could all work for such a monster as Hitler." "We elected Hitler to power because his promises of a Greater Germany were very appealing to most of us. We longed for the greatness of the Kaiser, and it seemed that this was what the Nazis were offering. I am going to be quite honest with you. We knew that they were transferring the Jews to work camps, but we never knew what they were doing to them until much later on in the war. When I found out, I was appalled. I had quite a few Jewish friends in Berlin before the war, but not a single one survived.

"But you worked for them."

"Don't be mistaken. I worked for Germany in the same way that you worked for Britain."

"Yes, but I worked for freedom, while you worked for a despicable and murderous State."

"Things are not always what they seem. I'm going to tell you a secret that I haven't told anyone. Two of my closest friends were Count Klaus von Stauffenberg and Erwin Römmel."

"The first name rings a bell, and naturally, one cannot help feeling a certain admiration for Römmel. He was a formidable enemy," I said, fascinated by the turn the conversation was taking.

"The Count was the mastermind behind the plot to kill Hitler and Erwin was seriously implicated. Klaus placed a briefcase with a bomb in it at a staff meeting. But it all went wrong. Hitler survived, and he ordered poor Klaus execution the next day.

He is a very tragic hero." "But not only was Field Marshall Römmel was never implicated in the plot, but he received a hero's funeral with full military honours, if my memory does not deceive me," I said.

"They forced him to commit suicide at the hospital in Ulm. Hitler knew that he was too popular to degrade his memory. Did you know, Rodney that poor Erwin was about the only German commander not to be involved in any war crimes? He was a real gentleman." Her tone of voice was one of certain nostalgia and sadness tone of sadness.

"We did hear in those days that during the North African Campaign, he often cut the water rations of his troops so that the prisoners of war could survive. He must have been quite a man. You are fortunate to have known such a man. Were you involved in the plot?"

"Yes. I was one of the few that escaped scot-free. By then, we were all very disgusted by Hitler and what he was doing to our country."

"I have to say I'm impressed. I thought you were nothing but a cold-blooded bitch. How did you manage to leave the service?"

"I stayed on until after the war, but gave them hardly any information or, at most, misleading tips. I had to pretend I still worked for them because my life was at stake. After the war, I managed to get to France, where a friend turned me into Mimi. My involvement in the plot to assassinate Hitler saved me from prosecution and landed me with a French passport." She fell silent, lost in thought.

"Gisella, I have hated you for many years. I was in Laszlo's apartment when you murdered him."

"I had nothing to do with his death. Yes, I was there when it happened. "But I must tell you that it was Vogel and one of his men who pushed poor Laszlo off the balcony. I was very fond of him." She said sighing.

"In that case, how come the diamond brooch was under a chair?

"When poor Laszlo realised, he was going to be killed, he struggled and held on to anything within reach, and that's when my brooch must have fallen off." Gisella was trembling as the memories of that incident flooded back, so I took her hand. "You see," she went on after the briefest of pauses, "Laszlo and I had been lovers.

If it could buy information, sex was just part of my job, but I did like him."

"And part of mine, too."

We both laughed, and it helped ease the pain of our memories of a time long gone.

"I'll return your brooch to you."

"No, keep it as a souvenir. I never want to see it again."

"But you can always sell the diamonds," I insisted.

"Rodney, Mimi St. Claire is a very wealthy woman."

"I've always enjoyed having rich friends," I teased with a wink, and she winked back.

"I have longed for you for many years," she said, turning flirtatious as she raised her glass of champagne, and we drank a toast to us.

"You have always been on my mind, Rodney. Sex with you is something a woman does not easily forget." She placed her hand on my knee and moved it upwards, and though I was flattered, it made
me feel rather uncomfortable but I did not stop her. "Had our circumstances have been different, I would have made you my lover, and you would have learnt some fascinating techniques!"

We both laughed at the idea.

"I have to admit that the sex we had was probably the best ever, but it all happened long ago. By the way, whatever happened to Francisco de Beaumont?"

"Do you remember the night in the houseboat?" She replied with a question.

"I have never forgotten. What did they put in the champagne?

"A very strong narcotic. It was all Francisco's idea, but sex was not part of the plan. It all just got out of hand. We were supposed to knock you out and try to find out what you were up too. I think we all got a bit carried away by the sensual atmosphere."

"Francisco nearly lost the plot. You know, he kidnapped me and tried to make me his sex slave!"

"Don't be absurd, Rodney. He saved your life. He was in love with you, and he would never have allowed any harm to come your way. The Germans wanted you dead."

"So, they knew?"

"Of course, we knew. First in Madrid, then in Cairo, and so well connected.....what else could you have been darling?"

"Where is Francisco now?" I asked with curiosity.

"He returned to Germany at the end of the forties. The pearl trade had suffered, and his mother was not well. I have seen him on and off throughout the years. Ever so charming, he always spoke of you as his long-lost love. You know, he never married. He died in his sleep just a couple of years ago."

"I'm sorry for him. I did find him extremely charming and entertaining. He was very refined, but, unfortunately, he was not my type! As you know I was never into men." We both laughed

"I know that, Rodney!"

"And the American spy, Paul Roberts?"

Gisella took a sip of her champagne. She now seemed to be enjoying remembering those long-forgotten days.

"He was not American. He was one of us in fact born in Berlin. He was taken in the same day they arrested Hekmet and handed over to the Americans. He was rather harmless the poor fellow."

"Not so harmless. He nearly killed me!"

"He was sentenced to death!" Gisella sighed.

We both took a sip of our champagne and then Gisella returned to her favourite topic.

"Well, maybe you and I could make love once again for old time's sake," she suggested seductively, "I am staying at the Marbella Club!"

"I think not, my dear. It would not be a good idea. I'm a married man now, and they say in England that it's not a good idea to heat a cold soup!"

"Too bad," she said, smiling. "At least I can still fantasize with the memories."

"You are quite naughty for a lady your age," I said jokingly.

"I'd never have imagined that a gentleman like you would say something so rude!" she pretended to blush, "We young girls have our needs, my dear, just like you boys do, I suppose." We laughed again
and refilled our glasses.

The bar was full of familiar faces, like Gunther Sachs and his wife, and Princess Soraya, the former Empress of Persia, but that night it seemed to both of us that we were the only people there.

"You must have been very pleased to have Jettenbach prosecuted," she went on.

"Well, it was a job well done and a stroke of naked luck," I said.

"He was an immoral crook alas with good manners. He gave me the creeps. I never liked him, and I was delighted when I heard the news. He was responsible for the deaths of a few of my Jewish friends. You see, my father was also a collector, and they all knew each other."

"You should have been an actress! You really misled me. I thought he was a friend of yours."

"That was part of the job…. Misleading the enemy. I was highly skilled at it in those days."

"I have to confess, Gisella, that during that trial, I felt sorry for his wife as she had no idea who her husband was. Poor woman! By the way, whatever happened to Vogel? I saw him once in a restaurant in Madrid before the trial, and I am certain he was harassing me at the time."

"You, and a few others!"

"What do you mean? "

"Hansi was a real monster. He was a sadist who loved his work. I have not heard from him in years. He escaped prosecution. The most prominent exiled Nazis would not admit him into Odessa. He became so obsessed with the survival of the Reich that he founded a small organisation with a few other hardliners. This, I know because he tried to recruit me. They acted in very bizarre ways and were a bunch of crazy and dangerous fools."

"But Laszlo told me that you two had been lovers."

"Poor Lazlo. He loved to gossip so much! We were only lovers for a few days until I discovered what a cruel monster he was."

"He should be history by now," I said. Then, realising it was close to eleven and that I had to hurry home, I added, "It's been a pleasure spending the evening with you, Mimi. I would love to see you in Paris and would introduce you to my wife if we were to meet again."

"What a lovely idea!" She said, passing me her card, "But you better make it soon, as, after all, I am not that young anymore!"

XXI

GHOSTS FROM THE PAST

I was soon to turn fifty-eight, and I felt terrific. My wife was planning a birthday dinner party at our home in the country, at which all my children would be present, and I was very much looking forward to the occasion.

A few weeks earlier, however, as I arrived one morning at the office, I noticed a very strange-looking old man swaggering about. He was wearing an old trench coat that reached down to his ankles and a hat that dated back to the '40s. He was standing on the corner, reading a newspaper, and trying to look inconspicuous. I presumed that he was just a beggar and never gave him a second thought.

That is until I saw him again as I was leaving Balmoral, my favourite bar, on *Calle Hermosilla*. He looked quite harmless, and I wondered if it was just a coincidence. I chose to think it was, and I pushed him from my mind, once again.

Nevertheless, the following morning he was standing across the street from my home, and it was then that I decided to call a friend of mine in the police. Inspector Vega asked me to go and see him in his office at the *Dirección General de Seguridad*. He was a charming young man who had the bad habit of chain-smoking. Having been a heavy smoker myself until I turned forty, other people smoking now bothered me, so I opened fire at once.

"I shall assign someone to protect you while we try to find out who the person is," he said reassuringly, "I'm sure there's nothing to worry about."

"I hope so too, Vega. Many thanks."

However, just as he had appeared, the mysterious man disappeared, and I did not see him again; so, after only a couple of days, my bodyguard was withdrawn.

The evening before my birthday, my youngest daughter Sandra came over for a drink. I always enjoy her company as she is in a permanent good mood and full of life. There is never a dull moment when she is around.

"Papa, there's a very odd-looking old man in the street. Is he your new beggar?" she asked jokingly. I looked out of the window, and there he was again, in the same old coat and hat, only this time his hair was white, and he wore a ridiculous fake moustache.

"Yes, he does look odd," I agreed, drawing the curtains closed.

I went into my bedroom and called Inspector Vega.

"He's back," I said.

"Who's back?"

"The stalker." I walked my young daughter to her car, but by then the odd man had disappeared.

The next day I dropped by the office for a couple of hours before taking my wife out to lunch. I was aware of the presence of the plain clothes police officer, which Vega had assigned to protect me, but once again the stalker was nowhere to be seen. It looked as if he had disappeared again.

After lunch, we went out to our country house to prepare for the evening's celebrations. At about half-past eight, the children arrived, and we drank to my health with champagne. We hardly manage to spend much time together, and it was a wonderful feeling to have all of my sons and daughters with me! However, about an hour later, just as we were sitting down to dinner, the doorbell rang, which was rather strange, as we were not expecting anyone. The maid went to open the door and returned a few minutes later.

"*Señor*, there is a gentleman who says he must speak to you immediately."

"What is his name?"

"I don't know, *Señor*. I shall go and ask him."

She returned a few moments later.

"It is Adolf Dumas, *Señor*. I think he is a strange person."

I got up from the table to find out who he was. I was stunned to see him standing in my doorway.

"Who the hell are you?" I demanded, "Why have you been following me?" I had no idea who he could be. His face was not at all familiar. Maria was right; he did seem unbalanced.

He started rambling on in German, and I realised he was saying something about Klaus von Jettenbach.

"I think you had better leave," I said, very annoyed.

The old man had his hands in his coat pockets. He looked

like a caricature of a detective in an American film and had it not been for the circumstances, I probably would have laughed

"Don't worry, I shall leave very soon," he now said in surprisingly perfect English.

Without warning, he pulled a pistol out of his pocket and pointed it straight at me.

"Happy Birthday, Herr Mundy."

I reacted in a jiffy and pushed him to one side. The gun went off, the noise alerting my whole family, who immediately rushed into the hall.

My assailant had fallen to the ground and my eldest son, who is an expert at martial arts, leapt on him and held him pinned to the floor. He had not much difficulty as the man was well past his prime. I immediately called Vega and asked for instructions, as I had given my bodyguard the evening off.

"Lock him up in a bathroom. We'll be there as soon as possible."

Therefore, with the help of my sons, I locked him into the small guest bathroom. It was rather tricky as though he was frail, he behaved like a wild animal. His strength was outrageous for a man of his age.

"I think we had better sit down for dinner until the police arrive," I said, as we trouped back into the dining room in a state of utter shock. The children and my wife wanted to discuss the incident and bombarded me with questions, which I avoided answering. We just left it to the act of a lunatic but I knew better. I would certainly never forget this birthday, for I had been reborn.

No noise came out of the lavatory. I had just managed to blow out my candles when Inspector Vega arrived with two other police officers.

"Where is he?" he asked.

I pointed him to the loo and gave him the key. He unlocked the door and found the man was lying on the floor. Vega knelt and examined him.

"I'm afraid he is dead. What did you do to him?"

"What do you mean?" He tried to kill me! We did not use any violence against him."

Vega called an ambulance, and before midnight, they took the body away to the morgue for an autopsy.

"I shall let you know who he was as soon as we find out. Meanwhile, Happy Birthday, *Señor* Mundy."

On October 30th, Inspector Vega called me and asked me to go to the police headquarters. I took a taxi and was soon sitting in his smoke-filled office.

"What did you find out?" I asked impatiently.

"Your friend was not called Adolf Dumas, although he did have a false French passport with that name. He had no fingerprints, and the only clue we have as to who he could be is this old photograph we found in his wallet."

"May I see it?"

The Inspector handed me the picture. It was an old black and white photograph of a young man in a SS uniform.

"Oh, my God!" I exclaimed.

"What is it?" asked the Inspector, lighting yet another cigarette.

"This man is Hans Vogel. He was an important member of the Gestapo in Spain during the war." I told him part of the story. "How did he die?"

I impatiently waited as Vega stubbed his half-smoked cigarette out in an already overflowing ashtray. The stench of cheap black tobacco was nauseating.

"Cyanide poisoning!"

"They all carried cyanide pills after the war. Death was considered preferable to arrest. What would I tell my family?"

Vega sensing my worries, said- "Don't worry *Señor* Mundy. The official story will be that Dumas was a deranged fool! No connection to you whatsoever. Trust me! it has all been taken care of."

"Thank you, Inspector." I was relieved.

XXII

CARLOS & I

24th December 1991 Cahuita (Costa Rica)

The dinner was delicious, and Carlos had listened to my story without a single interruption. When I finished, he remained speechless, his features soft and handsome in the flickering candlelight. He raised a glass of champagne and said: "To you, Papa."

"What do you think of my life?" I asked, at last.

"Why didn't you ever tell us? I can't believe you didn't share this with us."

"Well, some things are best left unsaid. It was a way of protecting you all, but under the present circumstances, I felt I had to."

"What present circumstances?"

"Carlos, I think that Martin Jimenez could be a Nazi. I never forget a face, and I know I have seen him before. I don't know. Maybe I'm just getting old!"

"Oh, come on, Papa. I am sure it is not that. It could just be a coincidence. You know better than anyone that people can be similar and remind us of others. It happens all the time. It all happened so long ago."

"Carlos don't ask me why, but I have the gut feeling that

he means trouble. Look at all the strange things that have been happening and let's not forget the shaman's warnings!"

"You heard Mauricio; the Indians are quite superstitious. Come on, Dad, don't worry! The guy gives me the creeps, but he can't be a Nazi. He is too young." Carlos tried to calm my fears.

"It looks as if we're in for quite an adventure. It would be best if you wrote a book about your life as it would make a great story. Your life story would do a fascinating reading! Promise me that you will write your biography one day."

"I'll think about it, but I won't promise anything. I'm just to upset right now to be able to think about anything except getting out of here."

It was past midnight and time to go; all the other guests had already gone. Miss Edith came out to wish us goodnight, giving us both a kiss on either cheek, and we set off in the direction of our hotel along a dark path beside the beach. The small beach bars celebrated their own Christmas parties, and the voice of Bob Marley blasted out from some rather second-rate amplifiers. I do not know if I was paranoid, but I had the feeling that someone was following us. I had always possessed a sixth sense, that of consciousness, and although I did not hear or see anything, I could feel someone was following us on our track. I told Carlos, and we decided to stop off in a bar called *El Ancla*. Ethiopian flags and posters of Emperor Haile Selassie hung on all the walls. I went to the loo, which turned out to be a shack in an open field. While I planned my next move, I somehow felt exhilarated, feeling young again.

Following my familiar old instincts, I circled the building and placed myself behind our pursuer, whom I could see hiding behind a palm tree and taking a good look at the table where my son sat. I edged forward like a sleuth to get a better look. He was quite tall, maybe six feet, and he held a machete in his right hand.

Suddenly, I leapt forward and fell on him with all my strength. At sixty-nine, I was still fit, agile and fairly strong. We fell to the ground, and I managed to pin his head down. However, he spun around with extreme ferocity, and I felt his fist crash into my jaw. As I fell backwards, I could taste the salty flavour of my blood. I saw him pick up the machete, but just as he raised an arm to strike, a large Negro stopped him from behind.

"Are you crazy, man? This gentleman is a friend of Miss Edith's."

By now, the people from the bar, including Carlos surrounded us who helped me to my feet. Taking advantage of the confusion, my assailant took off with his machete.

"We know who he is. He works for *Señor* Jiménez, the owner of a lodge. He was probably just after your money. There is quite a big drug problem here," said the big guy who had just saved my life.

"You don't need to cut someone's throat to get their money. Who are you, anyway? I owe you my life".

"I am Miss Edith's son. She asked me to keep an eye on you. I am glad I did. You see, my mother has premonitions and sees things before they happen."

"Maybe it would be a good idea to call the police," I said without thinking.

"We better not Papa. Don't forget the call and why we're here!" Carlos said with logic.

"Maybe we should all have a drink," I said, trying to sound cheerful. We all returned to the bar, where I put some ice on my painful jaw and invited everyone to a beer.

The next morning at dawn, we drove back to San José, and on the way, we stopped at a phone booth in a small village, and Carlos called our friends in San Jose. I thought our well-connected friends would know something about the identity of our protector, but I was wrong. Our story shocked them and said they would make some calls and try to investigate.

*

Back in San José, we checked again into the Gran Hotel. There was a message from our friends saying that they would be picking us up for Christmas lunch at 1.30 pm. We had an enjoyable meal at their beautiful home, answering all of their questions, but we left without a clue as to who our guardian angel was. Carlos decided to spend the rest of the afternoon with our hosts, and I ordered a taxi to return to the hotel and take a nap. I felt I needed a little rest and some time on my own. I was tired from the sleepless nights, and I planned to start packing, as we had to catch the next day a midday flight to Kingston. I had just begun snoozing off when I received a phone call.

Rodney Mundy in Madrid 1999

"*Señor* Mundy, I have a message for you," said the receptionist in the sweetest and softest of voices, "*Señora* Blasco will be waiting for you outside the hotel in fifteen minutes. She will be driving a red Range Rover. She insisted that you accompany her. It seems to be very important."

I was not sure if I was up for more mysteries; but I got up, dressed, and prepared to meet my blind date. The red vehicle was waiting outside, with a fragile dark-haired woman in her fifties behind the steering wheel. She was elegantly dressed and wore a string of excellent pearls around long, lovely neck. She had an aquiline nose and deep-set black eyes, her skin was translucent, and she looked anything but hostile. I got in and, without a word, she started the engine and we drove off.

"I must apologise for arranging a meeting in such an unorthodox fashion. My name is Rita Stern. I am the daughter of Simon Stern, whom you met after the war."

"I can't believe it!" I cried, "I last saw you as a little girl in London with your father."

"I am sure you have many questions to ask me, and I shall be happy to answer them." Taking my hand affectionately, she smiled, "My father always cherished your memory and was very grateful for what you did for our family."

"I know he passed away."

"Yes in 1961. His health never fully recovered after Auschwitz."

"I am terribly sorry to hear that. Your father was a good man, and I became very close to him. But what brought you here?"

"My father had a sister living in San Jose, and as we had so little money and nothing to keep us in England, we emigrated. We needed a fresh start, and this is wonderful country!"

"I agree.

The people are so friendly, with a couple of exceptions."

I waited for her reaction, but she said nothing.

"Why don't we have a drink at the Terrace Bar in the hotel?" I suggested.

"I'd love to." She turned the car around, and we drove back to the hotel. As the Avenida Central was closed to traffic because of some processions that were to take place shortly, we took side streets. When we arrived, Rita gave the car keys to the porter.

The Terrace Bar was in front of the Teatro Nacional. In a small flea market in the square, *ticos* and Indians sold their merchandise while a group of musicians played local tunes.

The weather was cool and very pleasant. We ordered some fresh papaya juice, and I settled comfortably into my chair, waiting for Rita to speak.

"And what bought you to Costa Rica, Rodney, if may I ask?"

"I am on holiday with my son. But how did you find me?"

"Let me explain. I have a son called Rodney. He is now twenty," she said at last.

"And I one called Simon."

She smiled at me candidly.

"My husband is a high-ranking official in the Police Force. As your name has been mentioned so many times at home, a couple of days ago he told me there was going to be a drug raid. A foreigner with the same name as yours was somehow involved. I was very intrigued. Was it possible? Was it you? For all I heard my father say about you, I could not believe that you could possibly be involved in drugs or any unlawful activities. I pleaded with my husband to find out if the man who reunited me with my father was the same, and if he was, to help you. I was so insistent that he investigated. Your embassy here confirmed you were above any suspicion and told my husband that you were up to no wrongdoing. He concluded it was a setup; so he took immediate action and had one of his men call your son and saved you from a very embarrassing and complicated situation."

"But why weren't we told what was happening? It would have saved us a lot of anxiety."

"Well. I understand, but that was not possible because it would have ruined the investigation as to why you were set up."

"I am so thankful, anyway. I can't even imagine the nightmare it would have been"

"It is we who can't thank you enough. You made it possible for my father to find me, and not only that, but I also became a very wealthy woman after I recovered his art collection."

"Rita, but who tried to get us framed?

"My husband is investigating that. When your room was raided this morning, they found 5 kilograms of marihuana and that is a big crime here."

"Do you know Martin Jimenez?"

"Yes, he is married to an acquaintance and is the owner of the Toucan Lodge. Do you think he is involved?"

"Well, I'm not sure, but it did all happen at his place."

"Why would he? You don't know him, do you?

"No, I don't, but his face is disturbingly familiar, and since we arrived at the lodge, strange things started to happen."

"What things Rodney?"

I told Rita about the snake, which now I suspected was an attempt on Carlos's life, and the attack in Cahuita by someone who worked for Martin Jimenez. Rita was horrified.

"I think you better tell my husband. This information might help
him in the investigation. I'll call him right now."

Rita took her mobile phone out from her handbag and made a call.

"He will meet us in a couple of hours at home. He took our son Rodney to his parent's home."

"Great. I will feel better to get this off my chest. So, tell me, what do you know about Martin?"

"Not much. He spends most of the time on the coast and seldom is in San Jose. I don't think he and his wife are very close."

"Do they have any children?" I asked.

"No. He is quite a loner. I would say an odd type and always keeps to himself. I heard that both his parents committed suicide when he was only a child. He has a reason for being so different, I suppose."

"But is he Costa Rican?" I enquired.

"No, I think he is originally from Paraguay. We don't really know much about him...it is his wife who has the money, though."

The mention of Paraguay hit the nail.

Could it be?" The pieces in the puzzle seemed to fit, "but why did their names not match?"

"Are you alright, Rodney?"

"Yes, sorry. I am just baffled.

"Rita, why didn't you go to the trial?"

"What trial? My question took her by surprise.

"Klaus von Jettenbach's!

"Oh God! I should have gone, but I was only a child when all those terrible events took place, and I could not face reliving all the pain." She paused and shuddered ever so slightly.

"Rodney, are you still in the Secret Service?

"Oh no my dear, I now work for my son Carlos as the financial director of his model agency, and for an old man, it's a wonderful job as I get to go to all the model contests. It's fun, and it keeps me young."

"I'm sure you do. Dad told me you had quite a reputation with the ladies!"

"When I was younger, I did." I was glad that Rita had allowed me to change the subject of the conversation. I preferred to speak to her husband.

"You still look like you can break a few hearts," she replied jokingly.

Now my hobby is antiques. I adore going antique hunting in England. The conversation was very friendly, and we both felt a sort of empathy. After all, we did know each other for many years.

"I love antiques too. Let us go to my shop now, and then we can go home to see Antonio, and you can meet Rodney, my son? The shop is closed today so we can have it for ourselves. It is just around the house."

"That sounds like a wonderful idea."

We drove off to an area with lovely houses, not too far from the centre of town, or that is what it seemed to me as we chit-chatted until we stopped in front of a lovely modern antique shop. Rita parked the car.

"We live in the house next door," she said as she got out and pointed to a magnificent wooden mansion, which had been designed by one of the most prominent young Costa Rican architects.

"Charming neighbourhood," I said.

Rita unlocked the door of the shop, and we passed through a lovely courtyard filled with flowers, and she invited me to come in, locking the door from the inside after her. She put on the lights, and I followed to the back of the shop where she displayed what she said was part of her private collection. The quality of her pottery collection amazed me.

"I really can't have it all on display at home!" She said, trying to justify her treasure cove. "And of course, most of these pieces I will one day donate to Costa Rica who always made my father and I so welcome.

"I'm very impressed. Where have you found such exquisite pieces?"

"Dad convinced me to start collecting. You know it was his passion.

My first piece was a gift from him and then I bought at auctions, private sales, and in my travels around the world. You know... by the way, I have a present for you. It was one of dad's favourite pieces. Here come... follow me.

We went to the far end of the room, and in a prominent place was one of the most beautiful pieces I had ever seen. The pale green and blue tones had an incredible intensity.

"Here it is. Do you like it?"

Rita was pointing to a beautiful 11th century Korean Celadon vase, which was worth a small fortune.

"I can't possibly accept such a treasure, my dear. But I'm touched and grateful by the gesture."

"It would have made daddy immensely happy. It is yours. I insist."

I kissed her on the forehead. Her gesture moved me.

"It's settled then! Look at the designs; the chrysanthemums symbolize health and well-being; the lotus, the sun and the mercy of the Buddha; the butterfly, happiness and harmony, and…"

"The phoenix symbolizes good omen!" I interrupted her, and we both laughed.

"You know your pottery, Rodney. I can say that. I will get it shipped to Spain. Do you have a business card?"

"I'm afraid I don't."

"I'll go to get mine and bring you a piece of paper and a pen."

Rita went to the front of the store while I admired the wonderful present I had just received.

As she was handing me the piece of paper, the doorbell rang. "It should be Antonio. He is early, though! I'll be right back."

Rita left and went to meet her husband.

I heard a scream and the sound of an object crashing and breaking into a thousand pieces. Rita entered the room in a state of shock followed by a man who I instantly recognized. It was Martin Jimenez, beyond himself and he was carrying a gun in his hand. Shouting, he ordered Rita to fetch a chair where at point-blank, I sat. Pointing his weapon at her, he ordered me to tie my hands behind the back of the chair and my ankles to its legs.

"Sit down beside your friend, bitch!" He was in a state of rage. Rita did as told, and she sat on the floor.

"Please Martin, put the gun down. I am sure we can talk this over. What is bothering you?" She pleaded.

"Close your fucking mouth!"

We were in real danger. The thought of Vogel on my

birthday came to my mind, and I gestured to Rita to say no more.

"I never thought I would live this day. You killed my father and mother."

"What are you talking about?" I finally said. "I don't even know you." Regretfully, by now, I knew very well who he was.

"Yes, you do, you son of a bitch! Does Klaus von Jettenbach ring a bell? I will never forget your smile of satisfaction when my father received his sentence."

Rita looked at me in disbelief.

"But you were only a child!" I exclaimed.

"You shattered our lives. My mother could not cope with the shame you brought on us, and she shot herself, you bastard. And now you are both going to pay for what you did to my family."

"Martin. Be sensible. You have done nothing yet and I am sure Rita's husband will help you get out of this. Rita is not responsible for
anything, so please be reasonable. You have a wife and a life. Try to make the best out of it. There is still time." I tried to reason with him.

"Yes, Martin. Rodney is right. I will speak to Antonio. "Just let us go, and we will forget this." Rita tried to reassure him but to no avail. He despised us profoundly. His wrath blinded him as his wounds were beyond healing.

"It's too late for that. Since that day in Israel, I have prayed every day to see you suffer the shame and the pain that we have suffered. However, as that won't be, I will have at least the satisfaction to avenge the death of both my parents. You deserve to die for what you have done to us!" He raised his gun and pointed it at me. His hand was shaking.

Please, Martin, please!" Rita pleaded.

Martin, full of rage, turned toward Rita and punched her with force on her face. The suddenness of his reaction took her off guard, and she fell backwards. She moaned as she sat up. A trickle of blood came out of her nose.

"I told you to close your fucking mouth."

Martin stepped back and, once again, pointed the gun toward me. He was beyond reason. I could see that he was about to pull the trigger. I heard Rita scream.

"No!"

My time had come. During my long life, I had been on the verge of death on several occasions, but my destiny was to stay alive. I had lived on the edge, and now I was sure that I could not be so lucky once more. However, for some reason that only God knows, Martin missed. I felt the bullet passing dangerously close to my head. It hit a shelf full of lovely glass pieces by Lalique that was behind me. They came crashing down, clangouring as they hit the floor.

Martin was astounded by the fact that he had missed. He was about to pull the trigger again when Rita sprang from the floor and punched him in the stomach. He fell backwards and a shot went off and hit the ceiling bringing a chandelier down that missed me by inches. Rita was now on top of him. She was a petite, delicate woman over a stocky strong deranged man, struggling to take the gun from him. I was most uncertain of the outcome of such an uneven fight, but I could not do much to help, tied up as I was. Then, she miraculously managed to pick up a small Tibetan bronze horse that was on the floor by her side, and with force uncommon for a woman, she hit Martin on the head. He lay on the floor, motionless.

"Oh my God, Rodney. I think I've killed him!"

"Rita, please untie me." Without taking an eye of the inert body,
she untied me loose. I got up and checked Martin. He was breathing, and his pulse was regular.

"Don't worry. He should be all right. I think you had better call an ambulance, the police, and Antonio. I will make sure he cannot move. Here, take the gun."

Rita and I waited lost in our thoughts. I wondered why life kept giving me more opportunities. I had been so close to death so many times.

The paramedics took Martin to hospital, and we both told the police inspector what had just happened when Señor Blasco, Rita´s husband, and a handsome young man, Rita's son Rodney, arrived. We all embraced each other.

"So, we finally meet. Merry Xmas Rodney!" Antonio said, "let's go home next door and have a drink. It seems that we have something to celebrate and lots to talk about."

"Indeed, we do," I said as I followed them out of the shop.

EPILOGUE

Madrid, 2nd January 2000

I had now lived long enough to be nearly part of two centuries. There was so much fuss about the Millennium celebrations that my wife and I decided not to travel anywhere. Carlos was in India with the Maharajah of Jaipur, and the rest of the children, now all grown up, were scattered around the world in some exotic place or other with their families. Such is life.

Those few quiet days gave me time to reflect on what my life had been and what my wishes were for the future. I am now 78 years old and have a splendid relationship with all my sons and daughters. Through an extraordinary bond between us, I have finally learnt to express my emotions. If there is one thing of my life that I regret, is not having yet met my granddaughter Carla, whose mother was a lovely Ecuadorian girl. I still hope to meet her before I die.

I have four other grandchildren. They are all remarkable children, and I am a proud grandfather. I am still happily married and enjoying my old age. I like meeting my children's friends, as I enjoy the company of younger people. They are so refreshing and always have something to teach you. I continue to enjoy life, though I feel there is too much competitiveness in the world today that individuals are lost in the competition.

Martin Von Jettenbach or Martin Jimenez or Echevarria was charged with attempted murder and sentenced to a psychiatric hospital where shortly after, he followed in his parent's footsteps and hanged himself. It was a tragic ending to a sombre family story.

I never called Gisella when I went to Paris. I assume she must be dead by now or close to a hundred, but one never knows, she was a tough one; so, she may conceivably still be alive. Whatever the case, I hope she finally found the peace of mind she yearned for.

For so many years, hatred for her and Vogel consumed me. However, later in life, I learned from the teachings of the Dalai Lama that my son, Carlos, explained to me, that hate, and revenge are negative emotions. In the end, we always get what we deserve anyway.

My life has taught me that it is a fool's game to mock the enemy.

I would not like to finish these memories of my life without reflecting on what happened in Spain on the 23rd of February 1981. I was no longer involved in the Secret Service. I followed in disbelief how some disaffected members of the Civil Guard took over the Congress. The plotters made the coup in the name of the King, but I knew from the start that was not possible. What I did not understand was how the CIA and MI6 had not prevented the coup in the first place. I did not doubt that they had to be aware of the machinations of the Army.

The CIA had been involved in the plot that killed Admiral Carrero Blanco, the consequence of which had been that the democratic process had so far been successful.

Those were agitated days as during the last twelve months; ETA[36] had murdered over a hundred innocent people, many of them members of the Army and the Security Forces. I, as most people in the social and business circles, knew that the army was fed up with these indiscriminate killings. The rumour that certain military circles, close to the old regime, believed that the only solution to solve the ETA problem was the military one was out. These nostalgic elements in the army thought that the democratic institutions were ill-equipped to cope with this state of affairs.

Finally, after a few hours of uncertainty at one in the morning, the young king addressed the Nation on television in what would be his most important speech ever. Wearing the uniform of Supreme Commander of the Armed Forces ordered the troops back to their barracks. With this act, the monarch saved the infant Spanish democracy. I felt proud of His Majesty! I am sure Spain will always be grateful to the Crown. Without any doubt, the positive effect of that disgraceful episode was that from the 24th of February 1981, never again democracy and the monarchy would be

---

[36] The Basque terrorist groups

questioned.

I have had my share of suffering, but then, who has not? If I look back on all the good times, I can only feel gratitude for the many gifts the Universe has given me.

H.M King Juan Carlos I addressing the nation after the *Coup d'Etat*. With this act
he saved the infant Spanish democracy and entered the annals of History.

Rodney Meynell Mundy died of a brain stroke in his sleep on January 18[th,] 2008 Sadly, Life did not grant him his wish of meeting his granddaughter, Carla Mundy Noboa.

ABOUT THE AUTHOR

Carlos Mundy was born in Spain. From an early age, he was fascinated by music and history. Skilled in Event Management, Public Speaking, Management, Corporate Events, and Networking. Strong business development professional graduated from Runnymede College (Madrid), Universidad Complutense (Madrid). Since 1975 he has been a contributor to different media including El Mundo (Spain), Hola Magazine and Andy Warhol's Interview. Between 2003 and 2005, he founded the magazine Metaphore: Creative Culture. He is currently writing for Vanitas magazine and Moral Moda

www.carlosmundy.com